In the Event
of
Murder

Also available by Cynthia Kuhn

The Starlit Bookshop Mysteries

How to Book a Murder

The Lila Maclean Academic Mysteries

The Semester of Our Discontent

The Art of Vanishing

The Spirit in Question

The Subject of Malice

The Study of Secrets

In the Event of Murder

A STARLIT BOOKSHOP MYSTERY

Cynthia Kuhn

NEW YORK

This is a work of fiction. All of the names, characters, organizations, places, and events portrayed in this novel are either products of the author's imagination or are used fictitiously. Any resemblance to real or actual events, locales, or persons, living or dead, is entirely coincidental.

Published in the United States by Crooked Lane Books, an imprint of The Quick Brown Fox & Company LLC.

Crooked Lane Books and its logo are trademarks of The Quick Brown Fox & Company LLC.

Library of Congress Catalog-in-Publication data available upon request.

ISBN (hardcover): 978-1-63910-070-5
ISBN (ebook): 978-1-63910-071-2

Cover design by Joe Burleson

Printed in the United States.

www.crookedlanebooks.com

Crooked Lane Books
34 West 27th St., 10th Floor
New York, NY 10001

First Edition: August 2024

10 9 8 7 6 5 4 3 2 1

For my family, near and far.
With special thanks and love to my
beautiful Mom.

Chapter One

Teacups were hoisted aloft as the women around the room toasted a very famous star of a very popular television show. Whitney Willton smiled brightly, brushing her long, perfect golden hair away from her impossibly smooth face and her celebrated blue eyes. She lifted her slender arm and gave a beauty-queen wave, a diamond bracelet sliding into the cashmere sleeve of her white sweater, which was the ultimate in California cool: luxurious yet casual, artfully slipping off of one slim, tanned shoulder. Her beach vibe was so strong you could almost hear waves in the background.

"Thank you for having me," she said into the microphone. "I'm thrilled to be home in Colorado, and I'm delighted that you've invited me to be your guest of honor this year at the gala."

The roar of applause filled the Grand Room, an oval space with a soaring ceiling, carved wooden beams, and arched windows. The library in our cozy mountain town of Silvercrest was located in what had once been the mayor's mansion, a perfect setting for this elegant tea. Friends of the library had been invited to officially launch Gala Week—the activities of which would lead up to a glamorous New Year's party and, we hoped, enough funds to ensure a robust budget.

A forty-something who looked twenty-something thanks to a steady stream of cash flowing into her plastic surgeon's bank account, Whitney could have passed for the twin of her niece, Lyra, a successful party-planner-to-the-stars. Lyra's career owed almost everything to the wild success enjoyed by her aunt: Whitney was a former child actor who, unlike many of her colleagues, had gracefully transitioned into dramas, then romantic comedies for several decades. Just last year, however, she had landed the lead role on *Chasers*, a humorous mystery show that had quickly gone to the top of everybody's watch list. Whitney had charmed the hearts of her fans all over again and picked up even more from the younger generations. Lyra, a mirror image of her aunt but clad in serviceable black shirt and pants, sent her a proud look from the side of the podium.

Whitney smiled prettily and stepped aside as my aunt, a creative writing professor and novelist, made her way to the stage, her flowing purple silk jacket flaring gracefully out behind her.

"Thank you, Whitney," Nora said, leaning forward to speak into the mic while turning her head to address the celebrity. I admired, as always, the white streak in the front of her dark hair, which had been pulled up into her signature twist, with curls spilling down here and there. "I'm Nora Haven, a member of the gala committee. We're so happy that you've joined us—the day after Christmas, no less. This morning marks the beginning of a terrific week of events. Hope you will attend this evening's special screening of an upcoming episode of *Chasers* that Whitney has kindly agreed to share with us. Let's show our gratitude, everyone."

The crowd clapped more as Whitney dipped her head gracefully.

Another blonde woman, whose locks didn't seem to rustle from invisible breezes the way that Whitney's did, stepped quickly across the room and ripped the microphone away from my aunt. From head to toe, she was technically flawless, but it was a hard sort of perfection.

"Now, you can do better than *that*," she said, pairing her evaluation of the crowd's muted response with a giggle. The members of the audience played along, providing a short burst of applause.

"I'm Tabitha Baxter," she announced gaily, "president of the library board and leader of the gala committee. This is the first time we've had a such a star-studded lineup. *Do* remember to dress up appropriately on New Year's Eve. Black tie only. And prepare yourself for the best Gala Week ever!"

Tabitha twinkled at the crowd and started to put the mic back into the holder on the podium. Nora edged over and whispered something in her ear. She frowned and whispered something back. My aunt shook her head. Tabitha reluctantly handed over the microphone.

Nora smiled. "We have a very special surprise for you."

A buzz of excitement swept the room.

Tabitha narrowed her eyes as she processed that Nora's announcement had received more enthusiasm than her own.

A tall woman in a long gray trench coat took the stage with a powerful dignity. She removed her matching fedora to reveal long salt-and-pepper hair, raking her fingers through the thick bangs to settle them properly. Her eyes were rimmed with black eyeliner and her lips were stained blood red. Even before she said a word, she had the attention of the whole room. Several claps broke out but quieted when she held up her hands, palms out.

"Greetings, friends. I am—though no doubt you already know—the author Calliope Nightfall."

The crowd, who did indeed know the popular local literature professor and writer, applauded as hard as they had for Whitney.

"What you may not know, my beloveds," she continued dramatically, "is that *I* am the author of the episode that will be screened this evening. It is based on one of my earliest stories, "The Spider's Web," published many years ago. It is a thrilling tale about what happens when dreams and desires come up against"—she struck a pose—"the *deepest* deceptions. Something you noir fans will surely enjoy."

No wonder she was dressed like an old-school private investigator.

"The lead character may have one or two things in common with your favorite literary goddess," she said, pointing to herself. The crowd cheered. "I'll let you be the judge of that."

She handed my aunt the microphone, bowed again, then swept off the stage and out of the room altogether. The palpable crackle of energy that seemed to accompany her presence began to dissipate.

"And Calliope will be joining me at our special Gala Week mystery panel at Starlit Bookshop," Nora said, inviting the crowd to visit the store our family owned. "You won't want to miss it."

Tabitha hurried over to reclaim the microphone as quickly as she could—she liked to have the last word, I'd learned over the years. As Nora and Whitney walked away, Tabitha moved the microphone up to her lips, then paused.

The audience waited.

"Enjoy your tea," she said, finally.

Light laughter swept the room.

Judging from Tabitha's expression, that hadn't been the response she was looking for.

Whitney followed my aunt over to where we were circled up at a white-skirted table set, like every other table in the room, for high tea. There was an empty seat that had been held for the guest of honor, over which Tabitha was hovering territorially. My aunt had confided that there had been a great deal of seat-arrangement bartering but Tabitha had ultimately claimed the seat next to Whitney and grudgingly allowed Nora, who had been the one to invite her in the first place, the other position. I was next to Nora, as her plus-one. Tabitha's best friend Melody Crenshaw was visibly put out, scowling at us from the other side of the table, especially since she knew about Tabitha's long-standing animosity toward Nora and me. However, we'd forged a sort of uneasy truce, and whatever Tabitha decided, her bestie accepted.

She didn't always like it, though.

By the time Whitney sat down, Tabitha, whose seasonally appropriate cedar green tailored suit was paired with marble-sized pearls, was back. Melody—who wore a suit identical to Tabitha's in a muted red shade—had accessorized with smaller pearls but added an extra loop so her necklace was approximately the same width. Other board members were similarly dressed, and many wore hats and gloves.

I tried to push a stray curl back into my braid unobtrusively. My dark mane typically didn't obey efforts to tame it. Perhaps I should try a hat too.

Ariel Salt, a slender brunette, came up and whispered something to Tabitha. She had the air of a skittish fox, and her blue eyes were watchful. She and Lyra were managing the tea service, and they were doing an impressive job so far.

"Thank you. We'll get started." She quickly shooed away some of the unseated attendees. They grumbled but did as she asked, sneaking glances back at Tabitha, who didn't seem to notice or care.

"Please help yourself," Tabitha said, indicating the metal tower in the middle of the table bursting with pastries. The ladies demurred until Whitney reached over and took a tiny morsel, then they all pounced like a shiver of sharks on the rest. By the time I got my hand into the mix, only one misshapen tart remained. The frustrating thing was that most of the women didn't really eat so much as breathe in the aroma of pastries they had grabbed. It was more about *having* than consuming them.

Or maybe it was about keeping *us* from having, at least as far as Melody and Tabitha were concerned. That certainly fit their general approach to life. Although I'd known the women in their country club clique since school, I could never figure out what made them tick, aside from doing whatever Tabitha wanted. Two of the original fearsome foursome who had basically run our high school—we'd graduated just over a decade ago—were no longer in Silvercrest; only Melody and Tabitha remained, which shifted the power and effect of the group. Melody could have stood up to Tabitha if she wanted. But she didn't. Was it affection or fear that kept her in line? Hard to tell. I was still trying to interpret what her pearls meant. They always dressed the same, so wearing anything different than Tabitha, even a minor variation, was new and surprising. In any case, the gala was one of their many services to the charity world. They were good at raising money—I'd give them that—and the library desperately needed the money to function.

"I'm a big fan of *Chasers*," Melody announced to Whitney. "My kids like it too, even though they're younger."

"Thank you," Whitney said graciously.

"The cast is hilarious," Melody drawled. "What's it like on set?"

Whitney smiled. "Exactly as you'd imagine. Mostly because Nat ad-libs all the time. In fact, most of the lines that the fans use for memes come from his mind and not from the scripts. But don't repeat that. We wouldn't want to take away anything from our writers' great reputations."

"I won't," Melody promised, her eyes wide, though I could tell she was itching to post that shiny new intel immediately.

Tabitha cleared her throat in the time-to-look-at-*me*-now way she had.

Melody opened her mouth to speak again.

"But *seriously*," Tabitha said, verbally elbowing her best friend out of the way and belittling the quality of her conversation at the same time. "The Silvercrest Library Gala is our biggest fundraiser of the year and very special. Have you ever attended before?"

"Sadly, no," Whitney said. "I was too young to go when I was growing up here, and now that I'm old enough, I live in

California." She clasped her hands together and her eyes lit up. "But I've always been dying to attend."

She *was* a good actor. Now I knew why she'd won so many awards. The gala was important to the townspeople, of course, but there was no way she'd spent two seconds wishing to be here instead of at some glamorous gathering in Los Angeles on New Year's Eve.

"I'm glad you'll have your chance. We have many wonderful things planned," Tabitha said.

Whitney smiled politely.

"You are going to be the belle of the ball, I promise," Tabitha said. "Have you been to the venue before?"

"Where is it being held again? I'm sure you probably told me, but I forgot."

A flash of annoyance crossed Tabitha's face, but she quickly covered it with a wide smile. "The new ballroom at Silvercrest College."

"Oh, right, the union," Whitney said quickly. "One of the oldest buildings on campus, right?"

"It *used* to be the union," Tabitha went on. "With the help of our Silvercrest College Cares Committee, we were able to raise enough money to build a new union, which was finished last year, then we transformed the historical building into a state-of-the-art event space. The renovations are finally completed, and the gala will be its first event. We're all very excited."

"You're on a committee at the college?" Whitney asked.

"My late husband was a dean there," Tabitha replied stiffly. "So I've been very involved for years with the Silvercrest College community, and that hasn't changed since we lost Tip."

Whitney expressed her condolences, which Nora and I had done many times before.

"He must have been the youngest dean there," she said. After a beat, she added, "Because you're so young, I mean."

"I'm thirty," Tabitha replied. "Tip was slightly older."

Tip had been twice her age and then some, but no one corrected her.

"And you're still an English professor there too, right?" Whitney said to Nora. "I remember when you used to babysit for us and you were always grading papers."

"That's how you knew each other?" Tabitha said wonderingly. "Nora was your *babysitter*?"

"Many years ago." Nora laughed.

Whitney nodded, and her gaze fell on me. "And did I hear correctly that you're a professor as well, Emma?"

Tabitha rolled her eyes and shifted in her seat impatiently while the spotlight wasn't on her.

"No—" I began.

"But she did just receive her PhD in English," Nora jumped in.

"Congratulations," Whitney said warmly. "That's quite an accomplishment."

"It *is*," Nora agreed.

"Yes, we're all so happy for Dr. Starrs and glad she's gracing us with her presence," Tabitha said in a syrupy sweet tone, then pretended to look puzzled. "Though why are you here? You're not on the gala committee."

"Our family has belonged to the Friends of the Library for ages," Nora interjected calmly. "I believe everyone in the group was invited?"

Tabitha pursed her lips.

"Thrilled that you could make it, Emma." A silver-haired gentleman in a tidy suit stopped at the table and greeted us. "Everyone, please applaud Emma *profusely* for putting together the fabulous mystery panel at the bookstore. So looking forward to it." Without giving her a chance to reply, he turned to Whitney. "Hello, dear. I'm Trevor Fontaine, the library director. Cannot thank you enough for your presence. It means a great deal to the future of Silvercrest Library."

"My pleasure," she said, beaming at him. He beamed back, then moved on to the next table.

Tabitha aggressively smoothed her carefully blonded hair while she processed her small defeat. After he was out of earshot, she leaned forward. "I'm surprised you were able to do that, Emma. You have many other demands on your time, like"—she hesitated for effect—"honestly, I couldn't *begin* to fathom what you do all day."

"It's for such a good cause," I said. "I'm happy to help—"

"As I was saying"—she focused on Whitney—"we have wonderful things lined up for you. The screening is tonight, there's a party Friday, and in between . . ." She trailed off as she realized that Whitney wasn't looking at her but smiling at someone else.

We all turned, following her gaze, to see Lyra crossing the room, a large tray full of iced cupcakes on her shoulder. As she drew closer, I noticed that she looked very pale and seemed to be struggling to keep the tray steady.

"I think she's coming to replenish our pastry tower," Tabitha said.

Whitney flinched as Lyra stumbled and hurtled her cargo toward us. Cupcakes flew off of both sides as I lurched forward with both hands out and managed to catch the tray before it hit anyone, but I couldn't catch Lyra, who staggered over to where we were sitting, twisted around as if controlled by unseen forces, and fell backward. There was a horrible thump when her head connected with the table, and she slid to the floor. After a stunned silence, Whitney pushed back her chair and ran around the table to help her niece. I set the tray down and followed her.

She knelt and cradled Lyra in her arms, calling out her name.

Chapter Two

"What happened?" Whitney looked wildly around the room.

No one said anything. The crowd of elegant women murmured to one another as several of them pulled out phones and started dialing 911.

At that moment, Lyra opened her eyes, then struggled to sit up. "What happened?"

"Oh, thank goodness," Whitney said through her tears. "You fainted, sweetie. Take some deep breaths."

Lyra nodded obediently and inhaled slowly. Ariel edged toward her but hung back, looking helplessly at Whitney.

Whitney assisted with Lyra's shift in position and kept her hand on her back. She peered up. "Is there a doctor in the house?"

"No, no. I'm okay," Lyra protested. "I just got a little dizzy all of the sudden."

"Dr. Belasco?" Nora called out. "Are you here?"

A wisp of a woman with a stern expression made her way to the front. She cast a look of annoyance behind her, as if it had been a struggle to get through the other women, but her features softened when she looked at Lyra. The doctor knelt and adjusted her glasses. "Let's take a look at you."

"Everyone, please make some space," Tabitha raised her voice and began shooing people away again. She loved to shoo. "We need to give the good doctor here some room."

At first, people barely edged away at all, drawn to the scene like rubberneckers on the highway. Nora sighed and gave directions to several of the women on the end, who took up the metaphorical baton and began to usher all of the looky-loos backward.

Some of them resisted, but not for long. Nora always had that kind of authority.

A small group was left staring down at Lyra.

"Move slowly. You may have a concussion," said Dr. Belasco. "I'll do a quick check here, but you might want to swing by the ER to have further tests done."

"We will if someone could please give us a ride," Whitney said.

Tabitha volunteered before anyone even had their mouth open.

"I'll come too, if that's okay," Ariel said shyly.

"Yes, dear. Go ahead. We'll clean up," Nora offered.

"Thank you," Ariel replied, as she and Whitney helped Lyra stand and move slowly toward the door.

Soon it was just Nora and me left to pick up the pieces.

And the cupcakes.

* * *

"Oh no. Poor Lyra." My sister Lucy's hand flew up to cover her mouth. I patted her other hand that rested on the dark oak dining table, where we'd gathered for lunch in the old Victorian house that we shared with my aunt. Lucy had two years on me, but I often felt as though I was the older one who was responsible for taking care of her. It's just how it had always been.

She picked up an elastic band and put her dark, shiny, shoulder-length hair into a ponytail, her gaze focused on the river outside the window. Lucy's navy cardigan brought out the blue in her hazel eyes, which were usually the same shade as mine, but I was wearing black, which made mine look greener.

"Of course I was working and missed everything," Lucy said. "But it's a big shopping day."

"I can come help later if you like," I offered.

"No, Em. You're not on the schedule today for a reason," Lucy said. "You've been working overtime planning the panel, and the tea was important. Plus," her tone turned teasing, "it actually sounds as though you were needed there to save the lives of our townspeople."

Nora set down a tureen of squash soup and began to ladle it into bowls. "True. If Emma hadn't *leaped* on top of the table—"

"It wasn't on *top* of the table," I protested.

"It was top-adjacent," Nora insisted. "If she hadn't had such good reflexes, that tray might have taken somebody's head off."

"I don't know about that," I said.

"Emma, it was slicing through the air at an *incredible* speed!" Nora shivered dramatically.

While Nora unfolded her napkin, Lucy and I exchanged a smile, knowing my aunt's tendency toward theatrics.

"The worst that would have happened was that someone might have been buried by cupcakes," I said.

"You always downplay your successes," Nora tsked. "You need to embrace them and own your power."

She launched into a familiar lecture, about how women needed to be proud of our accomplishments in a world that didn't always see our value. Lucy nodded in the right places while we listened. We'd heard variations of her powerful speech for decades now, and while we appreciated the advice, we probably could have said it back to her verbatim.

Finally, she coasted to a stop.

"Look at you two humoring me. Don't think I can't see it," Nora laughed. "But at least I never have to worry whether or not I've passed along the one thing I have learned over and over again on this green earth."

We thanked her, as always, and told her that she was our hero, as always.

I took a few spoonfuls of soup, savoring the warmth. Snow was falling hard outside the windows of the drafty old house; the cold felt as though it was coming from everywhere all at once, slowly and inexorably claiming the air surrounding us. We had heat, of course, but it was no match for the odd nooks and crannies here and there.

"She'll be all right," Nora said, dipping a cracker into her bowl. "Dr. Belasco said that she suspects Lyra has a touch of altitude sickness. They flew in yesterday and stayed overnight with friends in Vail before driving down early this morning, so there wasn't a lot of acclimation time. When Lyra started to faint, she tried to resist it by wrenching her body around, but all that did was make her hit the back of her head on the table instead of the front. She probably has a good-sized lump there. In any case, she's resting comfortably this afternoon and being monitored for a concussion."

"Good news that she's comfortable." My sister circled her spoon around the bowl slowly. "I thought she was the party planner. Why was she serving cupcakes herself?"

"You know planners have to be willing to do any job that's required," I said.

"In this case, it was at her own insistence," Nora said. "Lyra wanted her team to have time with their families for Christmas, which was very kind. They didn't hire a caterer either, because it was just tea and treats. She felt that she and Ariel could manage it. Perhaps she is rethinking the wisdom of taking that on so soon after arriving now."

"Not everyone remembers to take the altitude into consideration," Lucy said.

"Moving on, will you be joining us for the screening tonight?" Nora asked. "Whitney told me that we'll be seeing a future *Chasers* episode—we're the only ones who get to see it before the show comes back on air after the holidays."

Lucy's eyes lit up. "Really? I love that."

We were all fans of the show, as was most of the world. Having Whitney be our guest of honor was quite the coup for Nora. The tickets purchased for the gala had surpassed previous years by at least fifty percent. According to my aunt, Tabitha enjoyed taking all the credit at the committee meetings, but everyone knew that Nora was responsible for the most important aspect: The Big-Name Get.

"What else can I do to help this week?" I asked.

"Me too," said Lucy. "Max and Bella asked for extra shifts since they're on break from school and trying to earn some extra money, so I have a bit more freedom than usual." Our part-time student workers were like members of the family; we'd had a holiday party the week before at the bookstore and I could still remember their delighted expressions when they unwrapped their Starlit Bookshop messenger bags: the very first items in our branded "bookwear" line that we were trying out, made of environmentally friendly materials. In our new Book Nook Corner, we now offered satchels, backpacks, sling bags, and totes—along with tees, hoodies, and caps—embossed with the Starlit Bookshop logo, a shooting star.

As if reading my mind, Nora commented on how happy they'd seemed with their gifts this year.

"I hope you know how much I appreciate everything," Lucy said. "In a few months, we've gone from practically closing our doors to having record sales, an exciting lineup of future events, and even, thanks to your creative vision, merch."

"Merch?" I laughed.

"Yeah, that's how I talk now," she said. "But stop making fun of me so I can compliment you, please."

I shook my head. "We did it together. If Nora hadn't taken over the mortgage, and if you hadn't made managing it your priority, we wouldn't even have a store anymore."

"It feels like a fresh start since you've been back," she said softly. "And I for one am grateful. Thank you for coming home after you graduated."

"Thanks for having me. I'm so happy that we're together again."

There was a moment of silence. The absence of my parents hung, unspoken, like a gossamer web, over us. We all carried that pain, two years after they hadn't returned from a trip overseas—especially here, in the home we'd shared.

My eyes welled up, as they did during instances like this when the combined threads of our grief intertwined unexpectedly.

"Enough of *that*," Nora said briskly, with a swipe at her eyes. "Anyone want a cup of cocoa by the tree?"

Lucy raised her hand.

"I'll make it," I said.

Lights twinkled softly on the Douglas fir in the corner that we had decorated with the shining glass ornaments my grandmother had made over the years. My grandparents were artists of various mediums—like my parents. They'd settled in the charming, quirky Victorian on the edge of the Silvercrest River, drawn by the small town's reputation as a haven for artists. They opened Starlit Bookshop, which had been the main family business ever since, but continued their artistic pursuits on the side.

I cleared the table and washed the dishes, then poured cocoa mix into clean mugs while the kettle heated. As the water came to a boil, thrumming louder and louder, I thought of the teaching offer I'd turned down to come home and help Lucy get the bookstore on track. All I'd ever wanted to do was land a job on the tenure track and begin my college teaching career. Correction: All I'd ever wanted to do was become a professor at Silvercrest College specifically, which was right down the street. I'd grown up running around on campus; I knew it like the back of my hand. Nora had been there for thirty years, balancing her teaching with a very successful career as a mystery novelist at the same time. Admiring her beyond measure my whole life may have had something to do with my having chosen the same path. Although I no longer could see teaching in my future, I was working on my first novel nonetheless, which was still following in some of her footsteps. And I had always loved working at the bookstore, so perhaps it was the best of both worlds.

The whistle shrieked at the same time that I realized that I was supposed to be responding to pages from the members of the writing group I'd joined, West Side Writers. Cocoa first, though. I snatched the kettle up, poured water and stirred, then delivered mugs to my sister and aunt, who were on either end of the long couch. I sat down in the old velvet wingback chair next to the tree.

"So what's the schedule for Gala Week?" Lucy asked.

Nora blew on her cocoa, then set it on the table beside her. "Tonight is the screening, as you know. Tabitha wouldn't let any of us participate. Not sure what to expect. Could be fantastic, could be a disaster. You never know with that one." My aunt hadn't ever warmed fully to Tabitha, whose country club clique had made everyone's lives miserable for years, but the way she spoke about her now was definitely several degrees cooler than before. Working on the same committee was clearly taking a toll. "Same with the auction. And it's always difficult to know until we see the bills whether Lyra did the work since Tabitha claims it all, somehow."

"She was certainly surprised at the tea when Calliope took the stage," I said, smiling.

"What happened?" Lucy asked.

My aunt described Tabitha's reaction and soon we were all giggling.

"I would have given anything to see that," Lucy said. "I love when karma takes charge and pays her back for all her years of pushing everyone around. Though it's never enough, somehow, to stop her awfulness."

"Remember when she stole your butterfly painting that you were bringing home from art class in ninth grade?" I asked.

"She threw it out the window of the bus!" Lucy said indignantly.

"Maybe this tiny upset was payback for that. Though your painting was worth *way* more than that. It was gorgeous."

"Maybe she'll get a flat tire," Lucy said hopefully.

Nora laughed.

Lucy's eyes widened. "Sorry—I can't believe I said that. I would *never* wish anything bad on anyone."

"Not even Tabitha Baxter? And not even just between us?" Nora inquired with a straight face.

She shook her head miserably.

"Ok, darling, we'll stop teasing. And you didn't wish it on her—you just imagined a possibility—so you're fine." My aunt cleared her throat. "So in addition to the screening, we will host the mystery panel at the store, then there's a tour at the new ballroom, a run-through once everyone arrives in town, and a pre-gala dinner. Oh, and we'll need to pick up our gowns at the vintage store. Marlowe's holding them for us, which is good since everyone in town will be descending to find that one-of-a-kind piece, if they haven't already."

Lucy brightened. "This is going to be *so* much fun. I need to run back to the store, but please pick me up on the way to the screening."

"Will do," I said.

We toasted with our cocoa as the sun came out from behind a cloud, illuminating the snow falling quietly from the sky.

Chapter Three

A few hours later, Nora and I hurried along the icy sidewalks, pulling our coats closer to keep out the cutting wind, until we arrived at Starlit Bookshop and stepped gratefully into the warm, familiar space. The whimsical stained glass panel that my father had made, with a star representing each family member, divided the first and second floor display windows and never failed to make me smile.

My sister and I had grown up chasing each other around the bookshelves on the main floor and scampering up and down the ladder that moved along iron tracks on the side shelves. Now we ran the place. Sometimes it was hard to believe.

I waved at Lucy, who was finishing up her work in the office, and moved past the wall mirrors in white ornate frames and damask chairs in colorful jewel tones toward the back, where I climbed the spiral staircase and circled the second-floor mezzanine, open to the lower level. I'd left my scarf here, having been focused on getting to the library tea on time, and wanted to add it back into my cold-weather-shielding efforts. Once I'd located the bright pink wool material on a shelf near the front, I wrapped it around my neck, descended again, and joined my aunt and sister, now chatting near the register, with the row of famous authors captured in black-and-white photos diligently keeping their watch over the shelves from their frames.

"Hi, everyone!" Bella Perkins emerged from the stockroom and joined us. She was wearing a tunic-length Silvercrest College sweatshirt over leggings and ankle boots. Her blonde hair was pulled up in a high ponytail. "Have fun at the screening."

"Come by after closing if you have time," Lucy told her.

"I might do that. I don't have any homework, praise be, and I'd love to meet the actors." She smiled at a customer who placed a teetering pile of books on the counter, then began ringing things up.

The rest of us went back out into the arctic gale and hustled several blocks to Bluestone, a restaurant on the main drag of River Street. It was a popular location, and we could tell as soon as we opened the door, almost at capacity. Nora stopped to say hello to someone while Lucy slipped quickly through the crowd and just beat out a man with an unforgettably large and droopy mustache to snag the very last wooden table in the back, practically in the hallway that led to the kitchen. Her competitor looked disappointed and trudged away. I made my way past the other guests and more than the usual amount of large potted plants—the owner had famously described his décor style to a news reporter at the grand opening as "ferny"—then unwound my scarf, peeled off my coat, and joined her.

Our aunt appeared and piled her things unceremoniously onto an empty chair. "I'm going to say hello to Whitney and Lyra. Want to come?"

"Is Lyra handling the food tonight too?" I asked.

Nora laughed. "There is no food. Tabitha decided that we would all get popcorn and candy. You know, movie treats. For authenticity, she said. In any case, I believe Tabitha has the two of them stashed in the kitchen."

"Why are they in the kitchen?" I asked, confused.

"They wanted to stay out of the dining area until it was time for Whitney to be introduced. And since no one is cooking tonight, the kitchen was free."

"How did you even know they were in there?"

"I have connections." She winked. "Meaning that Whitney texted me."

"I bet Tabitha wouldn't like to know that you're communicating with *her* guest," I teased.

"Tabitha can lump it," Nora said firmly.

"I'll stay here," Lucy said. "Ryan will be joining us, and I want to save him a seat." She'd only been dating Ryan Mahoney for a few months, but it was serious. They'd been friends for a long time beforehand—we'd discovered that he had tried to work up the nerve to ask her out for a year before he actually did. They already acted like an old married couple.

"Be right back." Nora said.

We went down the long hallway and turned left. The double doors were swinging slightly, and she gave one a push inward. I followed her into the gleaming kitchen, which had white subway tiles on the wall, shining silver appliances, and spotless cement floors.

"Hello!" Whitney gave Nora a hug, then greeted me warmly. Although we'd grown up in the same town, she was at least ten years older and Lyra was almost ten years younger, so we hadn't really known each other. It had been a pleasure to connect as adults.

Lyra looked up from her phone and smiled. She pushed a trio of metal pots down the counter and hopped up to sit there, her legs swinging as she typed. The aunt and niece looked more like twins than ever, an impression helped along by the fact that they were both wearing white puffer vests over red sweaters, along with jeans and boots.

"Do you like my hair?" Whitney twirled around to show us a long plait tied with a black ribbon. "Lyra and I had a braiding session. I think it came out pretty well, don't you?"

Lyra laughed. She had the same healthy sense of well-being that Whitney exuded. Maybe it was something in the California air. "We had to figure out a way to cover the giant bump from my cupcake crash."

"Are you feeling okay?" I asked her.

Her cheeks tinged with pink. "Yes, so much better, thank you. Just embarrassed mostly."

"And she has a terrible headache," Whitney added. "Poor thing."

"Still can't believe I did that in front of everyone." Lyra's blush grew deeper.

"Don't worry about that," I said. "I constantly bump into things in public. People forget."

Lyra gave me a grateful smile.

"Do you need anything?" Nora asked them.

Whitney and Lyra looked at each other, then at Nora, shaking their heads.

"You know that I'm here for you all week. Text me anytime," she told them.

Whitney rolled her eyes. "Tabitha said that she wants to be my . . . what did she call it?"

"Primary point of contact," Lyra said. "And she stressed the *primary* part."

Nora, to her credit, didn't laugh.

"We meet people like her all the time," Lyra went on. "They want to get close to my aunt here and keep her to themselves as much as possible."

Whitney nodded.

"Would you take a picture of us, please?" She slid down and handed a large phone out to me.

They posed with big smiles, arms around each other. I clicked the camera button and then handed the cell back to Lyra.

"Thank you. I get a little tired of selfies," she said. "It's nice to have an old-school one."

Taking a picture of another person was old school? Okay.

Whitney peeked over her shoulder. "You are gorgeous, girl."

"Says one of America's Most Beautiful People."

Whitney shook her head. "It's all smoke and mirrors. Takes me hours of makeup to look like you do naturally."

Lyra rolled her eyes.

"I'm serious," Whitney told her. "Enjoy the magic of youth while you can, sweetie."

Lyra blew her a kiss.

"We'd better go back," Nora said. "Have fun tonight. Or maybe that's not the right word since it's work."

Whitney smiled. "Thank you. It's hard to relax sometimes, but I'll try."

"I can understand that," Nora said.

"*I* think it's fun," Lyra said.

"You don't have to go onstage in front of everyone," her aunt said. "It's so stressful. I always feel like I'm going to say the wrong thing."

"You never do," Lyra assured her.

"I'm better when someone has given me a script to memorize, you know? Like right now, I'm shaking." Whitney held out her hand, which was indeed trembling.

"It's the adrenaline," Lyra said. "No worries. You'll be terrific."

"We'll leave you to it, then," Nora said, catching my eye.

In the hallway, we passed Calliope, who was chatting with the mustache man from earlier. We said hello. Still in her trench coat outfit, she tipped her fedora.

Nora waved at someone and sped up a few steps ahead of us.

"Good evening, Raven," Calliope said, using a nickname she'd given me when we'd worked on the Poe party last fall. "Are you as excited to see my story come alive as I am?"

"We all are," I assured her. "You haven't seen the episode yet?"

"Oh no. But all my chakras are open and ready. I'm shaking with anticipation. As are my necklaces." She indicated the various chunky stones around her neck. "They are singing in harmony, though, so I have no fears that it will be anything other than sheer perfection. Enjoy." Calliope sailed away.

When we arrived back at the table, a weary young man with artfully messed brown hair was unloading three stemmed cocktail glasses, a large woven basket of popcorn, and boxes of candy from his tray.

"We didn't order these—" Lucy began, shaking one oversized box.

"Everyone gets the same thing for Cocktails and *Chasers*." He wiped his hand on the apron below the white button-down shirt and black bow tie combo and sighed. "And yes, I know that it doesn't make sense because a chaser implies *two* drinks per person—the main drink and the one following it. The following part is *literally* what chaser means. But I'm not in charge, and no one asked me. Also, we're not serving any other food tonight. I'm sorry, okay?"

We all nodded, and he left to deliver more cocktails with a side of legitimate complaints to other patrons.

"I'm fine with this . . . whatever it is." Nora held her glass full of opaque white liquid up in the light and peered at it, then brought it under her nose for a delicate sniff.

I went right ahead and took a sip. "Peachy."

Lucy tasted hers and smacked her lips. "That is heavenly. Peaches and cream, I think. But why isn't it more orange?"

"It's a mystery," Nora said. "But a delicious one."

"Welcome, everyone, welcome!" The amplified voice caused the crowd to fall into a hush. We looked toward the front of the restaurant, where a large movie screen had been draped across the red brick. Our host stood on a narrow riser that had been placed before it. "I'm Tabitha Baxter. Thank you for joining us for Cocktails and *Chasers*! We hope that you've already bought your tickets for your table at the gala to be held on Friday at Silvercrest College's newly renovated Baxter Ballroom!"

"*Baxter* Ballroom?" Nora said wonderingly.

"That's news," I added. "Did they announce that to the faculty?"

She shook her head.

Tabitha continued. "The president has decided to name it after my darling Tip, the previous dean of Arts and Humanities, whom we lost so suddenly in October."

I froze. Tabitha had accused my family before of having killed him. And although the murderer had since been revealed, she was not known for letting go of a grudge, whether the initial offense was real or imaginary. So whenever he was mentioned in public, we held our breath.

There was an awkward pause, then a round of respectful applause.

"Baxter Ballroom will be the home of many events in the future. Please be sure to subscribe to the college newsletter so that you won't miss any exciting announcements." She launched into a description of several activities happening in the spring.

"She certainly has a gift for never missing an opportunity to advertise," Nora murmured to us.

"And I bet she never changes her last name again," Lucy said. "Baxter will forevermore have the most status if it's carved on the door of that ballroom."

I considered this. "I'm not so sure about that. Tabitha Louise Saxton Lyme Harmon Gladstone Baxter clearly loves to get married."

"Perhaps the fifth time will be a charm," Nora added.

The bride in question told a rambling story about how she and Whitney were practically BFFs as a result of all the planning phone calls. Even she appeared surprised at where she'd gone to at that point and managed to reel herself back on track with a pivot toward Whitney's biography, including the many titles of films and television shows in which she had appeared. She went down the long list slowly, then defiantly added a "without further ado," even though the ado had gone so much further than anyone could have possibly wanted.

Tabitha did a little hop. "Come on up here, girl! Whitney Willton, everyone!"

Whitney joined her on the riser and waved to the audience. The clapping went on for a while, during which she maintained her same beautiful smile. She took the microphone from Tabitha.

"Thank you for the warm welcome. It means so much to me. And now I have a secret for you . . ."

Tabitha blinked rapidly. Clearly, she had no idea what Whitney was talking about.

"Here we go." Whitney waved at someone at a nearby table. A dark-haired man in a flannel shirt and jeans moved toward her. Before he stepped onto the riser, he pulled off the baseball cap that had been pulled down low and spun around. His strong body and shaggy hair brought to mind a friendly bear.

The audience went wild as Whitney said, "My co-host and dear friend, Nat Fabulous!"

Nat was grinning madly as he took a bow, then opened both of his arms and soaked up the applause and cheers. Whitney laughed and held out her own arms. He embraced her and lifted her off the ground in a twirl.

After they coasted to a stop, he took the microphone and said, "And please welcome the marvelous Stella Vane, co-host number three!"

A flawlessly made-up woman in a cloak and tall boots emerged from the shadows along the back wall. She leaped easily onto the riser to join the others, throwing back both sides of the cloak to reveal a sequined catsuit and tossing her long platinum hair over her shoulder before striking a power pose.

The audience went wild again.

"Hello, everyone! So happy to be here," she said brightly.

Tabitha slid over to Stella and held out her hand for the mic, nodding benevolently, as if she'd been in on the plan for them to promote each other to co-host with Whitney.

"Isn't that fantastic?" she said to the crowd, though her left eye was twitching. "Let's get on to the screening, shall we?"

Nora laughed. "She's not going to let them say anything else?"

"Guess not." Lucy shook her head.

"Typical," I agreed. Anything that took the attention off of Tabitha was not generally something she welcomed. I couldn't imagine what was going on inside her head at the news that her host was becoming a triad of co-hosts . . . it was probably a bubbling lava of fury in there.

The stars didn't seem to mind that Tabitha had basically snubbed them. They waved to the crowd and jumped off the riser as the lights went down. After a moment, the upbeat notes of the *Chasers* theme song began. There was a short, funny teaser followed by a title sequence, then the episode proper opened with Whitney, Nat, and Stella trading witty banter—soon the audience was laughing along with them. We all settled in for a very funny, very enjoyable viewing.

After almost an hour, I heard what sounded like a muffled thump behind me. It must have come from the back of the building. I looked around the corner and down the hallway, but no one was there. The rest of the audience didn't seem to have heard anything.

"I'll be right back," I said quietly to Nora.

I slipped down the hallway and through the double doors that led to the kitchen. Inside, Nat was supporting Whitney, who was leaning against him.

"What happened?" I asked.

Whitney pointed to the silver chest freezer on the far side of the room.

With a sense of foreboding, I moved closer.

I could just barely see four fingers visible below the lid, as if they were clutching the outer edge of the freezer.

From the inside.

Chapter Four

I ran over and flung open the top.

Lyra was lying there, motionless. Her eyes were blank and her lips were blue.

I gasped and stepped back.

"She isn't breathing and doesn't have a pulse." Nat waved his phone. "We already called 911. They said not to move her and not to touch anything."

"Not even try to warm her up in case—" I asked.

"No," he said. "It's too late."

"Hello?" A disembodied voice said. "Are you still there?"

"Yes. What are we supposed to do?" Tears streamed down Whitney's cheeks and she began to wail. "Please can I close the lid again? I can't bear to see her like that."

"No. Leave everything alone," the voice advised. "I'm sorry. As long as you're safe, we need you to stay there. You can turn around if you need to. The police are on the way."

As they talked to the dispatcher, I stared at Lyra, who was terribly beautiful in her stillness, like a stone statue.

My heart hurt.

I turned around and took in the scene. There were no signs of struggle; the windows were closed and the shades were down, so it didn't look as though anyone had come in through them. A pair of glass cutting boards and two pots waited next to the stove, the butcher block triangle that held the knives remained full, and every hook had either a ladle, spatula, or whisk on it. Nothing seemed to be out of place.

"Why is everyone in *here*?" Stella asked as she came rushing in from the hallway, followed by Ariel.

"Lyra?" At the sight of her friend, Ariel stopped short and her mouth fell open.

"What's going on?" Stella's gaze moved back and forth between Lyra's body and Whitney and Nat just standing there. She looked questioningly at me.

"They found her like this. The police are coming. We're not supposed to touch anything." I didn't know what else to say.

"No, we have to help her!" Ariel cried, running over to the freezer. She reached down and recoiled. "She's so cold."

"I'm sorry, sweetie," Whitney said. "She's gone."

Soon, the three women were huddled together, crying. Nat patted their backs, one by one.

I became aware of the fluorescent lights buzzing and flickering, and everything felt even stranger, if that was possible. My body wanted to flee, to escape this uncanny sensation, but we had to wait.

Eventually, the medical examiner and police arrived. After securing the area, an officer asked us to follow him to the dining room, which had been cleared of civilians. We were seated at different tables, facing the street; Whitney was next to me, and the others were at tables behind us. The officer checked our IDs and gave us forms to fill out our statements. He strolled around gazing suspiciously at us from time to time. It felt oddly as though we were taking an exam. Nora and Lucy kept texting me, but I didn't dare reply.

It was excruciating to see Whitney grieve so deeply. She was weeping, rocking back and forth with hands over her eyes. I heard multiple people sniffing behind us, as if they were also crying or at least holding back tears. I was shaky and my stomach wobbled every time the image of Lyra in the coffin-like freezer ran through my mind, which didn't seem to know what to do with it other than to show it to me again and again.

Movement through the front windows caught my eye. A crowd was gathered in front of Bluestone—Nora had her hands on either side of her face and was peering through the glass. She lifted her shoulders, asking what was going on. I pointed to our house and mouthed that I would see them later. She said something to Lucy and Ryan; all three turned to leave.

"Starrs." A tall man with short, spiky brown hair and what I'd always thought of as sea-green eyes slid into the chair across from me. He was wearing a navy suit over a light blue button-down shirt. His badge was around his neck on a chain, resting on a burgundy tie with small ivory medallions.

"Hollister," I said with relief, though I managed to temper my tone. Jake and I had reconnected, after I'd "helped" (his word) solve (my word) Tip Baxter's murder. He was both a detective and a thriller writer, and I had to admit that his feedback on my mystery in progress, delivered at the meetings of the West Side Writers group he'd invited me to join, had been very useful.

"What do you know about this?" He pulled out a rectangular notepad and flipped open the black cover. His cheekbones were as high as ever.

I shook my head. "Nothing, Jake."

He drew his eyebrows together. "Let's start at the beginning. What happened in the kitchen that made my colleagues think I should talk to you?"

"Lyra was in the freezer," I said, then I stopped.

"And?"

"And that's it." What else was there to say?

"How did you see her?"

"While we were watching the episode, I heard what sounded like a sort of muffled thump."

"What do you think it was?"

"Maybe the freezer lid closing after Nat and Whitney found her?" I guessed. "It was very heavy."

"Not the freezer lid closing after they put her in there?" he countered.

I shook my head. "If they did put her in, why would they then stand around and wait to be caught? Why wouldn't they take off?"

Jake took this in. "I mean, they could have been pretending. That's what they do for a living. Here's a question: Why didn't anyone else go running to the kitchen?"

"I can't explain that. Maybe it was because I was sitting in the very back and others didn't hear. Maybe I only did it because the last few times I heard an unexpected sound, bad things were actually happening, so I took it more seriously. It does tend to change your perspective on things."

"You mean with the murders last fall? Understood." He shifted in his seat. "So you were with Whitney and Nat in the kitchen. What was their demeanor?"

"Upset. Shaken. She was crying."

"Did you touch anything?"

I shot him a look. "No. Nothing other than the freezer lid."

"Because last time—"

"No. I didn't touch anything else, okay? And last time . . . never mind." I crossed my arms in front of me, then quickly uncrossed them again. I knew that trained officers read body language and I didn't want it to look like I was hiding something, even though I was merely annoyed. Jake could get under my skin faster than anyone else I knew. It had always been that way—I didn't know why. Maybe from all the competitions for editor of the paper and scholarships and other opportunities.

Maybe not.

He made a note, and I craned my neck to try and see what it was. He slowly raised the pad cover to block my gaze.

I coughed.

The corner of his mouth quirked up. "Was there anything unusual that you noticed in the kitchen?"

"Aside from Lyra?"

He nodded.

I thought back to the scene. Something was tugging at the back of my mind, some detail that registered as different, but I couldn't quite pull it forward.

He waited, his eyes fixed on mine.

"Sorry," I said eventually.

"More generally, is there anything else you think is important? I read your statement but—"

"You read it? Then why are you asking me the same questions I already answered?"

"It's what we do." He grinned.

"Because you don't trust me?" I crossed my arms, then wrenched them apart again.

"No, because sometimes telling the story more than once helps you think of additional details."

"You mean that it gives the suspect a chance to slip up."

"Or that."

I stared at him. "Suspect? You don't think *I* did something to Lyra."

He shrugged. "I don't prejudge things."

"Seriously, Hollister? You've known me forever. You don't think for one hot second that I could be capable of killing someone, do you?"

"Technically, everyone is capable." He looked over his shoulder on both sides, then leaned forward. "Starrs, I'm just doing my job. Questions must be asked. Boxes must be checked. There's a whole process."

"Please proceed, then." I tried not to notice how nice he smelled—it was a heady combination of forest and soap.

"How well do you know the celebrities?"

"Not at all. My aunt used to babysit for Whitney, from what I gather, but I only met them this week for the first time."

He dipped his head and scribbled something else down.

I couldn't imagine what.

"How many times have you seen them this week?"

"This morning at the tea, then again tonight."

"Anything unusual happen at the tea?"

I laughed.

He raised his eyebrows.

"You keep using that phrase. Maybe I should buy you a T-shirt that says 'anything unusual?' so you could pull open your jacket whenever you interrogate someone. You know, like a superhero."

Jake made a face.

"Sorry. It appears that I'm getting punchy now that the adrenaline is fading."

"No problem. Now . . . about the tea . . ."

"Right. Anything unusual." I tapped a finger as I thought. "Lyra fainted in front of everyone. She was carrying a tray and stumbled, then she hit her head on our table and sort of melted onto the floor."

"She hit her head?" He made a note.

"Oh, yes, good point. Nora said people were keeping an eye on Lyra in case of a concussion. Do you think it could have kicked in later or something?"

"We'll look into it."

"Word on the street was that it was altitude sickness," I told him. "By which I mean that a doctor suggested that diagnosis to Nora."

"Interesting," he murmured. "And how would you characterize the interactions among the three of them, from what you've observed?"

"Since this morning?"

Now it was his turn to sigh. "Whatever you got."

"I'd say that they all seemed to get along very well. Genuinely affectionate with each other. And Whitney was palpably grieving during the whole time."

He stroked his chin thoughtfully. "Again, she acts for a living."

"You don't seriously think—"

"I think anything is possible, Starrs."

Chapter Five

When I got home, I stayed up late filling Nora and Lucy in on what had happened. They asked question after question until we'd covered every aspect of the evening in detail. My brain still wanted to process everything during the night, though. I tossed and turned, and there was no sleeping because every time I closed my eyes, I saw Lyra's pale, still form. I stared at the ceiling, replaying the night in my mind. The shock had blurred the edges of my memories, giving me only fragmented images and uncertainty. What was it in the back of my mind that seemed important yet elusive?

The next morning, as I rinsed and put away my breakfast plate, my aunt's phone buzzed.

Nora looked up from her cell. "Will you come with me right now to an emergency gala committee meeting at the library? As our resident event planner, you may be able to see things that the rest of us can't."

"Oh, I'm sure Tabitha has it figured out."

"She doesn't. We need you, darling. Will you please help us?"

"Of course I'll help you."

Her smile lit up the drafty room.

"Want to walk over together?" I asked. "It's supposed to be warmer today."

She looked out the window and agreed. Winter in Colorado went from one extreme to another. Snowstorm one day, spring-like temperatures the next. The wind had died down and the sun shone on the drifts—by afternoon, they'd be melted. The river, which had been frozen over for the past week, had patches of melted ice through which the water underneath was slowly flowing. A tiny brown rabbit hopped along the crust of snow near our wrap-around porch, leaving footprints that would soon disappear in the sun.

But it could start snowing again at any time.

We both dressed in layers and donned our coats. Our destination was only a few blocks south, next to the community center on the east side of the street. It was cool enough that our breath launched little puffs into the air as we walked, but it was quite refreshing, in its own way.

The library roof was still kissed with snow. Inside, we climbed the long, curved stairs to the second level and moved toward the lovely room where the tea had been held. Just before we walked in, I touched Nora's arm and pointed down the short hallway on the right.

She had a quizzical expression but gamely swerved as I led her through doorway into the kitchen.

"Are we gathering snacks?" she inquired.

I laughed. "No. I want to have a look around. You know, because Lyra worked in here. Probably a long shot, but since we're here . . ."

She nodded and moved slowly with me around the bright space. It was filled with industrial-sized appliances—two stoves, two dishwashers, and two freezers. The stainless steel island had a dual-dish embedded sink. A large clock resided on the wall dividing floor-to-ceiling windows.

A quick scan confirmed that the counters were empty.

"It would've made everything so much easier if there was a bottle sitting out with a skull-and-bones on the label," I said.

"Or a treasure map."

"Are we pirates now?"

She pointed at me. "You're the one who brought up the skull-and-bones thing."

"I meant that as a warning symbol. For poison?"

"Ah. But don't pirates use that too?"

"You got me there. Let's dig around a bit." I checked the cabinets and drawers while she inspected the refrigerator.

"Anything?"

"No." She sounded as disappointed as I felt.

The last drawer I opened was what my grandmother would have called a "junk drawer" for odds and ends. I sifted through rubber bands, pencils, paper clips, erasers, and several rulers until I touched a piece of paper.

Nora appeared at my side. "What does it say?"

"It's a business card," I said, looking down at the cheery red bird graphic in the center. "No name or address, though."

She reached out her hand to take it and turned it over. "Ah."

"Did you find something? A number or, even better, a secret code?"

"A date and time—February first at ten AM. I know what this is. We have cards at school with just the crest on the front, so we can make notes for students during advising sessions, or jot down suggestions at college fairs. Sometimes we use them for appointments. Things like that."

"Why don't you just use notepads? Or use your own business cards?"

"Tradition."

"Carry on."

Nora looked down at it. "You'd think if it had been lying in that drawer for a while, it would have rubbed against the pencils and whatnot. Picked up some smudges. This looks like it just came out of the printing press."

I smiled. "Printing press?"

"Hush, you. I'm old." She returned the card, and I slipped it back into the drawer. "Wait, aren't you going to take it?"

"It doesn't belong to me."

"Well done, darling. Very honest. Though now that I think about it, sleuths steal things all the time in our beloved mysteries. How come no one ever complains about all the thieveries?"

"I don't know. Perhaps there's a special universal exclusion for genuine clues?"

My aunt tapped her cheek, as she often did while pondering. "But that raises the question: How does someone know if it's an authentic clue or only a potential clue?"

"Maybe the *belief* that it is a clue puts it into the acceptable-for-plundering category."

She laughed. "There you go with your pirate lingo again."

"It's wholly unintentional." I closed the drawer.

"Wait." She pulled the drawer open again. "Take a picture. Isn't that what you young people do to capture the moment every other second anyway?"

"I'm not really a selfie person. As you know."

"Not a selfie, Emma. A documentation of the drawer contents. In case you need to circle back."

"Good idea." I didn't know why I hadn't thought of that. Then I remembered that *she* was, in fact, a selfie person. Or at least an experienced selfie subject. Her social media streams were filled with pictures of Nora and her many reader fans.

I snapped a few shots, reaching in to swirl the items around several times like I was stirring a bowl of sauce.

"Ready?" She asked, brushing off her sleeves.

"As I'll ever be."

We went back through the swinging door and strolled in serenely, as if we hadn't just been rifling madly through everything in the next room.

Tabitha, Melody, and Trevor were already seated at one of the round tables, in animated conversation. As we drew closer, Tabitha looked up abruptly.

"Thank you for coming," she said, though she didn't sound very thankful. More like irritated.

I checked my watch. We were two minutes early, so it wasn't that.

"Please sit down and join us," Trevor said, smiling. "We're trying to make some decisions about what we're going to do."

We did as he said, draping our coats on the back of the chairs.

"I thought Emma might be able to help us think through this," Nora said.

"Excellent," Trevor replied.

Tabitha ignored us, but Paisley, her Yorkshire terrier, yipped hello from the giant bag on the ground next to her. Her bow was black, matching Tabitha's suit. When Tabitha reached down and patted her head, Paisley slid lower and lower until she disappeared from sight.

"Cannot *believe* that we are in this position. Not very professional," Tabitha said, as if she believed that Lyra had brought about her own demise on purpose.

"I don't think professionalism is the issue, exactly," Melody said.

"Thanks for the support, Mel," Tabitha snapped at her.

Melody looked down at the table.

"It's hardly Lyra's fault," Nora said.

"How do we *know* that?"

Trevor's eyebrows shot up in surprise.

"Sorry, sorry, sorry." Tabitha sounded passably contrite. "I'm beside myself. And it is tragic. Poor Whitney."

Trevor's eyes widened.

"And Lyra too, of course," she added quickly. "By the way, we are invited to Malina's house tomorrow evening. She wants to be with people who knew and loved Lyra, especially since Whitney and the other celebrities are already in Silvercrest."

There were nods around the room.

"*Anyway*," Tabitha said as a transition back to work.

Trevor took her up on it. "So we've lost our party planner and her entire team. They're not going to fly out anymore, right? Are we sure?"

"That's what their email said." Tabitha rustled through her folder and held up a sheet of paper. "But there's nothing in their contract that gives them an option to cancel on us if . . . "

"If their leader is no longer available," Melody inserted smoothly.

An attempt at tact was new for Melody. Good for her.

"We've already given them a down payment," Tabitha went on. "They can't back out now. As the leader of this committee, I can continue to do the heavy lifting—as you know, the overall management of a gala is quite an extraordinary burden."

I wouldn't have been surprised to see her pat her own back.

"While I could personally work with our caterer to keep things running smoothly, it's just *so much* to add on top of what I'm already doing. Lyra and her team were certainly earning their fee."

Which translated into doing the majority of the actual work while she took the credit.

Trevor scratched his chin. "How much did you give Lyra already?"

Tabitha showed him a page that must have had a shocking amount on it because he paled before our very eyes.

Melody tilted her head and Tabitha showed her the amount too. Her nostrils flared but she remained silent.

"I don't mind funding the costs up front," Tabitha said. "It's part of the process."

"It is a problem," Trevor said, "given that this is supposed to be a fundraising effort. We can't start over again, can we? Would they refund—"

"It says nonrefundable right there." Melody pointed at the bottom.

"But surely that can't hold true if they deliver nothing at all that was promised to us," Trevor protested.

"Have you spoken to anyone at the company on the phone?" Nora asked.

"That's so . . . old-fashioned," Tabitha said. "Planning is typically done by email and text these days."

"Do you have a number? We may as well give it a try," Nora said. "But what's the goal here? Do you want her team to come or not to come?"

"We want them to come and finish the project," Melody said irritably. "Obviously."

"But if they refuse, then obviously we want our deposit back," Tabitha said.

"Obviously," Trevor echoed.

"Let me see what I can do," Nora said.

Tabitha slowly shuffled through her papers and pulled out a single page, which she shook. Nora took the paper and her phone over to the window, pointedly away from prying ears and potential disruptions.

Trevor raised his hand. "I have a question."

Tabitha gave him the type of smile you give a child who has been babbling on for too long and you just want them to stop. "What's that?"

"Could we cancel the gala and do something else instead?"

Melody covered her mouth.

"Cancel? Of course not. It's *tradition*," Tabitha said firmly. "And very lucrative for the library's budget. You need this, Trevor."

"Couldn't we have . . ." He trailed off in the face of her disapproval, but she rolled her hand quickly around, urging him to continue.

"A potluck?" he finished.

Tabitha looked horrified.

"Or a pancake breakfast?"

Melody snorted.

Tabitha leaned forward on her elbows, invading his personal space. "I know you're new here, Trev, and I'm not sure if you understand how much money you need. The crème de la crème of Silvercrest will be in attendance at this gala, ready to shell out a great deal of money to keep your library here in tip-top shape. Do you even have any idea how much it would cost to repair just one of the chairs on the main floor? They are *antiques*. They should be in a *museum*. You are so lucky to have this job, surrounded by these jewels of Silvercrest *history*. So please don't tell me how to do the gala work, okay? I have been put in charge of it because everyone knows that I always raise the most money, and I intend to do it right."

He swallowed hard.

Melody watched him carefully.

"Tabitha, really," I said. "Was that necessary?"

She slowly turned her head in my direction, like the beast in one of those horror movies who realizes there is someone else to go after.

"Yes, it's *necessary*," she snapped. "We are in the throes of a crisis. And what does it matter to you, anyway? Isn't the library competition to your bookstore?"

I shook my head. "The library is not our competition—we are collaborators in the greater project of making books available to all, of encouraging readers everywhere. And I'm here because Nora asked me to come. I plan events, as you may remember, and she thought I could be of service."

Trevor began clapping, then stopped abruptly when Tabitha glared at him. He pulled out a cloth handkerchief from a pocket and mopped his brow with it.

"Do you mean *you* could take over for Lyra?" Tabitha asked.

"Oh no," I said, putting my hands up. "I just meant that I could help sort out next steps."

"Good." Tabitha tittered. "Because the gala is a much larger and more complicated event than your little bookstore launch parties."

"I've planned conferences before too," I said, shrugging.

She paused at that. "How many attendees?"

"We had five hundred or so at the last one."

Trevor looked back and forth between us. "How many people will be at our gala?"

"Two hundred, give or take," Tabitha said primly. "There are *millions* more who would kill to make the list, obviously, but we like to keep it intimate."

"Wouldn't having more people there increase the fundraising opportunities?" I asked.

"But then it wouldn't be the hottest ticket in town," Tabitha said through gritted teeth over which she attempted—and failed—to fashion a smile. "The limited number is what makes it so special. Simple economics, Emma."

"Whatever you think is best," I said.

"But why can't *you* do it, Emma? That's a perfect solution," Trevor said, rallying back from Tabitha's squashing of his ideas. "Granted, it would be a big job, taking over the planning—and we will pay you handsomely for it."

"I don't know if we need Emma," Tabitha said doubtfully.

"We were going to pay Lyra for doing the same thing," Trevor reminded her. "You surely thought you needed her."

Something moved behind her eyes, then she exploded. "You think you should take over one of *my* events, Emma? Last time I let you slide into a job, *my husband died*."

"But that wasn't her fault," Melody said. "You *know* who did it."

I gave her a grateful look. Maybe there were lines that Melody wouldn't cross, after all.

Meanwhile, her bestie was giving dagger eyes.

Tabitha sat up straighter and brushed something off her sleeve. "Be that as it may, you're not the person for this particular job, Emma."

"That's fine." I didn't even want the job.

Though the money from a successful gala would help the library.

And the bit I received would help the bookstore.

"Update time." Nora returned to the table and handed Tabitha the invoice. "Lyra's people are in no position to do this event. They've lost their boss, which means, as far as I can tell, that they've lost their jobs too. I spoke at length with her assistant, who finally agreed to take the cost of the tea—with a generous tip—out of the down payment and return the rest."

Tabitha nodded stiffly. "Thank you."

"And might I suggest that you do let Emma step up to the plate? As you noted earlier, you only have a few days to pull this gala off."

Trevor clasped his hands together, looking hopeful.

Tabitha's perfectly plucked eyebrows were drawn together. "Why do I need her? I already have a caterer. If Vivi Yang would just return one of my many texts, I could finalize everything. And if she doesn't, I'll find out where Silver Blossom Catering has moved and go there to confront her in person."

I opened my mouth to say that I knew exactly where Vivi had moved—right next door to Starlit Bookshop, in fact—but Trevor was already addressing Tabitha.

"Wait, you haven't even met in person with the caterer yet? And they've moved locations on top of that?" He sat back in disbelief.

"As I said earlier, Lyra conducted our planning work via email and text. She copied me on the conversations in case I needed to review them. But I trusted her, so I let her handle things." Tabitha replied. "I'm sure I could find the caterer's address online if I had to."

"I could tell you—" I began.

Tabitha waved my words away. "No worries. I've got this."

"Sounds good to me," I said, reaching below the table for my bag. I'd had enough.

"That's settled." Tabitha began gathering up the pages and tapping them on the table to align them before returning to her file.

"But I'm still confused. You had a party planner working with the caterer before," Trevor said, scratching his head. "Must have been enough work to warrant that. And now it suddenly isn't the same amount of work?"

Tabitha considered this, frowning.

"Here's an idea. *I* could take on the—" Melody tried again. Tabitha held up a don't-even-start-with-me palm in her face, and she fell silent again.

Nora elbowed me and stood. We put our coats on and walked to the door.

Paisley hopped out of the bag and seemed intent upon trotting out with us.

"Goodbye, all," my aunt said over her shoulder.

There was some frenzied whispering behind us.

"Wait," Tabitha called. "If you are *so intent* upon doing this, Emma, then you'll have to prove to us right here and now that you are the right person."

Peak Tabitha. She couldn't ask nicely like a normal person but instead had to throw down a challenge in front of the crowd.

"Please, Emma," Nora said. "We really do need you."

Tabitha hurried over and scooped up Paisley.

Without turning around, I texted my friend Vivi, told her that I might be replacing Lyra as event planner, and wondered if she had a window to chat. She responded immediately.

Yes, of course! Do you want to swing by here right now?

I faced the group, told everyone that Vivi had agreed to meet with us immediately, and invited them all to attend.

"That settles that," Trevor said, slapping the table. "Obviously."

Unhappily, Tabitha agreed.

But her eyes promised revenge.

Chapter Six

Nora and I rode over to Silver Blossom Catering, which had moved next door to Starlit Bookshop, with Trevor. He was kind enough to offer, unlike Tabitha and Melody, who jumped in the latter's fancy car and zipped off without a thought. Trevor had an old station wagon that smelled like cherry cough drops—just the sight of the wide vehicle brought back so many memories of my parents taking my sister and me to the drive-in near Denver when we were young. He turned the key as we were buckling ourselves into the bench seat in back. It coughed a few times, then sputtered to life, and crawled down the street at about ten miles per hour.

"I'm only driving because I need to go get some supplies for the library after we talk to your friend. Otherwise, I'd walk. That's one of the things I love most about this town, the ability to walk almost everywhere."

We agreed with his assessment.

"What did you do before you took this job?" Nora inquired.

"I was the director of a small library up north for twenty years."

"Up north, like Boulder?" I asked.

"Up north like Boise, Idaho. But I moved here to be closer to my kids. They live in Castle Rock. I'm a grandfather now." He radiated joy at the thought.

"How wonderful." Nora said.

"It's the best decision I ever made, to be with them."

After twisting his head to make sure no one was coming, he signaled and did a U-turn at a snail's pace on River Street, eventually parking in front of our store. Melody and Tabitha were tapping their feet on the sidewalk, impatiently waiting as Trevor's wagon shuddered to a stop. After we'd extracted ourselves from the vehicle, we entered the Silver Blossom Catering lobby.

I held my breath, waiting for Tabitha or Melody to comment on the location, as it had belonged to Tabitha's ex-husband Ian Gladstone at one point, but neither one acknowledged it. Instead, they gazed around the enormous space, which had movable walls that blocked out various zones. Through the door on the left, there was a small business section with an oversized desk, some filing cabinets, and a row of chairs. Behind the walls ahead of us, I knew from experience, was the kitchen and preparation area. The walls on the right hid the largest area, which was going to be used for events in the future, or at least that was the plan. The company had only been here for a month.

Vivi Yang, who had a bright smile that could lift anyone's spirits on even the grayest of winter days, came through a doorway and waved us in. Her white jacket had a flower embroidered on the pocket. "Hi, everyone—I'm Vivi. Welcome to Silver Blossom Catering."

She nodded at Nora and me, her friends and neighbors, and greeted Tabitha, for whom she had done an event this fall—the same event where we'd met—then said hello to Trevor and Melody. "Let me give you a tour, get you a beverage, then we'll sit down and chat."

"Could we skip the tour and the drinks, please?" Tabitha interjected. "I have a *super* full schedule today. All week, actually. I'd love to cross this task off of my list as quickly as possible."

Despite Tabitha's rudeness, Vivi's enthusiasm didn't diminish one bit. She led us to the office, took a seat at the desk, and invited us to sit in the chairs that had been arranged in a semicircle in front of it.

"So what can I do for you?" She smiled pleasantly.

"As you and everyone else in town knows, we have recently lost our party planner. Very sad news. You worked with Lyra on the library gala, right?"

Vivi nodded. "I'm so sorry to hear about her passing."

After a beat, Tabitha raced ahead. "Emma is taking over as party planner. Could you get us all up to speed on what's been done to date? I'd like to do some final approvals while we're here." Soon we were deep into options and requirements. Trevor kept raising his hand, and Tabitha kept telling him that he didn't need to raise it, which was awkward. I listened carefully, but I let Tabitha and Trevor say what they needed to say as the big bosses on this project. Once their needs had been determined, I'd go over everything with Vivi separately to make sure it all went smoothly.

Melody was scrolling through a social media site on her phone, totally checked out.

"Are you enjoying working on the gala?" I asked her.

She slid her eyes sideways, so that she was looking at something on the floor between us. "I've got nothing better to do, do I?"

I went with a sort of nonconfirmational confirmation sound.

"Charity work is my life." Then she added, under her breath, "Whatever Tabitha wants, Tabitha gets."

Uh oh. There appeared to be trouble in BFF paradise. After all these years, who knew it was possible? Melody had been Tabitha's devoted foot soldier for decades.

"Have you been involved with the committee for a long time?"

Melody put her phone down exaggeratedly slowly, making sure that I knew it was annoying her that I was interrupting her quality me-time. She rose from her chair. "Yes, Emma, I have been on the planning committee for this gala for years. Too many years." Then she spun around and walked out of the store.

Tabitha didn't even notice.

* * *

Once everyone else left, Vivi flipped her long dark braid over her shoulder and turned to me. "That was fun."

"How was the final menu discussion?"

"Tabitha had some add-ons, turns out." She smiled.

"Surprise, surprise. What were they?"

"She was demanding hard-to-acquire ingredients with extremely complicated recipes."

"And?"

"I am offering easy-to-make main dishes with simple sides. Plus drinks."

I grinned. "Did she go for that?"

"She did once I explained that we had to take what we could get during a holiday, especially in the quantity she needs."

"It's impressive how you handle her." I applauded softly. "I wish I'd known you years ago."

She scanned the menu with her phone and emailed it to me. "Sending now. Are you going to print individual menus for guests or put the food on the program or set up calligraphy slates on tripods?"

"I bet Lucy would love to do it. She took a calligraphy class with Ryan last month and fell in love with the art."

"That would be perfect."

My phone chimed with a text from Tabitha announcing that she would swing by Starlit after her current meeting ended.

"Oh no," I murmured. "I have to go to the bookstore and wait for Tabitha."

Vivi already knew that Tabitha and I were pretty much arch-enemies. I didn't have to explain any further.

Her eyes lit up. "Do you want some holiday cookies to take with you? We made a ton and have some extras."

"Cookies? You're so kind."

"The pleasure is all mine." She laughed. "I make cookies any chance I can get. They always make people happy. Pretty magical, yes?"

"I can't argue with you there," I said. "And I could use some magic dust right now."

Vivi went into the kitchen. I followed her and slid onto one of the stools near an oversized counter. Everything here, appliances included, was on wheels and could be easily moved. She rummaged around on one of the wire shelving units by the door and emerged with a cardboard box, which she handed to me. I thanked her, then stopped short when my gaze fell on the silver rack hanging down from the ceiling.

"What? You look like you've seen a ghost!"

"Tell you later—I have to go make a call." I held up the box as I backed away. "Thank you again for these, Vivi. We'll talk soon."

As I hurried toward the street, I scrolled down to Jake Hollister's number in my phone contacts and dialed. It rang, but there wasn't any answer. I left a message asking him to return my call as soon as possible.

With a few more steps, I'd gone out of Vivi's store and into Starlit Bookshop. It was quiet—just a few people browsing in the aisles. I waved at Max Melendez, who was at the register with a customer, and went into the office.

Lucy was working on the computer. She looked up and smiled when she saw the box I was carrying. "Oh, yum! Did you make something delicious?"

"From Vivi," I said as I set them on top of the desk. "So yes, definitely more delicious than anything I could make."

She peeled open the top and sighed happily at the array of stars iced in a rainbow of frosting colors.

I snapped my fingers. "Should we order a bunch of these and sell them individually? Star cookies for Starlit Books?"

"Yay for more merch! You keep coming up with one terrific idea after another. Brava." Lucy bit into a blue star cookie and closed her eyes blissfully.

I tasted a red one. "Oh, wow."

"They're sugar cookies, right?" she mumbled through a second mouthful. "How come ours never taste like this?"

"Because Viv's a professional."

I asked if Lucy would be willing to handle the menu calligraphy project and she enthusiastically agreed to acquire the supplies and begin the lettering.

As I was thanking her, we could hear the bookstore door close.

I poked my head out of the office to see Tabitha pulling off her gloves. Paisley popped her head up from the giant bag on her shoulder. As usual, she sported a bow that matched Tabitha's cream-colored wool blazer and looked downright adorable. Anne Shirley, our resident red tabby who had walked into the store and adopted us one day, looked down from one of her favorite perches high on a bookshelf, twitching her tail. Paisley caught sight of her and yipped once. Anne Shirley stared impassively ahead, ignoring her.

The hierarchy was pretty clear.

As Tabitha walked over toward me, Paisley slowly sank back down into the depths.

"You could let her run around if you like," I said, gesturing toward Tabitha's bag.

"Who?"

"Paisley." Seriously? Who else was in her bag?

"Oh no. She prefers to be next to her mummy at all times," Tabitha said. She cooed into the bag. "Don't you, scrumptious?"

Paisley didn't confirm or deny. I had my own thoughts about that, but it would probably be prudent to keep them to myself.

"I have a few things to cover," she said briskly. "First, Whitney, Nat, and Stella have agreed to come to your mystery panel, so we need to dump the local writers."

I stared at her.

"We have to pay all three of the co-hosts now, so they may as well give us a little more bang for our buck," she said.

I shook my head. "We can't just—"

"If you don't call them, I will," she threatened. "This is happening."

At least if I were the one to do it, I could provide some context and ask for forgiveness. "I'll take care of it."

"Good. Next, you asked for status updates on everything," Tabitha said, "but that seems unnecessarily time-consuming. I think the best thing to do would be to start from scratch, don't you?"

"No, I don't think that would be best. Not at all. Let's use whatever gala arrangements have already been made and build on those."

She kept going as if I hadn't said anything. "So we'll need a band, sponsors—"

"Wait," I said. "Don't you have those already lined up?"

"I just said we were going to start from scratch. I'm *extremely* busy, Emma. I don't have a single moment to be double- and triple-checking and hunting for all that information. I don't even know where it is."

I eyed her oversized designer-name-emblazoned tote. Pretty sure I knew where the information was.

She shrugged as if there was nothing to be done.

"Might it be in there?" I said it as pleasantly as I could. "You had a file at the library this morning. I'd be happy to look through it and sort things out."

The desire to refuse anything I asked was written across her face.

I cleared my throat. “Remember when you returned the Edgar Allan Poe book in November, and we had a little chat?”

“And remember when she saved your life?” Lucy added sweetly as she was passing by.

Tabitha squinted up at the ceiling as if she were thinking very hard but failing to locate the reference.

I went on. “My point is that we agreed to help each other out.”

She pursed her lips. “I thought it was more that we agreed not to get in each other’s way.”

“Well, *this* right here would count as getting in each other’s way. You’ve made arrangements. I’m stepping up to assist. If we could simply aim toward the same goal, we’ll get a better result.” I tacked on a comment about how it would take some of the stress off her too since she was, as she’d insisted at the meeting, already doing *so much.*

Tabitha straightened up sharply and put her pointer finger into wagging position, as if she were about to deliver a blistering lecture, then her shoulders sagged. “Oh, all right. Let’s get this done.” She reached into her bag and removed the file, then handed it over. “Do you have a copier here somewhere?”

Her tone implied that she suspected we were running the store on an inkwell-and-parchment system.

“Yes,” I said calmly. It took everything in my power not to reveal my surprise at her giving in, but I managed to keep it hidden as I accepted the thick file. “Do you want to browse and wait or come back for this?”

Her phone chirped and she dug around in her bag to retrieve it. A glance at the screen sent her eyebrows sky high. “If I don’t leave now, I’ll be late for my next—and obviously far more important—meeting. Go ahead and copy whatever you need, and I’ll swing by later.”

After she’d left, Lucy came over and grinned at me. “Well done, Em. Maybe she’ll stop being so horrid.”

“Oh, I doubt that,” I said. “It’s kind of her thing.”

“Sounds like she’s agreeing on a truce for the week at least.”

“We’ll see how long it lasts.” I wheeled around and hurried to the office.

* * *

A half hour later, I had spoken with the five panelists—all of whom were extremely professional and gracious about Tabitha’s un-vite. And because I’m a multitasker, I was also now the proud owner of a duplicate file. I didn’t have the time to sort through the pages individually, so I’d copied them all. Even a cursory glance revealed that she—and the committee—sure were spending a lot of money for an event that was supposed to *make* money. It seemed that it would be easier to give the library the money directly instead of using it for the fundraiser. But perhaps that just meant the amount they brought in was so great, it was worth the expenditure. The old spend-money-to-make-money idea.

Plus, I had to admit, the party sounded like it was going to be beautiful.

And everyone in Silvercrest would get to participate.

I just hoped that it was far less deadly than the screening had been.

Chapter Seven

Snow was falling lightly outside Starlit Bookshop's front windows, creating a picturesque backdrop to our event inside. The chairs in the back of the store had been arranged into rows facing the wooden tables set up for our presenters. Every seat was full, and attendees chatted excitedly among themselves as I walked to the front and picked up the microphone.

"Hello, everyone. We're so glad that you could join us, and we've got quite a surprise for you: our original authors have kindly agreed to appear at a future date, in order that we may present our new gala co-hosts: Whitney Willton, Nat Fabulous, and Stella Vane—the stars of *Chasers*."

The audience burst into robust applause as the actors came from behind the half-wall near the spiral staircase. Whitney wore a short white sweater dress with knee-high boots, Nat had a gray fleece with khaki pants, and Stella's black jumpsuit was paired with a long tailored jacket. The effect was casual but cool. I noted that many of the attendees, meanwhile, were wearing shirts featuring the show's logo, an open book with a red question mark in the center.

No one should ever underestimate the power of merch.

"The award-winning show *Chasers* is now in its fifth year. Each episode pays homage to a different mystery story and has received a warm welcome from viewers and critics alike for its humorous reimagining of plot and character. Who can forget the episode where Sherlock and Watson went undercover as film critics? Or when Miss Marple was recast as a high school principal?"

A hand shot up in the air. I turned to the young man in a Silvercrest College shirt who said, "I loved the one when Daphne du Maurier's Rebecca became a podcaster."

Appreciative chuckles broke out around the room.

"Tonight, our honored guests will be doing a brief reading from some of the original books that were adapted into episodes. Next to the register, you'll find them available for purchase after the question-and-answer period. The actors have kindly agreed to sign autographs with any purchase, so after you've paid for the books, just line up and you'll be able to meet your favorite star. In addition, please explore the nearby display table, where you'll see an actual *Chasers* script used for shooting the episode that was screened last night."

Her mention of the screening cast a pall over the room. Everyone in town knew what had happened there. For a moment, I couldn't believe it had only been a day since we'd found Lyra. It felt like so much had happened since then, yet we were all still processing her death.

Whitney was obviously struggling to keep her composure. I tried to send her strength vibes, which Nora always insisted was a thing. Earlier, I'd asked if she wanted to cancel the panel, but she said that pressing on with the activities was a powerful distraction from her grief, which she welcomed right now.

"If I may," Nat said. "We would like to acknowledge that we are heartbroken about losing our dear friend."

Whitney wiped away a tear.

Stella nodded sadly at him.

"So we hereby dedicate tonight's discussion to our dearest Lyra Willton." People perked up again at that and applause broke out. He did have a gift for evoking lightness, which was needed at precisely this moment.

"Thank you, all." I looked down at my streamlined version of the bios that the actors' representatives had sent in and gestured toward the trio. "Now we shall meet our panelists, but please hold your applause until the end. First, we have Whitney Willton, whose long list of television shows and films range from the very popular series *Maddie's Dream* to *The People Around Here*, for which she received a Golden Globe, and of course the Oscar-winning *Sunlight Over Aspens*."

No one paid any attention to my request to wait until the end: they clapped long and hard for Whitney as she put a hand to her heart and slowly bowed her head.

"Next, we have Nat Fabulous, who comes to *Chasers* straight from the hit sitcom *My Favorite Frenemies*, which was nominated for two Emmy awards. He has also sustained a successful stand-up career for over a decade."

Nat nodded, almost shyly, as the crowd rewarded him with applause.

"Finally, please welcome Stella Vane, who made her debut on Broadway in the smash musical *Ten Ways to Climb a Mountain*, which was followed by the critically acclaimed dramedy series, *All for a Rose.*"

After the next round of applause, I thanked the actors for being here and handed the microphone to Whitney. She held up the book in her hand—Agatha Christie's *A Murder Is Announced*—and started reading the first chapter.

I was impressed by her animated style. She could have had a career in audiobooks if she cared to. The audience hung on her every word.

Nat's book, which was Dashiell Hammett's *The Maltese Falcon*, showed off the actor's facility for physical comedy. He brought the characters in conflict to life with a variety of facial distortions and body positions.

Stella launched into a gripping reading of a particularly chilling section of *The Talented Mr. Ripley* by Patricia Highsmith. You could have heard a pin drop when she reached the end, the audience was so attentive to her every word and breath.

We rewarded their efforts with yet another round of applause, then I opened the floor for a question-and-answer period. The actors were funny and charming as they fielded questions about the show, their lives, and how to break into acting. They must have answered the same queries repeatedly during their publicity work, but they were so personable that it felt as though they were answering for the first time.

After a half hour, a hand went up in the back near where Nora was sitting. I called on the person to whom it belonged, a man in a mustard-colored wool jacket with a lumpy brown plaid scarf thrown around his neck. He had a thick shock of white hair and a long, droopy mustache. I recognized him—or, more precisely, his mustache—from the screening, where Lucy had been victorious in the race for the last table.

He stood up and cleared his throat. "I'd like to know why no one invited *me* to join this panel."

Heads swiveled toward him from all directions.

"I'm Dr. Gates Huddlesby, English professor, Silvercrest College. I've written an extremely important study of *Chasers*, which came out last year from a very prestigious university press." He frowned at me, as if I should have known that. "It was even summarized in a *Buzzfeed* list on the internet!"

The audience turned back to me.

I gripped the microphone. "Congratulations, Dr. Huddlesby. I'd be glad to chat with you in a moment—"

"No, I'd like to join the cast now, if you don't mind. I have some observations to share." He started to move to the right, in order to walk around the chairs. The actors appeared to be very uncomfortable with this turn of events.

Raising the microphone to my mouth, I spoke quickly. "Thanks again to our special guests for a wonderful evening. Everyone, I hope you had a great time here at Starlit Bookshop and please check out our books before you leave. Remember that Whitney, Nat, and Stella would love to give you an autograph with every purchase."

The crowd stood and began milling around. I managed to intercept Dr. Huddlesby before he reached the actors and invited him into my office. He reluctantly accepted, shooting another frown over my shoulder in the direction of his lost opportunity to take the spotlight.

Lucy smiled at me from the register in solidarity, and Nora hurried over to calm things down with the actors.

I pointed to a chair next to our large farmhouse table in the center of the office and took the one on the opposite side. "Please sit down, Dr. Huddlesby. I'm sorry, but I wasn't aware of any arrangements—"

"Precisely my point. No arrangements were made." He glowered at me.

I was at a loss.

The professor reached into the leather satchel he had been holding under one arm and extracted a book, which he placed carefully onto the table. "Behold," he said.

I leaned forward and beheld. The cover featured a shell-like fractal over which a title was spelled out in lurid red ink: *The Carnivalesque World of Chasers.*

"See? Written by Gates Huddlesby, PhD," he said, tapping his own name on the bottom. "That's me."

"Congratulations," I said again.

He accepted this silently.

"And did someone ask you to—"

"If they had, I would have been up at the panel table, wouldn't I?" The professor snatched his book back and filed it away carefully.

"So you're saying that you weren't invited to present on the panel but that you wanted to be included?" I didn't know how else to say it other than outright.

"That's correct." He made a sort of harrumph.

"I'm sorry," I said softly. "I wasn't aware of your study, which looks very interesting."

The professor pursed his lips. "Clearly you didn't do much research when you were organizing this event. Mine is the *definitive* book on the series."

"Are there many other such books out there?"

"Not a one," he said tersely. "Which is how I *know* without a doubt that mine *is* the definitive book on the series."

"I see."

His shoulders sagged. "No one thinks that books written in academia could possibly cross over into the mainstream, but they do sometimes. And I was sure that *this* one had potential. It's so strange how the rest of the world treats us. We are *experts*, you know, and we do have something to offer on the topics we study. When I heard about Gala Week, I thought surely someone would reach out to me, tap into my extensive knowledge. But that didn't happen. I tried to email Dean Baxter's wife, but she never wrote me back, and I even tried to talk to someone at the library tea, but the ladies wouldn't let me in because apparently I wasn't wearing the right hat."

"The right hat?" I repeated faintly.

"Pardon my little joke. There were just so many hats . . ." He trailed off for a moment, then regained his footing. "I simply meant that I wasn't on the guest list. I was already doing some research at the library that day, and when I saw the ladies flowing in all gussied up, I asked the librarian what was happening. When she told me, I tried to gain entrance and failed. But my point is, there was no invitation extended for me to contribute."

"I'm sorry," I said. "The gala planning committee wanted to focus on the actors this time around. But if we do an academic panel on *Chasers* or on film and television more generally in the future here, I will absolutely keep you in mind." He sat up a little straighter. "In the meantime, would you like us to put a few copies of your book in our local authors section? I'd be happy to order some, or if you'd like to work on consignment with us, we can do that too."

Underneath his bushy eyebrows, there was a discernible spark in his dark eyes. "That's acceptable to me. Can you put this one in your display tonight? So that it's part of this event at least *somehow*?" He reached back into his bag and held out his book with both hands.

"Gladly."

"Thank you," he said, in a slightly less gruff tone.

* * *

After everyone had left and I had cleaned up, I was doing a final loop to make sure I'd gotten everything. Anne Shirley was twining in and out of my legs, purring loudly, which was her version of helping.

Lucy, balancing the register, was humming something from an opera that I couldn't quite recognize.

I opened my mouth to ask her what it was but instead found myself saying, "Huh."

"What?" Lucy asked, darting a glance my way.

"The *Chasers* script is gone." I bent down and looked under the table, then turned around in a circle to see if someone had moved it aside, but it was nowhere in sight.

Lucy shut the drawer firmly and came over to help me look.

I moved the few remaining books that had been on the next table, but there was no script there either.

She walked along the aisles to see if it had been relocated. "Nothing here," she called back.

"That's so odd."

She grimaced as she came around the nearest bookshelf. "Are we in trouble?"

"I don't know. I'll double-check with Whitney. I can't believe we weren't able to keep it safe."

Lucy frowned. "Why would someone steal it in the first place?"

"Probably because it's memorabilia. There were so many fans here. Maybe someone simply wanted it. Or wanted to try and sell it online?"

"I just don't like to think that we have thieves in our charming little town."

"I think they're everywhere. Charming little towns included."

We both stared at the empty spot where the script had been.

Chapter Eight

"How was your talk with Gates?" Nora asked when we were all at home and settled near the fireplace. She was pouring her last cup of tea of the day, and I was nursing an ice water. Lucy was curled up on the sofa with Anne Shirley, who was staring intently at the Christmas tree, probably plotting an attack on the next ornament.

"It was a little uncomfortable at first, especially since we'd never met before—"

"Oh, he was on sabbatical last semester when you met the other professors," she said.

"—and he was extremely upset that no one had included him in the Gala Week events."

"It never occurred to me, though it probably should have. Now I remember that when his book came out, he had flyers put into the mailboxes of every professor on campus." She took a sip and sighed happily before putting the flowered cup back into the saucer. "Gates is not what you would call an email person. Or a technology person. He's old school."

"He said he tried to email Tabitha, but she never replied to him."

Nora smiled. "As I said. It may never even have reached her. He's famous for his email ineptitude. Always replying-all with every little thought and losing track of emails that you've sent him and sending his own emails to the wrong recipient. No judgment. It's *known* about him, shall we say."

"He said he expected someone to reach out to him. Meaning me, I think."

"Oh, darling, it's not on you. Not at all. Just because he wrote a book about the subject doesn't automatically earn him a place wherever he wants to go. That's his ego talking. Or more likely his overcompensation for what he considers to be an inadequate response to his genius. He was quite a star in certain circles back in the day. He's accustomed to people celebrating him. Plus, those of us on the original panel were rescheduled anyway. He would have been with us."

"Again, I'm so sorry about that."

"Emma, don't be. You did what you were asked to do—curate this panel carefully in response to the planning committee's desire to showcase their guests."

"Yes, but I don't like to leave anyone out. And he does have a point about professors becoming experts but not having many opportunities to share their knowledge outside of academia."

Nora laughed. "While that may be true, you can't take on the whole system."

"Can't I?" I mused. "I could do more panels at the store with professors."

"Yes, you could." My aunt smiled at me. "You have a big heart, darling. And honestly, if anyone can make things better in the world, it's you and your sister."

"Aw, thanks," Lucy said. "Is Gates the one who got into a yelling match with the trustees when they approved the online teaching initiative?" Anne Shirley reached up and patted my sister's face.

"He's the one. Like I said, he's old school." Nora got up and turned off the gas fireplace switch. The flames dropped down, and the cozy bubble of warmth they provided began to dissipate immediately. "But it's usually more fun to watch him kick up a ruckus. Tonight was a bit more awkward."

"The audience seemed to bounce back quickly, though," I said. "I hope, anyway. Any word from the cast members?"

"Whitney texted me a thank you for letting their panel replace our panel. If any of the actors were upset, she didn't mention it. I'm sure they've seen much worse from some of their events, with fans trying to get close to them in a variety of ways. And they seem genuinely excited to be part of Gala Week, as far as I can tell. So don't worry about a thing."

That was heartening.

"Someone did steal the script from the display table, though," Lucy said.

"Oh dear," Nora said in dismay. "Was it very valuable?"

"Not exactly sure. I'm going to talk to Whitney about it as soon as I can." I wasn't looking forward to that. What if it was priceless? How would we pay to replace it? I closed my eyes.

"Speaking of the gala," my aunt said, perking up, "will you two be bringing dates?"

"Ryan," said Lucy.

"I figured," Nora replied. "How about you, Emma?"

"Oh, I'll be working the whole time. *Not* bringing a date."

My aunt tapped her chin as she thought. "Maybe you could—"

"No, thank you," I said firmly. "I already have enough to deal with."

"What about you?" Lucy asked Nora, who smiled enigmatically.

"Oh! Who is it?" I held my breath. It could be any suitor, of which she had no shortage. She hadn't gone out on more than a few dates with each of them in recent years, however. I couldn't blame her—many of them had seemed dull, others had seemed self-absorbed, and some had seemed both dull and self-absorbed.

"Not George, please," Lucy said.

Nora laughed. "No. He only wanted to compare retirement funds."

"Not Elbert, either." My sister persisted.

"No. He was obsessed with plotting revenge on his wife's divorce lawyer."

"Not Hal," I said, throwing out my own least favorite of the bunch.

"No. He didn't want to talk *at all*, if you know what I mean." She did a little shimmy.

Lucy blanched.

My aunt went on. "As it turns out, I've discovered a new dating app created expressly for academics. There aren't even any real names or pictures at first. It's built to create a meeting of the minds. If we line up intellectually, we can choose to take it to the next level."

Lucy and I exchanged a look.

"Oh, don't worry. People date online all the time. You only live once, darlings."

"What is the app called?" I made a mental note to research it.

"The Faculty Lounge."

"That doesn't very romantic," Lucy said doubtfully.

"You'd be surprised." Nora winked at her.

* * *

After they'd gone to bed, I opened my laptop and looked up The Faculty Lounge. It appeared to be more of a social forum for academic conversation than a dating app, but maybe Nora knew something that I didn't know.

Next, I typed "Gates Huddlesby" into the search bar. All the usual professorial matter came up: faculty bio at the college, classes taught, and publications, which was an impressive list of articles and chapters plus a handful of books on assorted film and media topics. The *Chasers* book had the most academic book reviews, including several glowing ones in prestigious journals, but, as he had implied, there weren't many reviews posted at the mainstream sites. I dove a little deeper, taking a quick scan of my usual bookseller sites, which told the same story.

What if we could mention his book at the gala? I probably needed to ask Tabitha for permission.

Or not.

Chapter Nine

On Tuesday morning, I drove to the Silvercrest College campus to take the scheduled tour of the new Baxter Ballroom. Nora had already gone to her office to take care of some work first and said she'd meet me there.

I parked on the street nearby and walked over to where gala committee members and numerous volunteers were lining up outside the brick building, which had a thick velvet ribbon strung across the entrance. I was surprised to see a few other students and faculty members waiting with them. Tabitha was at the front on the top step next to the president, who had a long blue wool coat and a weary look. He repositioned his wire glasses with black leather gloves and nodded at someone in the crowd.

Nora appeared beside me. "Oh goody—I was in the *mood* for a spectacle."

The school band marched to the front, playing the peppy college fight song. Tabitha, in a scarlet coat, pillbox hat, and white gloves, gazed over them like a proud mama bird. A row of cheerleaders—who must have been freezing in their skirts—did a sort of Rockettes routine, then stood with their hands on their hips while a single snare did a drum roll. The president opened his mouth to say something, then realized that no one would hear what he was saying, so he shrugged and handed some scissors to Tabitha. A quick look of dismay scuttled across her face at the lost opportunity to make a speech, but she moved into position and completed the official ribbon snip. A cheer went up from the crowd.

"Welcome to Baxter Ballroom," Tabitha trilled.

As she stepped back with a sort of game-show-hostess wave, two students opened the large glass front doors. We followed the committee members up the stone steps and into a grand foyer that had the kind of hushed ambience created by thick, tastefully patterned carpets. Oil paintings of the campus from different angles, at varying times of day, lined the walls.

"There are meeting rooms on that side of the building." Tabitha pointed to the left. "And food preparation and housekeeping facilities on the other."

We swiveled our heads, though nothing much was visible since both of the wing hallways abruptly turned ninety degrees to run alongside the ballroom proper, which was in the center.

"Please come inside," she said, waving at the same students who had opened the door for her before. They performed the same action on the double doors ahead of us, which were wooden this time, and the crowd pressed on.

The ballroom was two stories tall, with a mezzanine level bordered by a curved wooden railing that floated above the immense dance floor. Sunlight streamed through the windows—a Tiffany-style floral design in the center pane on the upper level seemed to glow, providing a breathtaking focal point.

"Kind of reminds me of the bookstore," Nora whispered. "Both the general layout and the stained-glass embellishment."

I nodded. "Maybe she didn't do it intentionally."

"Maybe she did," she whispered back.

"I guess it's kind of flattering, if it's not a coincidence."

"We have made use of automation wherever possible," Tabitha enthused. "The performance space can be raised at the press of a button."

She signaled to Melody, who went running up the stairs to the right. A loud humming sound filled the room, during which we observed the floor lift itself into a stage, a set of stairs on either end unfolding once it locked into place.

"We also control every aspect of lighting." She nodded again at Melody, who was parked behind a large console on the second level. The shades along the windows above and below the balconies lowered at the same time, darkening the room considerably. Lights unfurled from a metal scaffold on the ceiling above and shone spotlights on the stage. Then a globe on a frame descended, lit up, and began to spin slowly, which cast dots of multicolored lights on every surface.

"We have projection capabilities for films or for a variety of backgrounds." A large screen descended noiselessly behind the stage and a cozy hearth scene appeared, complete with flickering flames in the fireplace.

Tabitha pointed to the shining floor under our feet. "The sprung hardwood floor has been perfectly crafted to follow in the tradition of early twentieth-century ballrooms. Go ahead, try it out!" When no one moved, she did a graceful twirl. Waltz music flooded through the loudspeakers, and Tabitha waved her hands at us to join her. People all around began to move, tentatively, then got into the swing of things and were soon whirling happily across the floor.

After a few minutes, Tabitha shook her hand sideways as a signal to Melody, and the music abruptly stopped. "And that was our sound system, for which we obviously spared no expense."

Applause broke out as the final dancers came to rest.

Tabitha smiled around the room. "I'm so glad you like it. I wanted to make something that the campus could use, and I wanted to honor my husband, who put in so many glorious years serving this community."

Melody cleared her throat lightly as she rejoined us.

"Of course, it wasn't just me. Everyone on the Silvercrest College Cares Committee deserves thanks." She didn't name any other names, however—she let the glory continue to shine on her.

That earned another light smattering of applause.

"And now, we'll explore the rest of the building so that you'll be able to find your volunteer locations easily when you arrive on Friday."

Melody stepped forward and opened her mouth.

Tabitha continued. "Emma, could you please run through the list of volunteer shifts already organized?"

Melody froze and stepped backward again, scowling at me.

That was weird.

I pulled out my cell phone and opened the list I'd pieced together last night after poring through Tabitha's unorganized files. "We have people signed up for shifts as door greeters, attendee list monitors, coat checkers, name tag helpers, silent auction setup and cashiers, swag bag fillers, and floaters. I'll send this out to the volunteer email list tonight so that everyone has a copy. If you have to cancel for some reason, please email me as soon as possible so that we can fill your spot with a floater."

"Melody," Tabitha turned to her friend, "will you please start the tour? I need to chat with Emma. Send half of the group at a time. The other half can go up to the balcony and check the incredible view from there in the meantime." She pointed to the staircase Melody had scampered up and down while doing Tabitha's bidding.

Melody's face lit up. She divided the group in two and motioned for half of them to follow her. The rest of the women drifted away toward the staircase Tabitha had indicated.

When they had left, Tabitha told me that the band had canceled.

The band that she had pretended not to know about at the bookstore.

"How did that happen?"

"When I returned the call, they said *I* had called and canceled. Which, of course, I did not do," she huffed. "But they had a waiting list, so they went ahead and made plans with someone else. Obviously, this is a problem. Do you happen to know any bands around town that might be free?"

No, I didn't know any bands around town.

She tapped her foot.

"How about the college marching band?" Judging from their performance out front, they were extremely talented.

"Oh, very funny. They'd take up half the ballroom!" She paused. "Do you know how to book a band, Emma?"

"What kind of band are you looking for?" My fingers hovered over the search box on my phone. Not having attended annual galas throughout my lifetime like she had, I didn't have the foggiest idea what type she was expecting.

"A *band*. Like we have at every country club event," Tabitha said exasperatedly.

"Mmm hmm," I said, holding up a finger and pretending to read something very important on my phone while my brain busily tried to translate her description into actionable information.

"Oh, that's right. You aren't a member, are you? What a shame. You should think about joining."

The exclusive club was almost impossible for anyone without a trust fund to get into—not that I would want to become a member anyway. I didn't remind Tabitha how she and her friends had made fun of me working the check-in table there as a favor to Vivi a few months back. There was no need. We both knew exactly what she was doing right now.

Her smirk faltered eventually, and she went on. "Anyway, we need someone to play dance music. Waltz, tango, foxtrot. You know, traditional stuff. A *ballroom* band."

"I'll get on it. Though it's such short notice, if I can't book one—"

"*Do* book one," she said sternly.

"But if they're all busy, we could—"

She blinked rapidly. "I really don't have time to keep saying the same thing over and over, Emma. Book a band. The end."

I snapped my mouth shut.

"And now, I need you to go to the basement and find a pair of art deco vases. They're blue glass with a fan design in relief. The box should have a peacock illustration on the side, and it will be in the locked part of the storage area, which is clearly labeled." She handed me a key. "An appraiser is coming over soon to do some paperwork."

"Where did they come from?"

"They were dropped off for the silent auction, and they are extremely valuable, so I locked them up. The box is on the shelf in the storage area."

"Sure," I said. "How do I get there?"

Tabitha led me down the hallway near the first meeting room and unlocked a metal door, then she bent over and positioned the little leg with a rubber stopper so that the door was propped open. She pointed into the darkness.

"Thanks so much and come find me as soon as you locate them," she said as she spun around to leave.

The stairway doubled back on itself, so I couldn't tell until I reached the bottom that there was another heavy metal door there. It creaked when I pushed on it, sending shivers down my back. I pulled down the little leg like I'd seen Tabitha do, then felt around for a light switch. Flipping that only increased visibility by about thirty percent, since any illumination was provided by dangling light bulbs that were pretty far apart.

I peered around apprehensively. The basement had definitely not been remodeled along with the rest of the building. Here were the ingredients required for any basic horror movie: vast areas of shadow, a hulking furnace in the corner, dripping sounds coming from who knows where, spider webs galore, and cold pockets of air that seemed to swirl up for no particular reason.

Sighing, I decided that this needed to be a quick retrieval operation. In and out. I didn't want to spend more time down here than was absolutely necessary. Moving forward, I scanned the room, finally catching sight of a spray-painted word on a board to the far right: *Storage.*

I made my way over, passing a pile of what looked like broken chairs and lamp parts. The silver padlock on the storage area gleamed dully—I unlocked it, then opened the hasp and the metal gate, which squeaked as loudly as the door had. It was as if someone had made sure to check *all* the possible boxes on their Creepy Basement 101 list.

The storage area was basically a metal cage filled with cardboard boxes on either side. A purple peacock was on a box that was exactly where Tabitha said it would be, directly across from where I was standing. Thrilled that I had found the object of my mission so quickly, I hurried in and pulled it carefully from the shelf. It was larger and heavier than I'd expected, but I was able to carry it outside of the storage area, where I set it down.

When I turned to close the gate, I sensed rather than felt someone behind me. The hair on the back of my neck shot up, but before I could turn fully around, I was shoved inside so hard that I crashed face down onto the cement floor of the storage area. Stunned and reeling from the pain, I lay there for a moment among the boxes, trying to get my bearings. There was a dragging sound and the gate clanged shut behind me, finishing with a click as the padlock was closed again. Although it hurt to move, I twisted around but didn't see anyone. My heart raced as I sat up and carefully bent my arms and legs. I would be sore tomorrow, but nothing seemed to be broken. I stood, went over to the gate, called out for help, and looked around. At least whoever had done this hadn't turned off the lights.

And I don't know why I was even thinking of it as Whoever Had Done This. Clearly, Tabitha had done this. She was the only one who knew I was down here. Heck, she *sent* me down here. Talk about a setup.

I yelled for help again, but no one answered. Turning my attention to the gate, I tried to insert the key into the padlock from inside, but my hands were too big to curve properly through the chain links. I rattled the gate as hard as I could, hoping to dislodge the padlock, but it held. Putting my hand on my hips, I surveyed the area. It was then that I realized the box with the vases was gone.

I pulled out my phone and called Nora since I knew she wasn't working at the bookstore today.

"Pick up, pick up, pick up," I chanted.

Her voice mail kicked in after several rings.

I immediately called her again but had the same result, so I left a message saying that I was trapped in the basement of the ballroom and could she please come rescue me.

Never thought I'd say something like that aloud.

I called my sister, who answered on the first ring.

"Luce!" I yelled. "Don't hang up!"

"Why would I hang up? I just answered."

Quickly, I told her what happened.

"I'll be right there. Don't worry. Take some deep breaths. Love you."

I told her that I loved her too and then clicked off, settling in to wait. The basement seemed even darker than before. If I looked at certain pools of shadows for too long, they seemed to shift. And now that I wasn't moving, the sounds around me were much more audible. In addition to the mysterious dripping, I also heard rustling, whirring, and squeaking sounds.

I couldn't wait to get out of here.

My legs felt like jelly and my arms were still shaking. Sinking onto the floor seemed like the only option—I didn't know what was in the boxes around me and didn't want to break anything, especially if it was going to be auctioned off. I drew up my knees and put my arms over them, rocking and trying not to think about what else might have been on the cement before I sat on it.

Was it possible that Tabitha actually wanted me to be hurt, or worse? Didn't she realize that it would mean more work for her on the gala? Or . . . what if it wasn't Tabitha at all? What if it was whoever had killed Lyra? And why had they killed Lyra, anyway? What could she possibly have done to put her in someone's crosshairs? I ran through the list of everyone who worked on *Chasers*. They seemed to be such good friends. No one stood out as having any particular motive to get her out of the way. And I couldn't summon any reason why anyone in Silvercrest would go after her, either.

Or me.

Other than Tabitha, which brought me back to where I started.

It seemed like days before I heard someone on the stairs. It sounded like an army, but just two figures came through the door: Lucy and Ryan.

"Here!" I called out.

They raced over as I scrambled up.

"Oh, Em—are you okay?" My sister tugged on the padlock.

"I think I'm fine," I said, pushing my fingertips as far I could through the chain link.

Ryan took the key. "Got it. Hold tight."

I've never been so happy to hear a key turn in a lock before. I stumbled out into my sister's arms.

"Oh, Em, I'm so glad that you're okay," she said into my hair. It sounded like she was choked up.

I couldn't let go for a long moment.

Ryan patted me awkwardly on the back, but as soon as I finished hugging Lucy, I hugged him too.

"Thank you both so much." My voice wavered.

"Of course," Lucy said. "This is horrifying. Let's leave."

Ryan closed the gate and pushed the padlock up the shank again, then tugged on it to make sure it held. "Good to go."

"How long were you down there?"

"Way too long."

Lucy and Ryan talked to me for a while in the hallway, gave me some bottled water, and made sure that I was okay.

I still had something to do, so they left to go back to the store while I went to hunt Tabitha down.

Chapter Ten

I found her in the ballroom. The two groups were still off taking the tour, and Tabitha was talking to Melody.

"Make sure her gown is ready," she said. "We'll be there Wednesday."

I strode toward her, growing angrier with every step.

She eyed my empty hands. "Where are the vases?"

"How dare you!" I said.

Tabitha took a step backward and put her hands up. "How dare I what?"

"If you wanted to get the vases yourself, why did you send me down there in the first place?"

"What are you talking about, Emma? And why are your hands all cut up?"

I looked down at my palms, which were indeed scraped raw. "That's what happened when you pushed me."

"Pushed you? I did no such thing."

I shook my head in disbelief.

"Calm *down*, Emma," Melody said, yawning.

Tabitha rewarded her friend's loyalty by rolling her eyes. "I will handle this, Mel. Go check on the tours."

Melody gave her an unreadable look but did what she was told.

Tabitha turned back to me. "I have been up here the whole time on the phone, taking care of Whitney's gown. We just hung up." She held up her cell and pointed to the length of her last call, which read 50:15.

If Tabitha didn't push me, then who did?

She scanned me up and down. "Let's try this again. Where are the vases you were supposed to bring up?"

"About those," I said slowly. "Someone took them."

Her screech set the birds on the branches of the tree outside the window flapping into the sky. "What do you mean, *took them*? Who was it?"

"I didn't see. They pushed me from behind."

"Find them."

"I'm sorry that they're gone, but I wouldn't have the faintest idea who did this. As I've made abundantly clear, I thought it was you."

"Why would I steal vases that I want to auction off?" Tabitha threw her arms up.

"Why do you do anything you do?" The words came out before I could check them.

Her face turned a mottled red.

"For the sake of argument, who else knew about the vases?"

"No one," she said. "Other than the donor."

"Then you should give them a call."

"You mean *you* should give them a call." She stamped her foot. "You're the one who lost them."

"I didn't lose them. They were taken from me." My palms were stinging even more now, and I gave my hands a shake to diffuse the pain. "If you'll excuse me, I really need to wash up. And then I'm going home."

"You can't leave."

"I am, though. Thanks for your concern, by the way."

She sputtered.

I left before I said something even more regrettable, something worse than accusing her of having stolen them herself, which actually made sense to me. She'd get to keep the vases, and no one would be the wiser. And I didn't want to take this argument public if I could help it: she'd be loudly pointing a finger at me while I was yapping on about some sinister figure locking me in a cage. A small part of me didn't think she was clever enough to set that up—if she had in fact been trying to frame me.

But I definitely didn't want any part of that conversation, and truth be told, I was angry that I'd allowed myself to be put into that situation too.

After washing my hands, I exited the building and crossed the parking lot. Nora came rushing outside and threw her arms around me. "My ringer was off because I took over one of the tours, so I just heard your message. You sounded awful, darling, positively awful. You're *not* awful, are you? You're fine? Yes? Please be fine."

She gave me another tight squeeze and peered into my face.

"Thank you. I am fine. Would you like a ride home?"

"Yes," she said, still sounding worried and relieved, all at once. "But I'm driving. No arguments. You need to take it easy."

I handed her the keys and went around to the other side. On the way home, she demanded to hear every detail.

"Hmm," I said, at the end.

"What?"

"After all of this, I still need to find a band for the gala. An event planner's work is never done, as they say."

She chuckled. "*Do* they say that?"

"They should, if they don't."

* * *

Two hours later, I had struck out with every ballroom band within driving distance that I could find on the internet. I took a sip of coffee and stared out the window at the river flowing past our house, which usually made me relax, but I was so keyed up from the day's events that I found myself clutching the mug too tightly. My wounded palms began to throb. As I tried to soften my hold without dropping the drink, a chime interrupted my efforts and I picked up my phone, glad to see my sister's name on the screen.

"Hi," I said.

"Wanted to check in. How are you?"

I smiled. "Much better, thanks to you and Ryan. Please convey my gratitude again." I didn't tell her that my muscles were complaining loudly about the fall in the basement. I'd done some serious stretching, and I still felt battered. A few more rounds of ice, though, and I'd be good as new.

She covered the phone and said something, but it was muffled. "Ryan says you're welcome."

"He's there at the store?"

"We're on our way to Riverside Coffee. Come join us? You could get a caramel latte. My treat."

I stared at the mug in front of me. The steam was no longer curling up. That was grounds for a refill, right? Or better yet, a replacement?

"Only if I could buy yours, though. You did save my life."

"I don't know about that," she said.

"You saved me from the cage."

"Deal."

I grabbed my bag, pulled on my boots and coat, and ran out the door. The sun had heated things up to the point that I didn't even need gloves. Following the riverwalk, I listened to the water as I covered the few blocks between our house and the café, which was right next to Starlit Bookshop. I pushed on the glass door and scooted over to the counter, where Lucy and Ryan were waiting for me.

"My heroes!" I said. Lucy and Ryan shook their heads.

"Their order is on me today," I told the woman behind the counter. Diandra Katz smiled at me. She had a graying bob that had never been an inch longer or shorter since I'd met her. I asked about her wife, and she caught me up on her latest culinary adventures. Ariadne wrote cookbooks and created new menu items for the coffeehouse that they'd owned for decades. She also ran the Etsy shop featuring the embroidered apron line that Diandra created when she wasn't here whipping up coffee masterpieces. Today, she wore one with a blue jay on a snowy branch. The two of them had more energy than anyone else I'd ever met.

We placed our orders and drifted toward a table at the window.

Diandra wasn't far behind, putting our piping hot drinks and a plate of scones in front of us.

"Need a taste test, please," she said. "Raspberry almond. Ariadne has been camped out in the kitchen perfecting them for days on end."

We thanked her and dug in.

"Oh my gosh," Lucy mumbled through a mouthful. "Delicious."

Ryan closed his eyes after he took a bite, which I think meant he was savoring the taste.

I went next and wasn't disappointed. Perfect texture and the right amount of sweetness. "Heavenly."

We chatted and sipped until Diandra returned.

"I saw the plate was empty, so I thought I'd check in. What's the verdict? She's dying to know." She held up her cell phone with Ariadne's smiling face on the screen.

We waved and said hello.

"No pressure," she said. "Just, you know, *casually* curious over here."

"They are the best raspberry scones I've ever had," Lucy said. "Aside from the other raspberry scones you've made," she added with a laugh. "I wish I could eat them for breakfast every single day."

"The best," Ryan agreed simply.

"And you, Emma? What do you think?" Ariadne clasped her hands together.

"They're my new favorite thing," I said. "Out of all the things."

She and Diandra cheered.

"Thank you," Ariadne said. "Hope to see you in person soon."

Diandra picked up the plate and smiled at us.

As she walked away, I heard her say, "I told you they'd love them."

"You never know," Ariadne replied.

"They are so sweet." Lucy twisted back to face me. "Which reminds me . . . do you have a date for the gala?"

I laughed. "A date? I'm working. We already talked about that."

"I know you're working, but you could still have a date." My sister was, without a doubt, the most romantic person in town. She was obsessed with romance novels—to the extent that Calliope had nicknamed her "Romance"—and she wanted more than anything to partner people up.

"No, I'm going to go by myself, thank you," I said. "And please don't do something you think would be sweet but which would be actually horrible for me like surprise-blind-date me at the event."

She put her hand on her chest and blinked, the very picture of innocence. "Moi?"

"Oh no." I knew that look. "What did you do?"

When she didn't respond, I turned to Ryan. He ran a hand through his red hair but wouldn't make eye contact.

"Ryan Mahoney. Tell me this instant: you didn't go along with some matchmaking scheme, did you?"

He laughed nervously and cast a beseeching look at my sister, then lowered his head practically into his coffee cup, making a big production of blowing on it.

Lucy sighed. "We think it's time for you to meet Gold. He's perfect for you."

"Did you say Gold?"

"That's his last name. His first name is . . ." She turned to Ryan, who finally lifted his head and engaged in the conversation again. "What is his first name?"

"Mackenzie."

She processed this. "Then why don't you call him Mac?"

"Mac is his father." Ryan grinned at her.

Lucy grinned back at him.

They sat there grinning at each other for a while. That was the phase they were in—easily distracted by the love cloud that had descended around them.

Eventually, Lucy shook her head and refocused. "Could you please tell Emma all about him?"

"He's a great guy," Ryan said.

We waited, but soon it became clear that he was finished with his overview.

My sister and I giggled.

"What?" He looked back and forth between us, confused.

"It's just . . . extremely concise," I said.

Lucy giggled again.

Ryan shrugged and took another sip.

"Let's see," my sister said. "He's super nice and unbelievably handsome, for starters."

"Not interested," I said.

"But think of the double dates we could have! We could go out for dinner at a candlelit restaurant, then ride home in a horse-drawn carriage together and drink hot cider as the snow falls around us."

"Did we fall into a holiday movie?" I asked.

"I *do* love holiday movies," she mused.

"I know—you've been watching them around the clock."

"What I'm trying to say is that I want you to be happy." My sister clasped her hands together.

"I *am* happy," I protested. "Very happy. I'm glad to be home."

"But you could be happier," she said.

I couldn't deny that. "Riding in a carriage on a double date sounds lovely. But I believe that relationships have to happen naturally."

Lucy nodded. "But it might happen faster if you let me introduce you to some people."

She had me there.

"Gold has a dog," Ryan said suddenly. "And he's a deejay."

The sudden pronouncement set us laughing again.

"His dog is a deejay?" Lucy asked, through giggles. "Wow."

"You know what I meant," Ryan said, chuckling.

But then I stopped laughing. "Wait, he's a deejay? Why didn't you lead with that?"

Lucy eyes started shining. "Oh, so *deejays* are your thing?"

I could feel her adding it to her mental list of Mr. Right candidates.

"No, not for dating. For event planning. I need to line up some music for the gala. What kind of music does he play?"

"Whatever you tell him to play. He also teaches music at the high school."

"Could you please give me his number?"

Ryan pulled out his phone and read the digits aloud. I tapped them into my contacts, thanked them, and told them that I needed to leave so that I could call him.

Lucy looked very satisfied with that whole turn of events.

Chapter Eleven

Later that night, Nora and I were wedged in the corner of a leather couch in a room full of somber people there to remember the life of Lyra Willton. The family home was beginning to show signs of stress: cracks along the ceiling needed filling, paint was chipping everywhere, and the wooden floors cried out for refinishing. After her parents died and Whitney left for California, Malina had continued living there for several happy years until her husband had left town shortly after Lyra was born. At that point, she'd burned everything he left behind in what she'd told people was a "highly satisfying" bonfire during a house party that she threw a week later. She bought the salon where she worked not long afterwards and had had a successful go.

Until she sold it unexpectedly.

The muscular man with an anemic ponytail and cowboy boots standing next to Nora swaggered away.

"Who was that guy?" I whispered.

"That's Tom Fordley—he's the one who bought Malina's salon last year. Don't know much about him, but at least he came to show his respects."

Malina Willton herself came around a corner. A bleary-eyed woman in a tight black dress with her dark hair coaxed into a beehive, she had a white wine in one hand and a ceramic tray in the other. She offered us a shrimp roll, tilting the tray so much that the food began to slide toward us. We both declined. She handed the tray to a young man I didn't recognize and sat down heavily.

"How are you holding up?" my aunt asked her.

"My baby girl is gone, and nothing will ever be good again." Malina took a big gulp of wine.

We expressed our condolences.

"Is there anything we can do?" Nora watched her closely.

"Find out who did this to my Lyra," she said through clenched teeth.

I left them to talk, ostensibly going to the kitchen to refill Nora's wine. Whitney was there, holding Nat's hand. Interesting. I didn't know they were a couple. Or maybe he was consoling her.

Flawless as ever, her blonde hair shining against her black sheath, she gave me a small smile. Nat, in a dark button-down shirt and khakis, couldn't seem to take his eyes off her.

"I didn't know you were coming tonight, Emma. That's so kind of you. My sister is beside herself, and the more humans around her right now, the better. I was getting worried yesterday. She wouldn't even get out of bed."

"I'm so sorry again for your loss," I said. We had talked privately before the panel, but it never hurt to say it twice.

"Oh." She looked down and sighed. "I still haven't come up with a good response to that, other than to say thank you."

"That's as good as anything," Nat said softly.

"Thank you," she said, looking deeply into my eyes. The blue of her own was startling—bright and deep at the same time. It was like looking into a corner of the sky or the depths of a pristine mountain lake. "I can't believe Lyra's gone. It doesn't seem real."

"I keep expecting her to walk up waving her schedules around," Nat said. "She was one of the most organized people in the world."

We all were silent for a moment.

"May I get you something to drink?" I asked, gesturing toward the bottles covering the granite countertop. I felt immediately foolish, as I had no business playing hostess. This was their family's home. But they both visibly relaxed, as if now we were in more familiar territory.

"Whatever is closest," Whitney said.

I picked up the nearest bottle and read the label aloud. "Whiskey?"

"Okay, maybe not the closest," she said. "Second closest?"

"Tequila?" I held out the bottle.

"That'll do." Nat removed two clean glasses from a cabinet and poured a healthy dose. They downed it like they were belly up to a bar. No salt or limes, just straight down the hatch.

Once that was done, Whitney pulled out two cans of soda from the refrigerator and emptied the liquid into the glasses.

"Do you mind if I ask you two something?" I desperately wanted to see what they remembered about finding Lyra, but it had to be done delicately, especially given where we were right now.

"Shoot," Nat said.

"Being here to honor Lyra is taking me back to the night of the screening. I'm so sorry that you found her like that."

Whitney stared at the floor and Nat gave her a look of concern.

"If you don't want to talk about it, I understand, but I keep going over and over it in my mind and have a question: How did Lyra get into that freezer? Was there anything you have remembered later about that night?"

They both seemed to be waiting for the other person to speak.

"Nothing new," Nat said eventually. "If anything, it's getting blurrier."

"Me neither," Whitney said, delicately patting under her eyes with the tips of her fingers the way people do when they don't want to mess up their makeup. "It's strange, how quickly it's gone fuzzy. My therapist says my mind is trying to protect me from the horror of the discovery."

"She's called you every day, hasn't she?" Nat said approvingly. "Checking in."

"Thankfully, yes. My therapist is the best."

"How about you?" I asked Nat.

"I'm ignoring my feelings," he said. "Like a man."

Whitney rolled her eyes.

"Just kidding," he said. "I've got a therapist too."

A group of people came into the kitchen and made drinks, chatting with the two of them. The mood changed completely over the course of a few minutes. When they left, I was trying to figure out how to dive back into the questions, when Whitney spoke first and changed the subject.

"How's the gala planning going?"

Great, if you didn't count everything falling apart.

But I didn't say that.

"Fine, thank you," I said. "But I wanted to let you know that someone appears to have walked off with the *Chasers* script you gave us. At the panel, I mean. Very sorry."

"That's too bad. I think those are pretty valuable," Nat said.

"I wonder how much someone would pay for it," Whitney said thoughtfully.

"Fans? A lot," Nat said. "You should check out the prices on the auction sites."

Whitney nodded.

"At least that's what I've heard," he added.

It certainly sounded like he knew about the market. I wondered if he'd ever taken anything from the set to sell. A little side hustle, if you will.

"I'll keep looking for it," I said.

She nodded absently. Nat took a drink.

"It's brilliant," I said, shifting gears, "how *Chasers* incorporates a different mystery story with each episode. You have people tuning in for the old material as well as the fresh take on it."

"All kinds of folks seem to like the show," Nat agreed. "For which we are extremely grateful, of course."

"How does it work, exactly? You have writers for the show, right? How do they find the material that is chosen? Or do people submit?"

Whitney shrugged. "No idea. Not really my area. We're given scripts and I memorize my lines. I haven't paid any attention to most of the stories that they're based on. I wasn't much of a mystery fan before I got this job . . . and to be honest, I'm still not."

"I see."

She stared into her drink.

"In other news, we got a deejay for the gala today." I didn't mean to blurt that out. Why would they care? But I was extremely relieved that Mackenzie Gold had taken the job, and it was nice to hear it out loud.

"That's great," Whitney said distractedly, her eyes on something in the other room.

I took a step forward and followed her gaze, to see Malina and the salon owner speaking intensely by the door.

"Everything okay?" I asked.

"Tom is . . ." She shook her head.

Nat went over beside her and observed the conversation, then spoke out of the corner of his mouth. "A first-class jerk."

"What do you mean?" I watched the couple with this new information in mind. Tom was towering over Malina, and she was talking earnestly upward to him.

"He bosses her around something awful," Whitney explained. "I can't stand it. And I don't know why she ever sold the salon to him in the first place . . . except that she's been dating him, and he probably pushed her into it."

Malina, who had owned the salon for years, was my aunt's favorite stylist, her go-to whenever she needed to do an event. My mom had also been a fan. I had some vague memories of when Lucy and I would accompany the two of them over to the salon when we were young—perching on the window seat and taking in the busy activities in front of us, which were equal parts gossiping and hair-styling. Scissors, pins, and combs were busily performing actions we didn't fully understand. It was mesmerizing.

And at the end, Malina would give us candy.

"All she had to do was ask me for the money and I would have gladly given it to her. But she's so stubborn. Or proud. Something." She set the glass down on the island without taking her eyes off of her sister. "Lyra told me that Malina had to sell either the salon or the house. I wish she'd sold this place instead, gotten herself a nice new condo somewhere. This place is too big for her to have to take care of, especially since it needs so much work these days, but she had this idea that Lyra would move back home and live here again."

"You tried," Nat told her. "You really did."

"And now Lyra's gone." Whitney's eyes welled up with tears. "I bet Malina wishes she would have sold the house now."

She turned toward Nat, who enfolded her in his arms.

After a moment, she turned back around. "People have been saying that you solved a murder case here last month. Is that true?"

"I suppose that's true," I said.

"How interesting." She rolled back into Nat's embrace.

I picked up Nora's glass, quickly filled it, and left them to it.

* * *

My aunt was alone on the couch again when I brought her the wine. She took a healthy sip and rolled her neck. "You just missed Stella and Ariel."

"They were here?"

"Not for long. Ariel was crying. Malina took one look and burst into tears too. Stella took it upon herself to escort Ariel out once the weeping intensified."

"Oh, that's very sad." A weariness pressed down on me. Poor Lyra. Poor Malina. Poor everyone.

"Did you see that Detective Hollister was here? In case you're interested." She waved her wineglass around in front of her. I couldn't tell what direction she meant.

"Where?"

"Over there, by the fireplace." I followed her finger that was now pointing to the right and caught sight of Jake's back. He was listening carefully to a white-haired woman who was gesticulating wildly. When she was finished, he gave her a card and turned around.

Our eyes met and he smiled. I couldn't seem to look away.

He crossed the room, pausing to catch a careening toddler whose speed had gotten away from her and pass the little girl safely back to the harried-looking mother who had been racing toward her with open arms. Once they were all situated, he took a few more strides until he was right in front of us.

"Good evening," he said.

It was more formal than usual, but this was a formal occasion.

"What was that about?" I asked, curiously, nodding toward the previously gesticulating woman.

"A recent cat-in-a-tree situation. I told her to call me if she needed any help in the future. How are you?"

"Did you get my message? I called because I remembered something about last week."

"Do you mean about Sunday night?"

Had it only been two days ago? It seemed like an eternity.

Jake smiled, waiting for me to speak.

I turned my head to see who was nearby.

He read my mind and hitched a thumb behind his shoulder. “Should we talk on the sun porch?”

“Sure.” I stood up to follow him.

The porch was only illuminated now by the moon, but it felt appropriate for the conversation I wanted to have.

He turned around sharply, so that I had to stop short or bounce off his chest. “I’m sorry that I didn’t get back to you. As you can imagine, it’s been pretty busy.”

“I’m sure. I can’t stop thinking about Lyra. Is there any update on the case?”

He didn’t move for a long moment, then he gave a brief nod. “It’s been confirmed that someone struck her on the back of the head and placed her in the freezer. And that a prior concussion may have made lethal what would otherwise have been survivable. That information was just shared at a press conference. Which you probably missed because you were here.”

“So you’re saying that if she hadn’t hit her head before at the tea, she might have lived?”

“Yes. At least as regards the assault.”

“Did you find the weapon?”

Jake shifted his weight. “So *that* would qualify as privileged information. Maybe we’d better move on. What was it that you wanted to tell me?”

“You asked if I had noticed anything unusual. And there might have been. When I last saw Lyra, she shoved a stack of metal pots away so that she could hop up on the counter—”

“I don’t follow.”

“Maybe because I didn’t finish yet?”

“Sorry,” he said.

"But later when I went in there and she was, you know"—he acknowledged what I meant with a dip of the chin—"there were only *two* pots on the counter."

I waited for his response, but he didn't move a muscle.

"Do you see? One of the pots was missing."

He didn't say anything.

"Before I just wanted to mention it to you as an oddity of the scene since you asked me to report anything unusual, but now I'm actually wondering if it could have been the murder weapon? Did you find a pot somewhere that you shouldn't have?"

"I can only accept information, Starrs. I can't expand on your theory."

"Yes, you can."

"What?"

"I am *bringing* you the theory. You could at least tell me if it matters. C'mon, Jake, it's me. We're friends."

"We are?" He raised an eyebrow.

The floor felt as though it was slipping away from under me. Did I just tell Jake Hollister that we were friends? That was weird.

"We're in the same writing group. Weren't you the one who said that writing groups are based on trust?" I didn't add a "ha!" at the end to emphasize the triumphant logic I was deploying, but I could tell he understood.

"No fair throwing that back at me, Starrs. It's a different context completely."

"Trust means trust." I didn't know if I believed that. I mean, I thought I did. But mostly I wanted to see him try and wriggle out of his pronouncement from before.

He rubbed his chin. "Thank you for letting me know about the pot. I'll share it with the proper authorities."

Really? He wasn't going to wriggle? That was no fun.

"Fine, good. See you." I was turning to leave when I felt his hand lightly touch my forearm, which translated somehow into a not-unpleasant tingle.

"How did you think of that saucepot theory?"

"I was at Vivi's and saw the rack hanging from the ceiling. It must have jogged the connection bar in my memory."

"I see. Also, about the friend thing. I'd like to revisit that. Remember when we made plans for coffee? We never did have it."

"You got called in to work that day, then you didn't reschedule."

"I wasn't sure you wanted me to."

"You invited me, Jake. If you wanted to have coffee, you would have called."

"Have you been mad about that the whole time?" He chuckled. "I'm sorry. You're right. I don't even have a good excuse. Except that this job is very demanding."

"Don't worry about it. Absolutely doesn't matter, Detective." I pulled my arm away and marched over to Nora, who said it was time to leave.

I agreed, in more ways than one.

Chapter Twelve

On Wednesday morning, I only had one eye open as I groped around on the nightstand hoping to hit the key that would make my phone stop buzzing.

It was a literal rude awakening.

When I saw who it was, I had no choice but to answer.

"Hi, Emma! It's Whitney," she said perkily. "I hope I didn't wake you up, but I know you probably have to get an early start. Could you come over to my sister's house now? We would love to get your take on Lyra's case."

Even though my brain was foggy, it was screaming the word *no*. I had about eight million things to take care of before Friday. "I would like to help you out—"

"Great!" she interjected.

"—but I'm very busy with the—"

"We won't take up too much of your time, I promise."

"—gala."

"Yes, I know you have a lot of work to do on that. Nora told me you were stepping into Lyra's shoes. Impressive. Anyway, you know where we are. We have some fresh strawberry tarts."

She hung up and I sat there for a moment, staring straight ahead.

Had I just been bribed with pastries?

I guess I could at least listen to what they had to say.

* * *

An hour later, freshly showered, I was knocking on Malina's front door.

Whitney answered, wearing another one of her magically elegant white off-the-shoulder sweaters over jeans. Even if I bought the exact same top, I'd never be able to duplicate the stylish effect it had on her. "Thank you so much, Emma."

"I'm not sure that I will be able to—"

She raised her hand to stop my protestations. "If you can come up with anything at all, we'll be grateful. The police haven't provided answers yet. Or if they have, they haven't told us."

"Do they think you're suspects?" I clapped my hand over my mouth, then apologized. "I didn't mean to say that. I haven't had any coffee yet, so I'm not thinking straight."

She gave me a warm smile. "No worries. Let's take care of the coffee part, and no, they haven't given us any indication that they're suspicious of us."

As I followed her to the kitchen, I reflected on her choice of words. Was it odd that she didn't simply proclaim innocence?

Malina was a vision in purple from head to toe, including a headband that matched her velour track suit. She pulled a casserole dish out of the oven, set it on the top burner, and removed the oven mitts. The air was filled with a tempting combination of melted cheese and coffee.

As I took the chair at the round wooden table near the window, Malina greeted me and brought over a coffee, along with a tiny pitcher of cream and a bowl of sugar. The table had already been set with a bright red cloth and stoneware dishes. The women sat down across from me, smiling as I took a sip of the delicious hazelnut blend. The caffeine began doing its work clearing away the cobwebs immediately.

Whitney passed me a tray of strawberry tarts that were almost too beautiful to eat.

I was more than willing to give it a try, though.

Once we had all been served, I waited until they'd taken a bite—just like my mom had taught us—then dug in.

"This is fantastic," I said.

"Oh, we're not responsible. Someone brought them over last night." Malina pointed her fork toward the refrigerator. "The house is bursting with casseroles dropped off by neighbors. We'll never eat them all. But let's dive right into the case."

"Thank you for having me over," I said. "But I do feel as though I need to stress that the police are on this case already. They'll surely have answers for you soon. I'm not licensed or qualified in any way."

"But you did solve a murder case before," Malina said firmly. "It was in the newspaper."

"More luck than anything else, probably."

"Determination, I should think." She nodded her head. "You've been a persistent one ever since you were little. I remember you made sure that the candy was given out at the end of every salon visit. If we forgot, you would stand in front of the register until someone asked what you wanted, and then you would very politely request that the candy jar be taken down from the shelf."

Whitney laughed. "Priorities."

"And," Malina continued, "you always insisted that your sister was allowed to pick out hers before you did. So sweet."

I blushed.

"We don't expect you to transform into Hercule Poirot, but whatever you can do as an interested party would be great," Whitney said. "You know, more of a Miss Marple amateur sleuth kind of thing."

Her comment surprised me, given that she'd confided last night that she didn't care for mysteries, which must have shown on my face.

"Whitney starred in those Agatha Christie movies a few years back," Malina reminded me.

Whitney nodded. "Loved every minute of it."

"I enjoyed those," I told her. "Pretty faithful to the books."

"Thank you. We tried." She dimpled prettily. "And, Emma, we respect your time. We aren't asking you to report back daily or anything. We just want to hear what you think."

I took another sip of coffee. "We could talk through possibilities, I guess."

"Oh, good." Malina's whole body relaxed. "The silence has been wearing on me."

"Do you have any theories right now?" I asked.

They exchanged a glance.

"No," Whitney said finally.

"Are you sure? You both looked at each other as if you were trying to decide whether to say something."

That made them exchange a glance again.

"If there's something that could be helpful, please share," I said. I didn't want to bring up anything about the missing pot that I'd discussed with Jake, which might be akin to leading the witness.

Malina looked down at her plate.

"It doesn't make any sense," Whitney replied. "Lyra was alone in the kitchen while we went out on stage and said hello to the crowd. She wasn't supposed to be looking at screens in case she did have a concussion but otherwise she was perfectly fine, aside from a headache, at that point. You were there, so you can confirm. That's why we looked at each other. It seems impossible that she could have ended up in that freezer."

I structured the next sentence carefully, not wanting to reveal that Jake and I had spoken about this. "The press conference mentioned the cause of death involved a head injury."

"I have to say, not much information came out of that press conference." Whitney shook her head.

"It was frustrating," Malina agreed.

"You don't think she did something to herself on purpose, do you?" Whitney asked sadly.

"Like hit herself on the head hard enough to kill herself and then climb into a freezer?" Malina stared at her.

"I mean . . ." Whitney chewed a nail. "She could have already been in the freezer and then hit her head? Or hit her head falling into the freezer?"

"Backwards? She was face up. You mean she intended to go inside that . . . that frozen tomb? How ridiculous." Malina used a that's-the-end-of-that kind of tone.

"It's not ridiculous," Whitney retorted, "if no one else was there."

"Maybe someone came inside after you left," I suggested.

"Or maybe there was a malignant force," Malina offered.

"Malignant force?" I repeated faintly.

"She means a ghost," Whitney interpreted, with a slight eye roll. "She watches a lot of ghost shows."

"They catch paranormal things on camera every day!" Malina protested. "How can you ignore that? You need to be more open-minded."

"Something to consider," I said, then tried to move us into less otherworldly territory. "Did you see anyone unfamiliar at the screening?"

Whitney shook her head. "No one came into the kitchen, and I didn't see any strangers in the hallway. The only people around were those of us who worked on the show, and certainly none of them would hurt her. We're a *family*."

I closed my eyes for a moment, trying to visualize the physical space. "Was there a window in the storage room or another door to the outside that we hadn't noticed? An entry that isn't obvious? Is there a way that someone could have slipped in and out unseen?"

"That's a good question," Malina said. "I'll mention that to the police next time they call."

"They're probably thinking about that already," Whitney said lightly. "Since they're professionals and all."

"I saw you talking to Detective Hollister last night," Malina said. "Did he have any other information?"

"Nothing beyond what we've discussed," I said.

"Have the two of you ever dated?" she asked.

"What? No. Definitely not," I proclaimed, loudly.

Whitney and Malina exchanged a look.

"What?"

"There's a . . ." Malina looked at Whitney. "How do I say it?"

"A vibe?" she suggested.

"Yes, a vibe between you two."

I shrugged. "We've known each other for ages. Went to school together. To be honest, we were kind of competitive for most of it."

They stared at me thoughtfully.

"Maybe you should . . . you know . . . cozy up," Malina said, executing an unexpected shimmy.

"Oh! That's not my style," I said firmly.

They looked at each other again.

"It could be," Whitney said.

"A little more makeup wouldn't hurt," Malina suggested, indicating her own brilliant purple eyeshadow application that had at least three shades artfully blended all the way up to the brow.

"Noted." I folded my napkin in half. "Did Lyra mention any tension with someone? Rivalry? Jealousy? Anything at all. Could be recent, could be long-standing."

Whitney poked at the crumbs on her plate.

Malina looked out the window into the backyard. "You know, she did mention something about someone being upset with her about something."

"So helpful," Whitney said, with a laugh. "Did she happen to mention any names or topics?"

Her sister shook her head "Sorry. I can't remember any of the specifics. It was sort of an offhand comment and then she said 'never mind' and went up to her room."

"Her room?" I asked.

"Her old room." Malina flushed. "I haven't changed a thing since she moved out west. I always figured that she'd be back someday, and I wanted to keep it ready for her. But when she came back to town, she decided to stay with everyone from the show at Silvercrest Castle, so it turned out to be a dumb idea."

"Not so dumb," Whitney said. "She might have stayed here on a future visit. It's just that her friends were all there—"

"While her mother was here all alone," Malina said, with a forlorn air.

Whitney stretched her arms over her head. "We *told* you that you could come stay with us at the hotel, Mal."

"Anyway," Malina said, ignoring her, "would it be helpful to look around Lyra's room? The police already did."

"Maybe."

"Why don't you show her, then?" Whitney asked, a slight edge to her voice.

Malina smiled at me without responding to her sister.

Although it felt as though they were trying hard to play nice in front of me, there was some kind of tension in the air between them. It only revealed itself in the most subtle ways. A look here, a pause there. Family business, perhaps.

Maline showed me upstairs to a pink, princess-themed room. It had obviously been designed with a young girl in mind, but I could see the appeal of keeping it the same. Do we ever *really* outgrow a princess theme? Or do we push that down deep inside?

Because my hands itched to try on the tiara lying on the white dresser.

"Feel free to look at whatever you want," Malina said. "But she took pretty much everything with her. I don't know why I thought she'd be coming back."

The four-poster bed in the center was draped with sheer netting and gathered with ribbons. Everything else was sparkles on top of sparkles, from the beaded necklaces hanging from a bar on the wall to an antique chair with carved wooden legs topped by a burgundy cushion in front of roll-top desk. I began with the closet, which held only empty hangers. I felt carefully along the shelf but didn't locate anything.

"Is it weird that we're standing here watching you?" Whitney asked. "I feel weird."

I paused. "I'm sorry, do you want to help search?"

"No," they said in unison.

"Then please feel free to watch away." I turned back to the closet and groped along the wall and floorboards to see if there was any indication of a panel that could lead to a stash spot, then twisted around to face them. "Are you aware of any places where she used to hide things?"

"No," Malina said, her eyes brimming with tears.

Whitney murmured something to her and led her away.

Relieved, I sped up my efforts, looking inside drawers and around furniture, lamps, and wall art. Finally, underneath the bed, I found an empty jewelry box. When I gave it a gentle shake, something moved inside. I felt along the inside seams until I touched a dip along the floor and pressed it. The other end popped up like a lever and revealed a small square of paper beneath. I carefully unfolded what turned out to be a piece of stationery, with colorful flowers along the top and neat cursive in the middle:

She won't help. Please tell me what to do. You know what I want . . . and I'll give you what you want.

There had been other words written then crossed out so hard that they'd created a hole in the page. I took a picture, then stood in the center of the room and slowly spun in a circle, performing a final survey. There was nothing else here.

Returning downstairs, I presented the jewelry box and letter. "Have you seen this before? Any idea what she means?"

They looked at each other blankly, then shook their heads.

"That's her handwriting, but it sounds kind of ominous," Whitney said. "*I'll give you what you want*? Yikes."

"And who does the *she* refer to?" Malina asked. "It's not me, right? I always helped. I did everything I could to help her. Everything!"

"Of course you did," Whitney said automatically, patting her back.

After a moment, Malina shook free and walked toward the front door to indicate that it was time for me to leave. She had a different energy than I'd felt from her before—tense or angry. Maybe she and her sister had been arguing while I was upstairs.

"If you think of anything at all, please let us know," Whitney said, from behind us. "Something might occur to you later, and we aren't going to stop asking questions around here until we get real answers."

"Thanks for trying," Malina said, then shut the door.

Not so softly.

* * *

All the way home, I turned the meeting over in my mind. It was strange that they'd summoned me and then excused me so abruptly. It was as if they'd decided that I could zip by for breakfast and figure everything out . . . and when I had failed, they were done with me. I knew they were grieving, but it still felt unsettling.

Back in my own bedroom—which was not princess-themed, alas, but beloved, with its lavender quilt and bright yellow embroidered pillows as well as a cushioned window seat overlooking the mountains—I pulled out my to-do list and began making phone calls.

An hour or so later, only one name remained on my list. I sighed and selected Tabitha's number. It went straight to voice mail, which was a breathy yet overly peppy version of Actual Tabitha promising to call back later if we left our information.

I hung up, figuring I'd try again later. My gaze fell on the laptop I'd plugged in to charge overnight, and I retrieved it.

Before I was even fully aware of what I was doing, I typed in Lyra's name. Her "party planner to the stars" website and social media streams featured beautiful event pictures, with shout-outs to various businesses that had provided food, gifts, décor, and more. I wondered what sort of kickback she got for mentioning them. What did they call the freebie cycle? Promotional consideration? Mixed in with those were selfies and group shots of Lyra with quite a few actors and film industry types. Several of the actors from *Chasers* were featured in many of them—at parties, dining out, on the beach.

It all looked so perfect. Who would have wanted to kill her . . . and why?

Chapter Thirteen

Tabitha called back later; she was already snapping at me before I'd said a single word. I snatched up a pad and pen to take notes about the many instructions that I sensed were coming my way. Couldn't anything just be normal with her? Why did it always feel like we were jousting?

"I'd appreciate it if you would leave a message when you call, Emma. I don't have time to talk to everyone and their dog right now. Tell me what you need to tell me and be done with it. Or, better yet, text me."

I didn't say anything.

"Am I being heard?" she sniffed.

It took some effort, but I kept my response calm and professional. "Yes, Tabitha. I will text you instead from now on whenever possible."

"So? What did you need to tell me?" I could practically hear her stamping her foot.

"We have music for the gala."

"Great. Which band did you get?"

I closed my eyes and braced myself. "He's a deejay."

"A *deejay*?" Her screech shot me straight up in the air. "You must be joking. This is a *gala*! Not a fraternity party. That's unacceptable."

I held the phone in front of me and turned on the speaker. Wasn't going to give her a chance to pierce my eardrum again. "There were no other bands available. And Mackenzie Gold is supposed to be the best."

"The best?"

The best deejay in the Friends With My Sister's Boyfriend category, anyway.

"Yes," I said confidently. "He knows what you want. And maybe this will work out better since you have that amazing new sound system at the ballroom."

There was a long silence, followed by a long sigh. Once we got through the dramatics, she issued a warning about how he better be the best deejay she'd *ever* heard or she'd take his fee out of my pay.

So that was a nice surprise.

* * *

I wandered downstairs, hungry despite the tart, about which I reminisced wistfully for a moment, then prepared lunch: a cup of peppermint tea and some apple slices paired with cheddar cheese.

Because cheese was what I needed right now.

Nora was at the table, proofreading her latest novel. I could tell by the ruler she was using to review the work line by line and the special red pen she used for corrections. When she was done reading through it, she would input the changes on her laptop, but she always printed the manuscript out for this phase.

With some thirty novels to her name, she'd found a process that worked for her. Someday, I hoped to have a tried-and-true method myself. I was ready for the gala to be over so that I could get back to my own revisions.

She pushed her reading glasses up into her hair. A steaming cup of tea sat at her elbow too.

Hooray for impromptu tea parties.

"Where did you go this morning?" She smiled.

"Whitney and Malina invited me over."

Nora tilted her head questioningly.

"Someone told them about the murders this fall. They wanted to see if it helped to talk about Lyra."

My aunt nodded thoughtfully. "Did you come to any conclusions?"

"No." I put a slice of cheddar on top of an apple and ate it. The combination always reminded me of coming home after school with Lucy and telling my mother how our days had gone. It was comforting to have that kind of connection, somehow. Missed my parents every day.

"I can't imagine who would want to hurt her," Nora said quietly.

"Maybe it was an accident?"

"Perhaps. But why wouldn't someone confess, if that's the case?"

"Maybe they're afraid people won't believe that it wasn't intentional?"

She moved the manuscript pages off to the side and centered her tea on the placemat in front of her. Just then, the doorbell rang.

I pushed back my chair and went to the front door.

Jake Hollister stood on the porch. He smiled at me, but it was his on-duty smile, I could tell right away.

"May I come in?" He took a step forward, and I moved aside.

"We're in the back." I pressed the door shut and led him to the kitchen.

He and Nora exchanged hellos, then she gestured toward the chair at the side of the table.

Jake settled himself and waved away our offer of a beverage. "Wanted to have a quick follow-up to our conversation yesterday. You said something about a pot in the kitchen. What did it look like?"

"Silver with copper on the bottom. And it had a handle."

"Do you mean a saucepan?"

"Okay."

He did a double take. "I thought you said it was a pot."

"Sorry. I'm not an expert on anything kitchen-related, so yes, I might have used that general terminology. On the other hand, I remember hearing a very important chef whose name escapes me argue on a cooking show that saucepans *can* be considered pots because of the high sides—"

"Never mind," he said, shaking his head. "You said it was on the counter when you found Lyra?"

"No, I said when I took a picture for her. She wanted one with Whitney."

"She called it an 'old school' picture, as opposed to a selfie," Nora added. "If that's helpful to know, Detective."

He appeared confused by her contribution but made a note, then looked at me expectantly.

"She'd pushed a stack of three pots—er, saucepans—down the counter to make room for herself. I suppose that's what brought them closer to the stove, where I noticed two later. They might even be in the picture, though if so, I didn't do a very good job of setting up an artistic shot."

"Oh, it's always best to frame things carefully," Nora agreed. "Or to edit them afterwards if necessary."

"Thank goodness for cropping, right?"

Jake tapped his pen on the pad. "At what point in the evening did you take Lyra's picture?"

"Before the screening. Nora and I both went to speak to Whitney and Lyra."

"Thank you for including me in your story, darling," my aunt said approvingly.

"Of course. It was your idea to check on them in the first place."

"Did you notice the saucepans?" Jake asked Nora.

She bit her lip as she thought. "No, I can't say I did."

"What, you don't believe me, Jake?" I said it lightly, but I wondered.

"It's always good to corroborate if possible," he told me.

"Why are you obsessed with the saucepans? Did you find the third one somewhere?"

He tried not to react, but his expression was like a kid caught with his hand in a cookie jar.

"You *did*," I said. "Where was it?"

"Outside."

"In the trash?"

"Nearby."

"Any prints?"

"Wiped clean."

"Any residues?"

"Testing now."

Once we had completed the lightning round, I nibbled on some cheese. "What conclusion are you leaning toward?"

"We're still investigating, Starrs. You'll hear when the time is right."

"It's frightening to think that whoever did this is out there, walking among us." Nora sounded genuinely alarmed. "They might even be coming to the gala."

"We'll have a police presence there," he said reassuringly. "We always do, actually, but we'll increase it this time considering what's been going on."

"Thank you, Detective," she said.

After an elongated silence, Jake stood and thanked us for talking to him.

At the front door, he studied my face for longer than was comfortable. "Should we get that coffee sometime soon?"

The air seemed to crackle between us.

"After the gala?" I suggested. "This weekend is going to be exhausting."

"Riverside Coffee? We can finalize the time later." He turned and began walking briskly to his car.

"I didn't mean, like, *immediately* after the gala," I called after him. "A different day."

He waved without turning around.

So infuriating.

"Is it my imagination working overtime, or is there a spark between you and Jake?" Nora inquired when I sat down next to her.

"What? Why would you think that?"

"Something I'm sensing." She couldn't hide her delight.

"Eww, no."

"This is the same Jake you've been talking about since high school, yes?"

"*Complaining* about. Not talking about."

Nora looked into her teacup. "He's grown into quite a handsome young man."

"But he's still the same stubborn, overconfident guy that he was back then."

"There's something to be said for a strong-minded partner. I've always found that those kind of people keep the energy up in a relationship. For me, anyway. May not be to your taste, so to speak." She took a sip.

I threw up my hands. "What is it with you and Lucy trying to marry me off to any guy who comes into my orbit?"

"We love you, darling. We want you to be happy."

"I am happy," I said crossly.

"Just . . . be open. Okay? Be open." She smiled and went back to her editing.

* * *

"Are you coming to the hotel?" Tabitha's edge was twice as sharp this time when I answered the phone later that afternoon. "My hands are full!"

"I'm almost there."

Tabitha had made arrangements for the celebrities to stay at Silvercrest Castle, which was fashioned after a famous one in England. The next wave of special guests—not actors, but special nonetheless—was arriving today. I didn't know why Tabitha had invited local people to stay at the most expensive hotel in town since covering that bill took away from what the library would receive. Some of her decisions were downright baffling.

More than some.

As I turned into the long driveway, I admired the flags snapping in the wind atop towers on both ends of the long stone building. Perched on a river bank facing the town, it commanded the grounds with authority. Most of the fancy events not held at the country club happened here, and it was a popular wedding destination that booked out years in advance. The library gala had been held at the castle many times in the past, but Tabitha's plan was to continue using Baxter Ballroom henceforth, which would be good for the college.

I pulled up in front and handed my keys to the valet dressed in a red blazer with a crest on the left side. At the top of the stone steps, another blazer-clad-and-crested man wearing a pair of white gloves extended a tray toward me. "Spiced mulled wine?"

I reached out and took one of the silver mugs. It smelled divine.

I should probably *check* it at least, to make sure everything was up to snuff.

After thanking him, I took a sip. The wine was so delicious and invigorating that I took a few more. In the lobby, another person waited with a tray to capture the used mugs, and I set mine down with more than a little regret.

Maybe I should check it again on the way out.

The man sneezed, twisting his head away from me at the last second and throwing one of his arms up so that he could sneeze into the crook of it. The other arm flailed and the mugs slid quickly to the end of the tray. Although he tried valiantly to catch it, everything tumbled off and crashed mightily on the floor. The silver mugs bounced, making merry chime sounds, and the wine flew in every direction.

He looked at me in horror. "I'm so sorry, miss."

"Not a problem," I said. "Do you want me to—"

"No, no. We'll take care of it. Please forgive me." He hurried over to the registration desk and returned with a roll of paper towels.

Another employee let go of the bellhop rack he'd been loading up with garment bags from a long rectangular mailing box and raced over to bark at the tray holder. "Get the mugs first. The *mugs*!"

I edged away and left them to it, then crossed the polished floor, past the gleaming dark wood check-in desk and shining chandeliers, stopping in front of Tabitha. She was wearing a navy tailored suit and a cream silk scarf and could have easily passed herself off as a company CEO or flight attendant.

"Way to make an entrance, Emma." She clicked her tongue in displeasure and shoved a clipboard toward me. I glanced at the first page, which appeared to be a list, but her scrawling handwriting made it difficult to read. "When I greet someone, please check off their name."

"Sorry, I'm having a little trouble reading this," I said, squinting.

"Are you sure you have a PhD? Because it *so* doesn't seem like it most of the time," she said. "Jot down their names if you can't read what I already took a great deal of time to write out for you. Just *listen carefully* as I say their names."

I looked down at the list again, closing one eye and then the other. Still no luck.

An extended limo pulled up in front of the entrance.

"Here we go," she said excitedly.

A group of people wearing sunglasses despite the fact that it was getting dark exited the vehicle and swept inside. They moved purposefully toward Tabitha, who had her best smile in place. There was air kissing, exclamations about how gorgeous everyone looked, and general flattery. Then they moved into the elevators, the doors closed, and it was quiet again.

Tabitha turned to me, flushed with joy. "Did you get everyone checked off?"

"No. You said to listen for names—"

She frowned and snatched back her clipboard.

"Would you like me to ask the front desk for a list of recent arrivals?"

Her lips twisted. "They will *not* give out the names of the guests who stay here. But no matter. I know who they are, anyway."

"If you know who they are, then why do we need a list?"

She ignored my perfectly logical question while making angry check marks down the page. "It's strange to me that you don't know them."

"I've already met the *Chasers* people," I said. "Just not all of their entourage."

"That wasn't anyone from *Chasers*. That was the photographer Zander Flyte and his social media team. They're extremely important *influencers*. Really, Emma, popular culture matters. You should try to keep up with what's trending in the world, instead of having your head in a book all the time."

"I *like* having my head in a book all the time."

"Well, it's not working for me."

I reminded myself that I wanted to get the paycheck at the end of all this, so I dialed my tone way down. "Just asking you to be more respectful, please. I did recognize Zander, but you asked me to check off the names you said aloud. Then you didn't say any names."

"You know what? This conversation is boring."

"For both of us, I assure you."

She stared at me, and I stared right back. That might have gone on for hours if the person who was in charge of taking photos of The Beautiful People hadn't approached us.

"Where do you want me to set up?" he asked. I understood why Tabitha was so excited about having Zander Flyte, who had a reputation as the best photographer for high society functions—he may have even been on retainer for the country club events—not least because he deleted unflattering pictures and airbrushed things to within an inch of their lives. No one needed to be worried about how they'd look in the society columns or magazines when he was around. It helped people relax, knowing they'd not be caught appearing too awkwardly posed or excessively jowly.

Zander himself was a slim man perpetually clad in a uniform of black tee and jeans; at formal events, he'd add a tuxedo jacket to blend in better with the crowd. He had shoulder-length dark hair that he pulled back in a ponytail. His brown eyes were always moving, always gauging the next shot, even if you were speaking to him. Everything about him said "artsy," which was a label he both cultivated and cherished.

"Oh, Zander. Hello." Tabitha modulated her voice appropriately and walked him over to the elevator. "We're going up to Stella's suite."

A bevy of Zander's people scampered behind him toting lights and rigs and camera bags. It was a lot of gear.

"Allons-y, Emma!" Tabitha warbled, her tone ten times sweeter than when it was the two of us.

I hurried over and pushed the button on the wall. When the doors slid open, the assistants parted to create a path that would allow Tabitha and Zander to enter first. They didn't even try to go inside. Tabitha waved at me impatiently, and I took the spot next to Zander, who smelled like oranges and alcohol. I certainly wasn't going to judge him, given that I probably carried a petite cloud of mulled wine myself, due to the necessary checking at the door just now.

He gave me a quick smile, his eyes darting around the elevator, perhaps taking in its spatial measurements and wondering if he could do a group shot with the VIPs.

"Zander Flyte, Emma Starrs," Tabitha said, proving that she did have some manners, much to my surprise.

Before I had a chance to speak, she launched into a monologue about how excited she was about his being there. Zander nodded distractedly, like someone wearing earbuds as they walked down the street. When we reached the top level, she waited for him to leave and quickly shoved herself between us, so that I'd be last person out.

I wondered idly if she congratulated herself each night about all the ways she'd tried to put me in my place. She wouldn't bother if she knew how little it mattered to me in a general sense. Bad behavior was what I expected from her at this point.

We moved down the short hallway to a door made of burnished wood, which was slightly ajar. Tabitha leaned forward and knocked, then pushed it open. The suite was luxury all the way: elegant wallpaper, marble counters, and modern light fixtures. Sliding glass doors along the right wall offered a breathtaking view of the river and mountains, and plush sofas and chairs were arranged in an enticing configuration next to the fireplace.

Ariel came toward us, gesturing toward the seating area and murmuring that we should make ourselves comfortable. As we followed her directions, she disappeared down a hallway with several closed doors. Not long afterward, Stella Vane emerged, with her posse. They moved in unison, like the part of a movie where everyone's walk goes into slow motion to emphasize their coolness.

Her suit today was bright red and nipped in at the waist with a wide black belt. Someone else might have been put in mind of Santa, but Stella's ethereal slenderness and high-end accessories knocked any potential for that sort of interpretation aside. Every bit of her screamed *chic.*

She strutted around—there really was no other word for it—then, when she had almost reached us, held a pose with her head twisted to the left and her arms up high so that we could admire her. "I've *arrived,*" she said.

Caught up in the big response from the rest of the room, I joined in the applause. Stella laughed as she made her way over to the opposing couch and sat down, looking expectantly at us. The rest of her people draped themselves over nearby furniture like a pack of vampires waiting for a signal from their leader.

"Allow me to introduce you to Zander Flyte, photographer extraordinaire." Tabitha reeled off a list of honors that he'd received, as he sat there pleasantly. Stella professed to be familiar with his work, which visibly gratified him.

"This is my team," Stella said, waving languidly around the room.

No one moved a muscle.

She pointed to them one by one. "Rico, my hairdresser supreme; Brielle, the world's best makeup artist; Trey, an unrivaled stylist; and Ariel, the best assistant ever."

"And that's Emma Starrs," Tabitha said, jabbing her pointer finger at me.

"I'm helping with the gala," I told the room. "My family owns Starlit Bookshop."

Stella gave us all a big smile. "Thanks for the panel the other night. That was fun. And remember . . . Stella is a star too."

"That's right." I smiled at her.

"You're a *huge* star, Stella," Tabitha said hurriedly. "Did Emma say something to suggest otherwise? I'm so sorry if she offended you."

She threw back her head and laughed. "Not at all."

"The name Stella means star," I explained. "It's etymology."

Tabitha blinked. "Can we eta-whatever on the balcony for a few? The light outside is perfect and Zander wants to take some shots out there."

"Are Whitney and Nat coming?" I asked Stella.

She consulted her diamond-encrusted watch. "They're late. I don't know why, exactly—they're staying on this floor too. We all have suites. Would you please give them a call?"

There was a knock at the door, and the couple appeared. Greetings were exchanged all around and they were quickly shepherded out onto the balcony so that Zander could make the most of the setting sun over the mountains. The two stars posed in various configurations while Zander clicked away, moving from one crouched position to another. He must have had thighs of steel from doing that all of these years.

Stella watched for a moment, then stood up and wiggled her fingers. Her team leaped to attention, readjusting her outfit, spritzing something on her face, and tucking in various wisps of hair. Then she waved them away and headed outside to join the others.

"Magic hour, here I come," she breathed.

Chapter Fourteen

After the balcony photos and a few more in the living room, the stars went downstairs with glam squad in tow to shoot more around the picturesque grounds.

Tabitha and I stayed behind and took advantage of the quiet to talk about the run-through that was scheduled for the next day at the Baxter Ballroom. We had a surprisingly efficient conversation for once. Maybe our little standoff had been productive. Then she left to sort out the billing with the hotel manager, and I was left alone.

It struck me that I could take a quick look around, see if there was anything that could assist Whitney and Malina in finding out what had happened to Lyra. This group worked together so often, there might be something helpful lying around. Although I was against trespassing in theory, I nonetheless found myself drifting down the hallway toward the bedrooms. It wasn't snooping if there was a good reason for it, I told myself. It was *investigating*. I was *helping*.

I took a deep breath and pushed open the door to Stella's first room, which clearly served as a receptable for an explosion of clothes. Items were strewn about on the bed, chairs, and floor. I didn't know how Stella could take such pains to look impeccable yet blithely fling the expensive items hither and yon the instant she was done wearing them. Then again, they were her clothes. She had the right to treat them however she wanted. I circled the room and opened all the drawers, but nothing caught my attention.

I backed out and moved on to the second room, which was tidier but had suitcases and a pile of scarves on the bed; a container on the desk filled with makeup reminded me of the fishing tackle box my father used to use. Another box was filled with an array of vitamins and herbs, painkillers prescribed by a Dr. Cardinal, and expensive breath mints. The cut-glass perfume bottle on the nightstand had such a pretty flower pattern that I paused to smell it, expecting something sweet and floral to match but getting instead a snootful of a heavy earthy scent. Rubbing my nose to try and clear it, I refocused, then gave the suitcase, makeup box, and drawers a quick scan. They were serving their intended container purposes but didn't yield anything exciting. A flat iron, curling iron, and blow dryer lay on the dresser next to an issue of *Variety* open to a story about *Chasers*, which I quickly skimmed. The article was about how popular the show was, how talented the cast was, and how the executives were risk-takers who liked to keep things fresh. It didn't tell me what I needed to know, like how close were they all, really? Who was involved with whom? What motives lurked beneath the surface of their relationships?

I paused. Everyone who knew Lyra—sister, mother, and friends—genuinely seemed to care about her. Maybe Lyra was simply in the wrong place at the wrong time. Maybe she didn't even know her killer.

Time was running out, so I hurried back to the sofa and was going over my gala list when the group returned to the room. They quickly had me laughing at their description of how Zander had almost fallen into the pond trying to get a shot of them with geese in the background. Nat was vigorously reenacting Zander's flailing when there was a knock on the door of the suite. We fell quiet, waiting for someone to identify the visitor.

"I gave my glam squad the rest of the night off," Stella said. "Maybe they forgot something."

"Don't they have a key?" Nat asked with a grin.

"Maybe that's what they forgot," Stella said, elbowing him.

Whitney giggled.

Ariel opened the door. That seemed to be one of her primary job functions as Stella's assistant, aside from getting coffee and telling her that she looked fantastic at all times.

Melody strolled in, waving hello. "How's everyone doing?"

Tabitha did a double take. "I didn't know you were coming."

Her bestie took a seat next to me and gave a wide smile to the celebrities lined up on the other sofa, who politely acknowledged her. "I'm Melody Crenshaw from the gala committee . . . and a Silvercrest High School alumna."

That was weird. Usually she highlighted her society standing. Maybe she added the high school affiliation to bond with Whitney as a hometown girl.

"Go Cougars!" the star said gamely.

"I'm sorry, that's the *college* mascot," Tabitha said, as though Whitney were a contestant on a game show who had guessed the wrong answer.

"Oh, right. Sorry! I didn't go to high school in Silvercrest." Whitney explained that she'd graduated from a well-known performing arts school in Denver.

"Me too," Ariel said, from beside Stella.

"Oh, wow," Whitney said. "I never knew that! Why didn't you tell me?"

The young woman blushed. "I thought I did?"

"You definitely told *me*, honey." Stella laughed.

"So sorry. If I knew that, I've forgotten." Whitney said. "You must have gone through with Lyra. I had already been out in LA for years by then."

"Yes. That's where we met," Ariel said.

"And where did *you* go to high school?" Melody asked, trying to bring the conversation back to her arena. She was looking at Nat, but everyone started proclaiming which high school they'd attended at the same time. We had started in on colleges when we heard a sharp rapping and Ariel jumped up to answer the door again.

This time, it was the bellhop I'd seen downstairs unloading the garment bags. "Delivery from Sabine Saturn," he announced, pushing the luggage cart behind the sofa where I was sitting. He remained hovering there until Ariel rushed up and put a tip into his hand. He touched his red hat and withdrew.

Tabitha and Melody quickly scurried over to the rack. Getting Sabine Saturn, an uber-hot fashion designer in New

York, to send clothes for the stars had been something they'd prattled about endlessly over the past few days, when they weren't snarking at Nora or me.

I twisted around to watch the big moment. The gold bags each had a name written on the outside.

"This one's for Stella," Tabitha removed the bag hanging on the rail carefully, as if it were constructed of eggshells.

"And here's Nat's," Melody lifted the next one, giving it a loving look.

They both reached for Whitney's at the same time, but from different sides, and for a full minute, they clutched the bag and glared at each other until Tabitha moved her stiletto-shod foot slowly and poked Melody in the calf.

"Ow!" Melody yelped, stepping backward. Tabitha triumphantly snatched Whitney's bag and held it aloft.

The high sofa back had prevented the others from seeing what Tabitha had done, but I would never forget it. It was a solid metaphor for every interaction I'd ever had with her.

If she wasn't careful, she would end up without any groupies—and then how would she function?

Not my problem, I reminded myself.

"Do you want to try them on in the back?" Ariel asked.

The celebrities enthusiastically took their bags and went down the hallway. The minute they were gone, Tabitha pulled Melody out onto the balcony, closing the door behind them. I could see them arguing through the glass but I couldn't make out what they were saying.

Ariel moved around the room, gathering plates and napkins.

I picked up glasses from the end tables on either side of my sofa and carried them over to the sink.

She gave me a grateful look. "Thank you," she said shyly.

"How do you like working for Stella? Everyone from *Chasers* seems like a fun group."

"I love it," she said, rinsing out the glasses and putting them into the top rack of the little dishwasher that was cleverly disguised as a cabinet. "She's been very kind to me. Though it was more fun before—" She broke off, a stricken look on her face. She turned away briefly, then rotated back while wiping her eyes.

"Lyra?" I asked softly.

"I miss her," she whispered.

"I'm so sorry," I said, knowing the words were never enough.

"Ahem," said a voice nearby. Stella was standing in another elegant pose, arms skyward, hands curved beautifully. Her gown was deep green and covered with shimmering sequins, with a sheath along the top that turned into a flare near the very bottom. I'd never seen anyone look more mermaid-like.

Ariel and I dutifully gushed as the balcony door slid open so hard that it slammed along the end. Tabitha and Melody sprinted over and provided a chorus of oohs and ahs.

Nat emerged, strutting down the hallway in his perfectly fitting tuxedo. It had a patterned lapel and matching vest. He did a little twirl, and we were all applauding when the door at the end burst open and Whitney came out, looking unhappily down at the material in her hands. "Does Sabine hate me or something?"

"What's wrong?" Stella asked. "Doesn't it fit?"

Whitney held the dove gray gown up by the shoulders so that we could take in the front of the dress, which had numerous jagged slashes from top to bottom. Additional gashes were visible on either side. "Maybe I'm just misunderstanding the style. Is this how it should look?"

"No!" Tabitha cried, moving swiftly toward it, arms straight out as if she wanted to hug the injured garment. "It's not. Not at all."

"I mean, I don't know much about dresses," Nat said, "but isn't it supposed to be in one piece?"

"Definitely," Melody said.

"You all know that I never mind showing a bit of skin," Stella gestured toward herself, "but that is unwearable even for me."

Tabitha accepted the material from Whitney and placed it over the sofa. She inspected it carefully. "I saw the original sketches. This is all wrong. Someone attacked it!"

"Why would she send it like that?" Nat asked, scratching his chin.

"She wouldn't have," Tabitha replied. "It must have happened later."

Whitney looked around the room in dismay. "What should I do?"

"I could loan you something," Tabitha mused.

"Me too," Melody offered.

"She's *much* smaller than you are, Mel," Tabitha laughed. "But seriously, Whitney, please come over tonight and see if there's anything in my closet you'd like to wear."

"I guess so," Whitney said, but she didn't sound thrilled with the idea.

Stella stepped closer and inspected the tears. "We could call Sabine and ask her to overnight another gown."

"Oh no. I don't want to be a bother," Whitney said. "Also, didn't you say she started working on these masterpieces months ago?"

"That's true," Tabitha said. "But I do need to call her and let her know about this. She's expecting you to wear it, be photographed in it."

"I do *not* think you should," Stella replied. "She'll freak out for sure."

"We could go to Mulligan's—" Melody ventured.

"The *department* store? That's hilarious." Tabitha laughed again. "She wouldn't be caught dead in ready-to-wear at a *gala*. Would you?"

Whitney shrugged.

An idea occurred to me. "Do you like vintage?"

Her eyes lit up. "Who doesn't?"

"Let me call my friend Marlowe Markson, who has a great shop here in town. She specializes in one-of-a-kind pieces."

Tabitha gasped. "Surely *that's* not the direction we want to go in."

"Ooh, I love vintage couture too," Stella said, putting an end to Tabitha's objections.

"Marlowe is an incredible curator," I said to Whitney. "She finds amazing things all over the world."

Tabitha frowned so hard I could almost hear it.

"Do you have another idea?" I waited.

She crossed her arms in front of her. "We could commission something. My seamstress might be able to repair this . . ."

"Have you *met* Sabine? She would throw a *fit* if something altered was attributed to her," Stella said.

"Not altered. Mended," Tabitha said.

"Even worse," the star replied.

"Or my seamstress could make something completely new." Tabitha went on desperately.

"That doesn't make sense. She's not even a designer," Melody said flatly.

Tabitha recoiled at her public betrayal, visibly at a loss for words. She thought it was fine to denigrate Melody when she felt like it, but she demanded total loyalty for her own ideas at all times. I didn't know what was going on between the two of them, but I was glad to see Melody sticking up for herself. Not that she was a friend of mine in any way, shape, or form. It was just nice to see other people standing up to Tabitha.

I pulled out my phone and texted Marlowe, explaining the situation.

She wrote back, inviting us to come by immediately, which I shared with the group. I didn't mention the row of smiley face and heart emojis.

This was her cup of tea, exactly.

* * *

I was happy that Whitney was the only one coming with me to Riverside Vintage. The last thing I needed right now was more energy spent running counter-maneuvers to whatever Tabitha did.

I glanced at her in the passenger seat. She was looking out the window at the scenery. I couldn't tell if she was feeling nostalgic, simply taking in the stores as we passed by, or worried.

"Are you okay?"

"Sure." She produced a brave smile and stared out the window again.

It was a charming sight: the stores on River Street were still decorated for the holidays, all wreaths and ribbons and tinsel. Lights twinkled in window displays and in the trees that dotted the sidewalks. The snow had melted away from all but the biggest drifts.

"It's a little weird, right?" she said, as we stopped at a red light.

"The dress thing?"

"Yes. And Lyra. Everything is so surreal. It seems wrong for me to still be here when she is not. It seems wrong that I'm walking around talking to people when she cannot. I have a job to do, so I have to shove my grief down in order to function, and that feels disrespectful to her." Her voice wavered. "On top of that, it feels like someone is after us."

"I'm incredibly sorry, Whitney."

"Thank you," she said in a small voice.

"Have you gotten into any confrontations lately? Anyone with a grievance out there?"

"Not that I know of. I mean, my agent takes care of the business part, so I don't have to fight for stuff myself."

"How about fans?"

"They've been very sweet. Haven't had any stalker issues or anything, like some people have. Thank goodness."

The light turned green and traffic surged forward.

"I'm worried," she said.

"Why?"

"Because I can't wear Sabine's beautiful dress, and she'll be offended."

"Don't worry," I said. "Tabitha will handle Sabine. You didn't do anything wrong."

"You really don't think it was supposed to be like that?"

"No," I said firmly. "No one thinks it was supposed to be like that."

"Who could have done it?" She shook her head.

"Those bags were hanging in the lobby when I got there. They may have been unattended for a period of time."

"Why would it have taken them so long to bring them up?"

"There may have been an incident," I said.

"With scissors?"

"No, I mean that there was a guy holding a tray of wine mugs nearby and they spilled all over the place. Some of the wine may have splashed on the bags. Maybe they were doing triage. Don't mention it to Tabitha, please. She'll call the manager and try to get them all fired."

"She's kind of awful, isn't she?" Whitney said. "Just between us."

"No comment," I said, nodding.

We both smiled.

I continued thinking aloud. "Or perhaps they were just distracted by the rest of the cleanup that was required and didn't have eyes on the bags for a while. In that case, the real questions would be, first, who took advantage of the unattended clothing to destroy the dress and, second, did they know it was yours, specifically?"

"The names were on the bags," she reminded me.

"That's true. And come to think of it, everyone was down there walking around for that photo shoot. All of you actors, the photography crew, *and* Stella's team. Lots of potential folks and plenty of time to do the deed," I said. "If it wasn't a random attack."

"I don't know who would have done that. And I hope we can find something good at the vintage store," Whitney said. "But if not, I'll wear jeans. I don't care what anyone says. It would be more comfortable, anyway."

The more I got to know her, the more down to earth she seemed. Her otherworldly beauty interfered with that perception at first glance.

"It's strange," she continued. "I grew up here, but I left right after high school, and everything seems different now. I'm sure the vintage store was here when I was little, but I don't remember it."

"Maybe you never went there. Marlowe's parents owned it before she took over."

She nodded, chewing her lip.

"She's taken it in a new direction, though. It has more of a boutique vibe. Every time you go, there are more one-of-a-kind items you haven't seen before. She consigns clothes from people in Silvercrest, but she's very picky about what she takes in. The bulk of her items come from tracking down treasures online. She also supports local artisans, so she'll blend handmade jewelry and accessories in with everything else."

Whitney nodded. "Sounds wonderful."

"And don't worry, everything is dry cleaned before reaching the floor too. That might be an uncommon practice, but her parents always did it and Marlowe says she can't imagine any other way, even though it costs her money. She wants customers to be able to wear things right out the door if they want to, while they're excited about their purchases."

"Tell me more about Marlowe," she said after a moment.

"She's amazing. We've been best friends since elementary school. She is a genius at styling customers. If she lived in LA or New York, she'd probably be one of the most popular stylists ever."

"Has she ever thought about moving there?"

"No. But she has thought about moving to Denver and training to be a private investigator."

"Um . . . that's a *completely* different career path," Whitney said.

"She's always had a dream of tracking down bad guys in the big city. Meanwhile, she's writing PI mysteries, which I think helps her imagine what it might be like."

"Nora told me you're writing a mystery too?"

"I would love to follow in her footsteps."

"You know, I'm not a huge mystery buff, but I do love Nora, so I've read all her books. They're great. Has she ever thought about adapting them into film?"

I turned on my blinker as we approached the parking lot. The line of cars coming toward us seemed to be never-ending.

"It's been discussed, but for one reason or another, they haven't been developed yet."

"It's tough to get a deal going," Whitney agreed. "Some people will do anything for that to happen, though."

"Anything?"

"Absolutely. They'll sell their very souls."

Chapter Fifteen

Marlowe greeted us at the door, dressed in a plum suit and gorgeous boots. Her opal necklace was a perfect accessory, shining softly against her dark skin. She always looked totally pulled together—not a surprise, given that the store was like an enormous closet from which she could select the best pieces. Perk of the job.

I knew she was excited to meet Whitney, but she played it cool and was her usual warm and friendly self. I made formal introductions, and they chatted about the gala for a few minutes.

"Em here says that you need a gown. I've pulled a few ahead of time. Right this way." Marlowe led us back to the corner near the dressing cubes, which were painted in bright pastel colors with floral designs. She had moved a rack of dresses next to the one on the end.

Whitney quickly skimmed the glittering rainbow of offerings and pointed to a bronze off-the-shoulder, sequin-and-crystal long gown. The shade shifted from lighter at the top to darker on the skirt. "May I try on that one, please?"

Marlowe laughed. "I appreciate a customer who knows what they like. The ombre piece is very special. One of a kind and direct from an important closet. Apparently, someone sent it to her hoping she'd wear it to a ball, but she didn't think it suited her." She identified a famous designer and socialite whose names were in the news so much that even I knew who they were. "It's been a few years now." She paused. "Wait—is that a problem? It's not, you know, *right* off the runway. But nobody has ever worn it."

"Not a problem at all," Whitney said. "In fact, I'm intrigued by the backstory."

Marlowe removed the gown and handed it to Whitney, who disappeared into the pink dressing room with daisies.

"Your favorite cube!" Marlowe said to me. "By the way, Nora and Lucy came by earlier and got all three of your gowns. Your aunt paid for yours."

"That was so nice of her . . . and you. I can't wait to wear it."

My gown was black velvet and taffeta; I'd fallen in love with its tailored bodice and bell-shaped skirt that almost brushed the floor. Marlowe had picked out some long gloves and a stunning vintage pearl collar necklace. It was all very Cinderella. Or more precisely, Cinderella-meets-noir-film-heroine.

The door opened and Whitney stepped out, beaming.

Marlowe and I gasped.

The dress fit like a glove, and the deep bronze color could not have been more flattering. Whitney's lightly tanned skin was luminous, and her blue eyes were even more striking than usual, which was saying something. It suited her in every way.

"It's good, right?" she asked, twirling.

"It's great," Marlowe said.

"Beautiful," I agreed.

"I'll take it," she said, swishing the skirt back and forth happily. "I love it even more than the one I was supposed to wear!"

Marlowe moved over to a shelf nearby and brought back a box full of jewelry. "Do you want to try on some accessories?"

"Yes, please," Whitney said, not taking her eyes off of herself in the full-length mirror on the wall.

The two of them were exploring different combinations while I answered a call from Tabitha, who started by shrieking in my ear.

"Are you trying to ruin everything? Did you imagine I wouldn't find out? What were you thinking, Emma?"

"What are you talking about?" My mind reeled. Had I forgotten something? I thought I'd completed every task on the list so far.

"You canceled the reservation for the pre-party!" Her indignation was approaching nuclear level.

"No. I haven't canceled anything."

"Well, I got an email from Le Chateau confirming the cancellation, so I called them immediately. They said that earlier today I had changed the reservation."

I waited.

"So what do you have to say for yourself?" She yelled.

"Nothing?"

"Why would you do that to us?"

"Wait, you think I did that? It wasn't me. They said it was you."

"They said it was a woman's voice," she said suspiciously.

I laughed. "That could be half of the population, Tabitha. And why would you think I'm the one who did it? That doesn't make any sense. I *want* everything to go smoothly. I want what you want."

Not always. But as it pertains to the gala, I think it was a fair statement.

Tabita wailed. "Le Chateau is IT. It *has* to be there. There is simply no alternative."

"So did you straighten everything out?"

"No," she snapped. "We lost the venue. The manager said they'd already gone to the next person on their waitlist. And he was really snippy too, saying that I should have known there was a five-year waiting list. How dare he? Doesn't he know who I *am*?"

I ignored her sputtering and tried to come up with an alternative. There was almost no chance that we'd be able to find something that large and that elegant in Silvercrest at such a short notice. "Are there any places in Denver you could call? Or the metropolitan area?"

"You mean *you* could call. Since you—"

Here we go again.

"I'm *not* the one who canceled the reservation, but I would be happy to help figure something out."

"Help? No. Every second of *my* calendar between now and the gala is booked up solid. There are errands to run, treatments to be had, styling to be done. I'm going to let you take full rein here. The country club and the castle are booked solid through the holidays. You need to think of somewhere fresh, Emma. If there ends up being no pre-party whatsoever for our guests, you can kiss your payment goodbye." She hung up.

I took a deep breath and reminded myself that I was doing this for the Silvercrest Library and for Starlit Bookshop—fundraising for the former and contributing any paycheck to the continued existence of the latter.

Just a little longer and I could go back to *not* talking to Tabitha Louise Saxton Lyme Harmon Gladstone Baxter every single day.

"Everything okay?" Marlowe came up beside me. Whitney was right behind her, back in her regular clothes, carrying a garment bag and Riverside Vintage shopping bag.

I explained the situation.

"How about the community center?" Marlowe asked, then shook her head. "Strike that. They're doing a film festival that starts tomorrow and runs through the weekend."

"How about the gym on campus?" Whitney suggested.

"Big basketball tournament this week," I said. "Nora gave her season tickets to Ryan to give to someone is the reason I know *that* bit of sporting news."

We ran through a list of nearby locations and eliminated them one by one for various reasons.

"Don't worry about it," I said. "Would anyone be genuinely sad if we didn't have a pre-party?"

Whitney blew out her breath. "Do you want me to answer honestly?"

"Maybe not. Yeah, definitely not." I pulled out my car keys and twirled them around my finger. "But thank you very much for your assistance."

* * *

After I dropped Whitney back at Silvercrest Castle, I stopped at Starlit Bookshop. Lucy flipped the sign on the door to "Closed" as I poured out my tale of woe.

"Sorry, Em. This makes me even more mad at Tabitha." She shook her fists in the air and went over to the register to tally up the day's sales. I picked up a duster from behind the counter and brushed it along the shelves. It was oddly soothing, so I worked my way to the back, to the sound of coins being dropped into the drawer as Lucy counted them.

Anne Shirley came marching down the spiral staircase and meowed, tail up as she assessed her next move.

I sat on the bottom step and waited for her to curl up next to me.

Or walk by. You never knew.

Tonight was a curl-up night, turned out, and I petted her back and head. Her purr increased in volume, and I tried to push my quest for a location out of mind and focus on being in the moment. Five minutes of purring later, I had an idea. When Vivi had moved her company in next door last month, she had offered to let the bookstore use the extra space in the future. We hadn't taken her up on it yet, but now was the time, if ever there was one.

I hurried up the aisles toward the front.

"I'll be back in a sec," I said over my shoulder to my sister and ran to Vivi's. Her door was open, and lights were on in the kitchen—thank goodness—so I jogged back there.

Vivi was tossing something in a saucepan like it was no big thing. I'd tried to mimic her graceful motion at home once and ended up having to clean not only the floor but the walls too.

She put it on the gas burner and angled the handle toward the young woman standing beside her, who tried it to duplicate Vivi's movement. She did better than I would have, but some of the contents still slipped out.

I said hello, and she smiled when she saw it was me.

"That's great—keep practicing, Taryn," she said, then came over to where I was standing, wiping her hands on her apron.

"Sorry to bother you," I said.

"No problem. We were doing a little technique work. She's heading out in a minute. We're done for the night. How are you?"

I made a face.

"What's going on?"

I indicated the large, dark portion of her store. "Is your event space up and running yet?"

"No. We just store tables and chairs in there. Why?"

"We're in a pinch. Could I please use it for a gala pre-party?"

"You're welcome to it."

I almost cried with relief as I explained what had happened but slowed to a stop when I saw the expression on her face.

"I can't cater it," she said apologetically. "We're doing full-on gala prep work from now until Friday night."

"That's fine," I said. "Tabitha didn't say it had to be a dinner, just a party. Which means I can buy a keg of beer and a stack of cups. I'll even fork out the cash for some chips."

Vivi laughed. She had firsthand experience with the endless list of detailed demands that tended to accompany anything Tabitha managed.

"I'll deal with her and the food." I'd have to anyway. "For now, I just need a space."

"It's yours."

"Are you sure we won't be bothering you?"

"Not at all. Once we move the walls into place, we won't even know you're there. You might smell some food cooking, but I'll tell everyone to keep it down otherwise. By the way, we have plenty of plates, utensils, and everything you might need in that regard here, so I can at least contribute those."

"Thank you, Viv. You've saved me. I owe you."

"Actually, it will be a fantastic way to let people know that we can hold events here. Helps us both out. We make a good team."

"We do indeed."

* * *

Back at Starlit Bookshop, I made two quick calls. The liquor store was thrilled to receive my wine and beer order, agreeing even to deliver it, and the grocery store assured me they'd be able to put together the multiple hors d'oeuvre trays and other items by tomorrow night and offered to deliver as well. With relief, I moved on to the music, pulling out the store's backup Bluetooth speakers; I could use one of our existing playlists.

Then I emailed the volunteer list an invitation with the updated information.

"Perfect," I said aloud, sinking into a nearby chair. "Done with that."

Lucy walked up with Anne Shirley in her arms. "What can I do to help?"

"Thanks to Vivi, we've got a party."

"Applause all around."

Anne Shirley meowed in support. Or maybe she was hungry. Hard to tell.

"It's not going to be anywhere near Le Chateau fancy," I said. "More on par with the parties we threw for the literary journal at school."

"I'm sure Tabitha will appreciate it."

"Doubtful."

"How are you going to decorate?"

"Oh no," I said, deflated. "I forgot about that."

"What if I pulled Ryan into the project? He has all kinds of stuff in the theater storage rooms."

"I don't want to impose—"

"Are you kidding? He's been asking how he can help with the gala."

"If you think so. But I don't want to put him out in any way. He's such a great guy."

"Don't I know it. I'll text him right now."

While she was doing that, I went around and turned out all of the lights.

"He's in," she said. "Could you please let Vivi know that he'll be coming by tomorrow afternoon?"

"Thank you both so much."

We locked up and climbed into the car out front. I was glad to have it tonight, as it would have been a chilly walk home. While the engine was warming, Anne Shirley stood on Lucy's legs and peered out the window.

"How'd it go today?" I asked my sister.

"It was busier than I expected. Max and Bella came in and we did inventory, but one of us was ringing up books the whole time. I guess people are spending their holiday gift money, and I'm thrilled that they're spending it here. All of the events you've been doing have reminded them about us."

"I'm so glad. Did Nora come in?"

"No, she's still editing." She gave Anne Shirley a kiss on the top of her head and was rewarded with a purr.

I backed out of the spot and turned toward home.

"Allison Colt told me that everyone in book club is extremely jazzed for the gala." She stopped. "Did I say jazzed? I must be hanging around Ryan and Gold too much. Speaking of whom . . ."

I laughed. "Luce, no. No Gold. Please stop."

She shrugged and chattered on about Ryan this and Ryan that. "Oh, and Allison also mentioned that they are narrowing in on a suspect. Must be nice to be married to the chief of police. She always knows everything before the rest of the town."

"I don't think he's supposed to tell her."

"She actually said he talks in his sleep. But you didn't hear that from me."

I laughed. "Mum's the word. Any idea who it is?"

"He didn't give her a name, unfortunately."

As we passed under the glow of a nearby streetlamp, I wondered: was it wise to go ahead with the gala when a murderer was on the loose?

Chapter Sixteen

I wasn't looking forward to the Thursday general run-through with volunteers, followed by the program rehearsal with the celebrities. The thought of wrangling all of the enthusiastic volunteers, who had been tripping over themselves trying to get close to the stars all week, was almost more than I could handle.

But I'd signed on for this, so wrangle I would.

It was a bright day verging on warmish, so I decided to walk to campus. My backpack was full of copy paper, tape, and markers, so that I could make signs to help everyone know where they'd go to volunteer. Tabitha was bringing everything else, including the items for the silent auction. At least I didn't have to lug all of the donations around. It did seem like something Tabitha would love to assign to me, but for some reason, I'd escaped it.

Nora had mentioned having breakfast with her best friend and agent Delilah, which made me worry just a touch. The two of them had been known to jet off to faraway destinations on a whim thanks to the money Delilah's last husband had left her. She was a true lady of leisure, aside from her part-time agent work—she had whittled down her client list to a very select few—and could afford to do whatever entered her brain at any given moment. On the flip side, she was also the one who had to deliver publishing news to Nora. It was usually positive news, but it often meant more work. My aunt already worked harder than most people. She was always coming and going, writing or teaching or working at the bookstore. I secretly loved when she went off on one of her spontaneous trips—she deserved to have adventures and to relax. But I hoped she'd wait until after the gala this time since she was the one who pulled me into the whole thing.

The walk turned out to be a good decision. By the time I arrived, I was calm, cool, and collected. The scene resembled an anthill, with volunteers streaming up to join the lines in front of the ballroom doors. There was a festive mood in the air. I skirted the lines out front and slipped inside. Circular tables were set up on the ballroom floor, waiting for the tablecloths to be added. Tall pedestal candle holders lined both walls, and large urns in between awaited their bouquets.

Tabitha was near the stage, probably in her glory getting ready to boss everyone around.

"There you are, Emma." She gave me a look of reproach, even though I was half an hour early. Melody saw and duplicated her expression.

I ignored their shaming tactics. "Do you want me to start posting the signs?"

"I'm not sure you'll be able to get them up in time, but you can give it a try."

Rather than waste time trying to reason with her, I went back into the lobby, where I wrote "Welcome Desk" on one of

After confirming that the *Chasers* stars would be at the pre-party and taking the opportunity to let them know that it was a casual, not fancy, gathering for drinks, not dinner, I wrapped things up. Walking over to the front doors, I opened one and bid them adieu until this evening. It took a little while for them all to clear the premises, but clear they did.

The silence was peaceful, if momentary.

There was a knocking sound coming from the side of the building. I hurried over and found Whitney, Nat, Stella, and her team hiding among the tree trunks.

I laughed and opened the door.

They traipsed inside.

"Sorry," Whitney said. "We came too early but wanted to be unobtrusive."

"We were almost to the front when the door opened and a crowd came pouring out, so we ran to the side," Stella explained. "No offense, but once we get started signing autographs and taking selfies with them, it can go on forever. We knew you had a tight schedule for rehearsal today."

"It was my idea," Nat said proudly.

"That was smart." I took them down the hall and showed them where the green room was. It was a large rectangular room connected to another space holding a row of mirrors with marquee-style lights around the frames so that makeup and hair could be done easily. We passed through them both and moved into the ballroom proper.

A tall Adonis type was in the center of the floor. Tabitha and Melody were nearly standing on his feet, they were so close to him. He was looking down bemusedly as they chattered up at him. I hurried over.

". . . and so now I'm single," Tabitha was saying. Not very subtly.

". . . and I'm *newly* single," Melody added. That was news.

Poor Adonis.

He lifted his head and made eye contact. "You must be Emma. You look like your sister."

If Tabitha and Melody could have shot arrows from their eyes at me, they would have.

For the second time that day, I ignored them. "Are you Mackenzie Gold?"

His hair fell over his brow when he affirmed his identity: it was the gilded shade of sun shining on a cornfield. His eyes were deep blue pools, and his teeth were as white as a pristine snowfall. His defined pecs, to which his shirt was clinging, were like—

I shook my head, then turned around and introduced the *Chasers* gang, all of whom widened their eyes and seemed to have the same reaction that I had. Meanwhile, Tabitha and Melody were still visibly drooling over him. In addition to his astonishing good looks, he exuded so much charisma—or was it pheromones?—that it was hard to concentrate on anything else. Maybe he should be a movie star.

Stella sidled up and hooked her arm through his. "I'll show you where to set up, honey."

"Do you know where to go?" I asked her, out of the side of my mouth.

"Send me in that direction," she whispered back.

"The sound and light boards are on the second level."

Everyone watched as she sashayed him across the floor and up the stairs.

Tabitha leaned forward, as if she was going to run after him, then stopped herself. She made a show of examining the floor, pressing on the wood with her toe. "I thought I saw a crack," she said loudly.

Melody smirked but wiped it off her face before her friend turned around.

Whitney and Nat strolled across the floor toward the stairs. Stella's team scurried up behind their boss, and so did ten women who were weighed down with armfuls of bulging bags. One woman was hurrying so fast that she surely would have won the blue ribbon for her fifty-yard dash.

"Why are the gift bag folks heading upstairs?" I asked Tabitha. "Is everyone going to follow Mackenzie around?"

She turned her head sharply, perhaps measuring the likelihood of that being a jab about her own visible inclination to follow him that we'd all just witnessed. I meant no such disrespect, but it was somewhat agreeable to see her squirm. "They're going to fill the bags up there."

"Why up there?"

She sighed. "Do you see the doors at the bottom of the stairs?"

I took in the gold doors, which were open and flat against the wall. I'd actually thought they were decorative, with their rounded tops and beautiful metal filigree pattern.

"The doors lock at the foot of the stairs to protect the light board that controls every fabulous special effect. Anyway, we can leave all the bags up there tonight, so they are locked up tight but close for tomorrow. It's better because the women won't have to lug the bags in after their blow-outs tomorrow."

"After their blow-outs tomorrow?"

"You know what I mean. After they've been to the salon and finished dressing themselves up. Also, I *may* have owed Susanna a favor—don't ask—and she collected. She met Mackenzie before and wanted to be here when he was, so I figured there was no harm in putting her to work at the same time and place."

"Is she the sprinter?" I asked.

Tabitha giggled, probably despite herself. "Yes."

"Sounds like a plan," I said.

"Ready?" Melody materialized beside Tabitha, who startled.

"Come *on*, Mel, you know I hate it when you sneak up on me."

Melody pouted. "I wasn't sneaking. I was walking like I always do. Maybe you should be more aware of your surroundings."

Tabitha stared at her. "What is your *problem*? Why have you been so rude to me lately?"

Questions I myself had wondered many times, but mostly about Tabitha.

"I could ask you the same thing."

"If running the light board is too much to ask, I'd be glad to find someone else, Melody."

The subtext was clear: get back in line.

Tabitha continued, her tone growing dangerously sweeter. "If *anything* related to this gala is too difficult for you, then don't worry about being part of this committee. I would *never* want to ask for more than you can give. Don't worry. We can manage without you. In fact, if that's the case, you shouldn't even bother to attend the gala at all."

Melody cut her eyes to me, then back to Tabitha. She inhaled, then smiled widely at Tabitha, matching her syrupy tone. "That won't be necessary, Tabs. So sorry. It's been a little tough lately because of everything with—you know."

Tabitha, her lips pressed into a thin line, nodded curtly.

"I'm here to help however I can," Melody proclaimed. She angled her head toward the stairs. "I'll head up there right now, shall I?"

"Bless your heart," Tabitha said, though it didn't sound at all like a blessing.

Melody's eyes narrowed at this, but she left without further comment.

I was transfixed by the exchange.

"Everything okay with you two?" I inquired innocently.

"She and Bruce are getting divorced," Tabitha said. "You didn't hear that from me. But rather than taking my generously offered advice, as I *do* have some experience in that area—"

She paused, perhaps expecting me to comment on that, but I remained silent. Wisely, I think.

"—she's keeping me at arm's length. On top of that, she seems to be acting out. Against *me*, the one whose shoulder she has cried on forever. I cannot understand what she's thinking. You don't throw away a friendship of so many years—" She stopped short, probably realizing that I was the one she had been confiding in, whirled around, and stomped over to the stage area.

I followed, not stomping.

After I'd climbed the stairs to stand beside her, she pulled two headsets out of her oversized bag, switched something on, and handed me one. It looked like a wire closet hanger that had been bent into shape, with a round microphone piece glued onto the front. I wedged it gingerly on my head and heard Melody flirting with Mackenzie. The remote-controlled window shades came down, turning the ballroom pitch black.

Tabitha listened for a second, clicked her tongue in annoyance, then snapped, "Go for lights, go for music."

Not mentioning the flirting showed some self-control, anyway.

Drums, first joined by trumpets, then joined by strings formed a confluence of sound that surrounded us. The music swelled and swelled—and just when it reached its crescendo, there was a shriek and a series of rapid thumps. A pink light suffused the room, growing stronger, revealing the body of Stella Vane in a twisted heap at the bottom of the stairs.

Chapter Seventeen

"Stop!" Tabitha yelled. "Turn on the lights!"

I took the stage stairs two at a time and was already running across the room when the white overhead lights switched on. When I reached Stella, who wasn't moving, I knelt down next to her and felt her neck. Her pulse was fast but strong, and she was breathing on her own.

Everyone came thundering down from the mezzanine. Nat was the first to reach us, and he went to gather her up, but I told him not to touch her. She was face up but the rest of her was crumpled sideways. If something was broken, we didn't want to make it worse.

"I called 911," Tabitha said. "They're on the way."

We all stared at Stella for a few minutes, watching her breathe. Her face was so pale that her lipstick and blush grew garish.

"Does anyone have a blanket?" I asked. "We should cover her."

"And lift her feet," Whitney added. "For shock, right?"

Sirens were audible in the distance. I willed them to come faster.

"Don't move her," I said again. "If she's broken her neck or back, it could cause further damage. Let's find a blanket."

"I have a poncho," said a woman next to me, who ripped it right off over her head and handed it to me so that I could drape it over Stella.

A few minutes later, the paramedics burst into the ballroom and took over. We gratefully stepped back but still surrounded Stella, watching them work.

"That was fast," Melody said admiringly.

"We were nearby," said one as she whipped out various instruments.

"Could you give us more space, please?" said the other in a tone of voice that meant he wasn't offering any choice in the matter.

"Yes, let's go to the other side of the room," Tabitha said.

"In the lobby would be better," the man said firmly.

"Of course. Yes, sir," Nat told him. He began making swooping motions with his arms, herding us away from his co-star and out of the ballroom altogether.

We formed an uneasy circle in the lobby.

"What happened? Does anyone know?" I asked.

Everyone looked at everyone else.

"Did Stella say where she was going when this happened?" I asked Ariel.

She shook her head. "We were all standing together near the top of the stairs when the lights went out, and it didn't feel like anyone moved."

"We were on the other side of the light board, stuffing bags," Susanna said. "That tissue paper is so loud, I couldn't hear anything else."

"I had my headphones on, so I didn't hear anything," Mackenzie said. "And I didn't see anybody move, either."

"Oh, we can confirm *your* whereabouts, Mackenzie. You were in our line of vision the whole time," Susanna said, staring at him adoringly.

Mackenzie bobbed his head in thanks, but he was obviously uncomfortable.

"I wish I'd brought the lights up faster," Melody said plaintively. "But I was following Tabitha's directions."

"Oh sure, blame me. I was responding as quickly as I could, Mel," Tabitha retorted, then softened her tone and looked around the circle. "What should we do now?"

The glam squad shrugged but didn't contribute any theories.

"Why don't we finish the gift bags tomorrow?" I suggested. "Could you come in the early afternoon before the gala? Would that leave you enough time to get ready?"

Heads began nodding, so I went on.

"Melody, could you please sort things out with the group and oversee that, please?"

Tabitha shot me a look but didn't object for once.

Melody also shot me a look, but it was a grateful one. Clearly, she just wanted to be in charge of something. "Yes, I can," she said brightly. "Let's go outside and make plans."

"My poncho is in there," cried the woman who had donated the handmade creation.

"Leave it, Peggy," said her friend.

"But it's my favorite one," Peggy protested.

Her friend made an exasperated sound. "You could knit another one tomorrow."

The knitter allowed herself to be swept out with the rest of the women, though she did cast one longing glance backward.

I turned to Stella's team, who remained ashen.

"Are they taking her to the hospital?" Ariel asked.

I looked back into the ballroom. They were loading her onto a stretcher. I could hear Stella moaning faintly. "Looks like it."

"Someone should go to the hospital with her," Ariel replied.

"I'll go," Whitney said. "We're practically sisters."

I thanked her and turned back to Stella's assistant. "Do you think you could make sure everyone gets back to the hotel?"

"Of course," Ariel agreed. "But you'll keep us posted, right?"

"I'll call you as soon as I hear anything," Whitney promised.

The dejected glam squad followed Ariel out the front door.

"I don't want to go back to the hotel alone," Nat said. "I'll end up pacing the whole time. Is there anything I can do here? Are you going to stay? Give me a job, please."

Tabitha looked down at her clipboard. "We still need to set up the auction," she said softly, then cleared her throat and increased her volume. "Want to help us do that?"

He brightened. "Yes. Keep me busy."

The sound of wheels scraping across the ballroom floor made Tabitha wince, but I was glad to see that they were getting Stella out of here. I held open a door and Nat hustled over to open the other one, giving the paramedics plenty of room to move the patient out of the building. Stella was still moaning quietly, eyes closed. They loaded her into the back of the ambulance and slammed the doors shut.

"We're taking her to Silvercrest Hospital," the stern paramedic said. "It's not far."

"I'll follow you in my car," Whitney said.

"Don't try to keep up with us," he warned as he climbed into the back of the ambulance. "Use your phone maps instead to find the emergency room."

Whitney nodded and ran over to the driver of the town car that Tabitha had arranged for the weekend. He listened to her, then quickly opened the back door, and she ducked inside. He jogged back, dove into the driver's seat, and was near the exit by the time the ambulance turned on its lights and took off.

Tabitha told us to follow her. We went down the left hallway to a large, sunny room with a sign in calligraphy on the door that said "Silent Auction." Inside, rectangular folding tables had been set up in rows. She opened a cardboard box and removed a stack of table pads, white with a silver embroidered snowflake pattern.

"First, we'll put these on top of each table, then we'll bring up the items from the basement. You already know where those are, right, Emma?" She pretended to cover up her a smile with one hand.

I accepted the stack of table pads without acknowledging the kick she got out of My Special Time Locked in the Basement Cage and began laying them out. Nat worked beside me, smoothing them after I'd placed them on the surface. We made it around the room in no time.

"Those look great," he said. "Very festive."

Tabitha opened another box, removed a stack of clipboards, and began sliding in empty bid sheets from a pile nearby. When she finished, she asked us to follow her downstairs. It was easier descending the stairs and walking past the creepy spiderwebs and shadows as part of a group, though I still would not have wanted to stay in the basement for very long no matter how many others were down there. She unlocked the gate of the storage area, and for the next two hours, we carried box after box up to the auction room, unpacked them, and set the items to be auctioned out on the tables. For each one, there was a description card in calligraphy waiting in the proper spot. It was a compelling array of items, with everything from spa days to cruises to gorgeous antiques.

I moved the last box to the final table and opened it. When I looked inside, I caught my breath. There, nestled among a pile of shredded paper, was a blue vase that fit the description of the one Tabitha had originally sent me to get. Carefully, I removed it from the box and shifted aside the paper strips to see a second matching vase underneath.

Tabitha came over, counting all of the items on the table.

"I knew it!" I pointed at the box.

"Hold on," she said distractedly, as she finished jabbing her finger at objects one by one.

"You did steal these!"

"And now I have to count everything again. Thanks, Emma. Is it your dream to be more of a hindrance than a help? I swear."

"Look."

She focused on what I was pointing toward and frowned. "The vases are back?"

"Very funny, Tabitha."

She shook her head. "I thought they'd been stolen."

Her tone sounded sincere. I didn't know what to make of that.

Pulling out her cell phone, she began scrolling through call records. "I need to let the police know that they've been found."

"Are you sure they're the same ones? You barely looked at them," I said.

She made an exasperated sound, jammed her phone back in her pocket, and came closer. After lifting the vase, she examined it carefully, flipping it upside down to point out a mark on the bottom. "Yes. These are the same."

As she returned to her call, Nat came over and lifted up the vase. "What's so special about this?"

"It's by a very important artist," Tabitha advised him. "It's also rare to have a complete pair, and these are about a hundred years old. Be careful, please."

He made a show of moving slowly to put the vase down, then he backed away, hands in the air, signaling his disengagement from the object.

I retrieved the second one from the box and set it next to the first. Clearing away the packing materials, I studied the art deco vases, which were stunning; the fans down the sides in relief were exquisite. I wouldn't mind bidding on these, though I was quite sure I wouldn't be able to afford them.

"I'm not much of an art guy," Nat confided to me. "What would something like that run, normally?"

"A lot has to do with whatever the market will bear, how much demand there is for work by a particular artist or period or style or technique. Also, the fewer there are, the more expensive they'll be."

"Give me a ballpark . . . a couple thousand for these?"

I shrugged. "Depends on how many people want them and how much they're willing to pay."

"Far more than a couple thousand, I should think. A complete pair is very rare." Tabitha had finished her call and was opening a cabinet at the end of the room. When she returned, she was carrying a glass box that she set carefully over the top of the vases. "People will have to bid on *these* without touching them," she said with satisfaction.

"Are you going to leave them out all night?" Nat asked.

She looked at him as if she thought he was plotting a heist. "Why do you ask?"

"They're very valuable, aren't they?"

"This room locks securely," she said with a sniff. "It was designed with intention."

"Why not lock the vases back up in the basement?" I asked. "You're one of the few people with a key to that area, right?"

Nat nodded in agreement with my plan.

"Only the *most* trusted people on the renovation and college teams have them." Tabitha lifted her shoulders slightly and spoke haughtily. "You've seen my last name on the door of this building, right, Emma? It's the *Baxter* Ballroom. So yes, I have a key. To everything."

I was surprised that she was speaking like this in front of Nat. While Tabitha had no problem making snide comments to me, she usually controlled herself better when other people were around.

She may have had the same thought because she relaxed her shoulders and smiled at him. "I'll take your ideas under advisement. You two can go. I'll finish up."

Tabitha gave the description card for the vases a tender pat. "This is going to be my most successful gala yet," she murmured.

* * *

I gave Nat a ride back to the hotel, then raced home to change for the pre-party. Vivi had texted that the drinks and food had arrived safely and that Ryan had been working in the space all afternoon. I had given him carte blanche to use whatever props he thought would work. At this point, a beach ball in the corner would have been fine. I just wanted to get this whole thing over with.

Chapter Eighteen

The sun was setting over the mountains. I hurried along the riverwalk, taking in the fiery oranges and reds lighting up the summits that would soon turn to pinks and blues. I never tired of seeing the play of light and color along the Rockies.

My phone rang, showing Whitney's number. When I answered and we exchanged greetings, I could barely hear her, there were so many people talking in the background.

"Stella's going to be fine," she said, sounding relieved. "Nothing is broken, but she sprained her ankle and will be on crutches for a while."

I sent up thanks that she was okay.

"But she won't be coming tonight, unfortunately," she said. "I wanted to let you know so that you weren't disappointed. Also because I told you I'd keep you posted. Did that make sense? Sorry, I'm distracted. I'm in Stella's room—I know that's not normal for a sprained ankle, but I suppose it's a celebrity perk—and we're trying to get her comfortably situated. Lots going on over here. Nat and I will be at your party, though. Not sure when

Stella will be leaving, and in any case, she'll be heading straight for the hotel."

"Whatever you need—and if you can't make it, please don't worry about it. Stella's care is more important, and you all must be exhausted." If Tabitha got mad about anyone not showing up, I'd deal with her later.

"We'll do our best."

"Thank you, Whitney."

Turning the corner at Starlit Bookshop, I braced myself against the cold wind and hurried to Vivi's. Inside, I gasped: what had been a blank slate yesterday had been transformed into a garden wonderland. White columns lined the sides, and wrought-iron patio chairs and benches were everywhere. Flowers burst from the tops of tall vases, and elegant ferns were stationed at either end of several long, skirted tables. The first table held beer and wine bottles lined up next to glasses and napkins; the second had a stack of plates, reserving the rest of the space for the forthcoming trays of food. A third was at the far end of the room providing a place for the celebrities to sit while meeting their fans.

"It's amazing!" I exclaimed.

At my pronouncement, Ryan popped up from behind a fern at the other end of the nearest table. He said hello and waved a roll of duct tape. I gushed about the decorations for a long while, during which he blushed more and more. Then I asked if he needed any help.

"No, I'm all set. But I did see someone delivering food." He inclined his forehead toward the kitchen.

"Thank you for everything, Ryan. This is even better than Le Chateau. You've saved the day. Hugging you later."

He bent back down, and I sped to the kitchen. When I went through the door, Vivi was talking with one of her employees near the back. She saw me, smiled, and pointed to a stack of boxes on a table. I took off my coat, hung it on one of the hooks along the wall, and washed my hands. Then I unpacked the fruit, veggie, cheese, and charcuterie trays. Vivi helped me carry them out, marveling at the decorations.

"Ryan, you're a genius!" she called to him.

He grinned and gave a little wave.

After we'd arranged the trays and added silverware, glasses, and napkins, we took a step back and surveyed our work.

"That's *much* better than a keg and a bowl of chips," she said.

"Yes. Thank goodness for delivery service."

We turned on the music in the nick of time. As she went back into the kitchen, people began to arrive. I went over near the front door and welcomed attendees, pointing out the rolling coat racks that were set up by the wall as well as the wine and refreshments tables. Before long, the room was full.

It was, perhaps, the most rewarding to see Tabitha's reaction when she arrived. She froze for a full ten seconds, her mouth falling open.

"It's pretty," she admitted, shoving her coat at me.

I pointed to the nearby rack where she could hang up her own coat, which made her mouth fall open a second time.

Ryan appeared, this time holding hands with Lucy, who took one look and threw her arms around him. "I've never seen anything so beautiful, Ry."

"I think I may have undersold the elegance of this party with my 'casual' label," I said. "It's breathtaking."

Whitney and Nat came through the door; I introduced them to my sister and her boyfriend, then took a few pictures of them with my phone. I knew Lucy would get a kick out of that. Like everyone in America, she was a huge *Chasers* fan. The four of them drifted into the party, still chatting.

The door opened again, and the glam squad moved toward me, led by Ariel.

I did a double take—Ariel's hair had gone from short and dull brown to long and golden. She caught my eye and touched her hair self-consciously.

"Looks great," I said.

"Thank you." She blushed. "I've never had extensions before. But Stella said I should shake things up and Malina offered to do it, so . . ."

"I heard about Stella. How's she doing?"

"She kicked us out. Said she wanted to sleep, which I'm sure she'll do given the painkillers they gave her. She just wants peace and quiet and didn't even ask for a touch-up, so I know she's serious about it," Stella's makeup artist Brielle said.

"Is she in pain?" I worried.

"Not at the moment," her hairdresser laughed. "She's feeling fantastically good from the meds. I may even ask her for any leftovers, she was having so much fun."

"Rico!" Brielle elbowed him.

He elbowed her back.

Her stylist Trey watched the others, entertained by their antics, then asked if it would be okay if they came in without Stella.

"Yes, please do—and help yourselves." I gestured toward the food and drink tables.

"I'm not going to stay long," Ariel said. "I came over to have a drink and then I'll go back."

"That's fine. Would you mind if I asked you all some questions, though?"

"If it's about anyone on the *Chasers* show, we can't say anything," Brielle informed me. "We all signed nondisclosure agreements."

"What if you didn't *say* anything but . . ."

"Seriously. We can't. I don't even know if we're supposed to tell you about the NDAs." He gave Brielle a pointed look.

So much for that.

"I understand. Enjoy your evening."

They thanked me and moved on.

Melody was the next to arrive, accompanied by none other than Mackenzie Gold. Score one for Melody: they made a gorgeous couple.

Tabitha was going to lose it when she saw them.

I trailed behind them to witness the realization, pausing only to grab a glass of wine and a napkin from the table. Mackenzie started to drift over toward the food, but Melody yanked on his arm and marched over to where Tabitha was holding court with some volunteers. He went along for the ride, obviously not knowing what he was in for.

Melody called out her best friend's name. Tabitha stopped midsentence. Her eyebrows drew together into a straight line as she excused herself, then said something to Melody that caused her to let go of Mackenzie's arm and huddle up with Tabitha in the corner.

The fury emanating from both of them was so palpable that people in their vicinity started to look over their shoulders as if sensing that something was wrong. The two women began to argue, and Mackenzie did a 180-degree turn and walked, to my surprise, up to me.

"Hello, Emma," he said warmly. "I'm glad that we are finally able to chat. Your sister and Ryan have told me so much about you. You're every bit as lovely as they said."

"Thank you. You too." My cheeks heated and I found myself dipping my head awkwardly. I've never been good with compliments. And I was excruciatingly aware that what I'd said could refer both to finally meeting him and to calling him lovely back. While I weighed the likelihood of making it worse by explaining versus leaving it alone, he spoke again.

"Appreciate your hiring me. Looking forward to working the gala. Too bad we didn't get to finish the whole rehearsal, but I think I'll be able to deliver what you need."

"We're grateful that you were available."

He took a step closer. "So Lucy says that you're avail—"

"*There* you are," Melody shoved her arm through his. "Shall we find some wine?"

"Sure," he said to her. She tugged to get him moving more quickly, but he said to me with a wink as he passed, "I hope to speak with you later."

Had he come here with Melody? Or was he what my mother would have called "a smooth operator"? Seemed weird to flirt with one person while attached at the hip to another. Lucy and Ryan had vouched for him, hadn't they? As I watched them walk away, I felt a touch on my shoulder.

"This is a *such* a nice party." Malina smiled at me, slurring her words slightly. Her hair, which wasn't tucked into a beehive but piled into a sort of messy tower, was starting to lean to the left. I resisted the urge to straighten it for her. "Did you do the decorations?"

I gave proper credit to Ryan, then asked how she was doing.

She looked around, nodding slightly. "As well as can be expected. Still broken-hearted and don't have anything to live for. That's how I'm doing."

Oh dear. "If I can help, now or in the future, please don't hesitate to call on me."

"Thank you." Malina sipped from a very full glass of wine. "Is Nora here? I've been looking for her all night."

"She's coming later," I said. My aunt had wanted to finish her edits before coming to the party. She said she wouldn't be able to relax until that was finished.

"Your sister is here, though," I said, craning my neck and trying to pinpoint her location.

Malina snorted. "I don't want to talk to *her*."

"Is everything okay?"

"Not really. Whitney thinks she's such a big deal around here." She waved her glass so quickly in a circle that some sloshed over the side. "But nobody knows the real her."

"What do you mean?" I surreptitiously dropped a napkin on the spill and wiped it slowly back and forth with my shoe. Safety first.

"Everyone thinks she's *so* nice." She made a face. "But let me tell you something: she's not. She always had to have the best *everything* when we were growing up, and then she stole my daughter from me. She took Lyra out to California without my approval and then made her stop speaking to me. What lies did she tell her? I can't even imagine. I was a *good* mother! I worked my tail off to provide for Lyra."

People started to look over at Malina as her voice grew louder and she began gesticulating more widely. I enlarged the scope of my cleaning operations, moving my blotting foot in bigger circles. It probably looked like I was performing a spontaneous dance routine, like a Fosse flash mob of one.

"Did Whitney bother to ask my permission? No." She narrowed her eyes. "And did I even once get invited to go to California for any movie red-carpet or party anything? No."

"I'm sorry—"

My aunt appeared and put an arm around Malina, whose hairdo was now sliding sideways on her head. "Mal, do you want to come sit with me?"

"Nora!" she said joyfully, turning to embrace her. "Yes, I *do* want to sit with you. We need to talk."

I mouthed a thank you to my aunt and picked up the napkin that had sopped up Malina's overflow. The floor seemed dry and not hazardous, thank goodness. Quickly, I went into the kitchen to wash my hands and to bring out the final cheese tray.

After I ate some, that is. For strength.

* * *

At the official party close, Tabitha made a thank you speech, then not so subtly conveyed that it was time to leave. The crowd had thinned out, leaving the celebrities, a few stragglers, and those of us handling the gala events. From what I'd observed, everyone had a good time. Nora had managed to calm Malina down and now she even seemed to be enjoying herself, chatting up a gentleman by the fountain. I was turning over what she'd said in my mind when I noticed that Stella was outside the door, struggling with the handle. I ran over and pulled it open, and she gave me a grateful smile, then moved slowly on her crutches, finally getting inside. She panted slightly as she scanned the room.

"Thank you, Emma. How are you?"

"Fine. I heard you were resting," I said. "Are you okay?"

She curved her lips upward. "Oh, I'm *dandy*, doll. Better than I've felt in ages. Could you point me toward Whitney, please?"

Whitney and Nat had spent most of the evening at a table in front, receiving visits from eager planning committee members who wanted them to sign autographs and take pictures together. They'd been extremely generous with the fans. Now they were having a glass of wine and sampling the food on the plates that we'd set aside for them.

Stella clomped over and positioned herself in front of Whitney, who looked up and gave her a bright smile. "Stella! So nice to see you. How are you?"

"Alive, no thanks to you." Stella readjusted her grip on the crutches but maintained an intense stare. Her glam squad came from somewhere and positioned themselves behind her in a show of solidarity.

Whitney's smile faltered. "What—"

"What are you talking about?" Nat asked, speaking over his co-star.

"I know you pushed me," Stella hissed.

Whitney threw down the fork she'd been holding and brushed off her hands. "Wait one second. I didn't push you."

"Someone did," Stella spit at her. "And everyone knows you want me off the show."

"What would make you think that I want you off the show?" Whitney inquired calmly.

"You're jealous of me. And I can't even blame you for that, honey. I mean, *look* at me." Stella gestured up and down in front of herself. "We both know that I'm getting all of the attention."

"Because you're a plastic Barbie doll?" Whitney picked up her wineglass and toasted her.

"Takes one to know one," Stella retorted.

Nat laughed, then got pinned by Stella's glare, and started coughing instead. "Sorry, I thought it was a joke. You know, because we *all* have gotten little tweaks. No matter how discreetly, word gets around. And you know what? We shouldn't be ashamed. It's part of the job."

Whitney shook her head.

He stopped talking.

"Stella, if I wanted you off the show," Whitney said calmly, "you'd be off the show already."

Nat gave her a surprised look.

"You don't have that power," Stella sneered.

"Oh, but I do." Whitney took a sip of wine. "It's in my contract."

"Hey, that's not in *my* contract," Nat said, eyebrows furrowed.

"So you're saying that we have to keep you happy if we want to keep our jobs?" Stella asked, sounding legitimately surprised.

"Something like that." Whitney set down her glass carefully. "So you might want to be careful about coming *at* me, sister."

Stella studied her face. "I don't believe you."

"Try it and see." Whitney met her eyes.

"Whit," Nat said, "that can't be true. You never mentioned that before."

She shrugged, picked up a grape, and took a dainty bite.

Stella regrouped. "And don't call me sister."

Whitney swallowed. "What are you talking about?"

"You just said it. Also, Ariel mentioned that you told everyone we were like sisters before you came to the hospital too."

"Is it not true? Are we not like sisters?"

"Trust me, you don't *want* to be sisters with Whitney," Malina said loudly, tilting forward as she came up to the group.

"Stop it, Mal," Whitney said. "You're drunk."

"So what if I am? I can have a drink now and again. I'm a *grown-up*."

Whitney turned her head back to Stella, but Malina launched herself forward between them, putting both hands on the table and leaning toward her sister. "You took my daughter away."

"Because you weren't taking care of her! For you, having a drink now and again means all the time. You were more interested in your vat of wine than your own daughter!"

"How dare you!" Malina pulled herself up tall and shook her finger at Whitney. "You are such a *liar*! And everyone is going to find out that you're not as nice as you pretend to be." She whirled around and grabbed the table behind her briefly to steady herself, then lurched over to where my aunt was standing. Nora once again put her arm around her friend's shoulders and led her away.

"Let's get you home," I heard her say.

Stella laughed, but it was mirthless and cold. "Hmm. Maybe we *are* more like sisters than I thought, if that's what you're like with your real sister."

It was so beyond time to call it a night.

Chapter Nineteen

Back at home, I had just settled down in my room to go over my to-do list one last time when Nora tapped lightly on my open door. "May I come in?"

"Of course." I pushed aside the papers I'd spread out all over the bed and made enough room for her to perch on the side.

She picked up the thick manila folder of materials I'd copied from Tabitha. "What's all this?"

"Invoices, lists, and whatever else Lyra had already done for the event when she was working with Tabitha. Most of it has been superseded by this point, so I haven't had much cause to revisit it."

"Want me to recycle everything?"

"No," I said. "I was going to take a quick look tonight to make sure that I have completed every single possible thing that needs doing."

"Ah. Good idea." She sat down and gave me a kind smile. "How are you? I can't believe how hard you've worked this week."

I took a deep breath. "Well enough. Looking forward to the other side of tomorrow night."

"It's going to be divine. And the library will have a healthy budget. I wanted to stop by and let you to know how much it means to me that you were willing to jump in at the last minute. Especially since it meant working with Tabitha Baxter. I've been impressed with how well you've worked with her too. Very professional."

"That's kind of you to say."

"Just being honest."

I brightened. "Hey, at least Tabitha didn't accuse us of murder in front of everyone again."

"The weekend is young." Nora laughed.

I asked how her book project was going.

"Done!" She clapped her hands lightly. "Off to the publisher. Now I can enjoy the gala. Do you need anything from me, darling? I am completely available to help."

"Congratulations on finishing your book! And I'll let you know, but mostly I just want you to have a great time."

"Lucy and Ryan were talking about connecting you with a friend of his who sounded pretty delicious," she said, pretending to look out the window at something else.

"Oh, Mackenzie is dreamy, no question. But I hired him to do the music and I'm keeping things professional. Not to mention that everywhere he goes, a pack of admirers follows."

"Really, Emma? What a waste. Don't you want to dance under the stars with a handsome fellow?"

"Sure. But if I hadn't hired said handsome fellow to do the music, there wouldn't be any dancing in the first place for all the rest of you."

"Touché, darling."

"Thank you, by the way, for helping Malina tonight."

Nora's face turned somber. "She's in such a bad place right now."

"Is it true what Whitney said about the drinking?"

"Malina has always been fond of drinking wine and having a good time, but I never heard about it causing any problems. And she is grieving right now. But I haven't seen her as drunk as she was tonight, either. No idea what's happening on a regular basis."

"Maybe Whitney was exaggerating? Malina was giving her a pretty solid read in front of people she was already arguing with."

Nora held up one finger: *pause please*. "A read?"

"Calling her out."

She nodded. "I like the literary quality of that."

"If Whitney was telling the truth, though, perhaps that shines a new light on the relationship between Lyra and her mother."

"They got along very well, as long as I've known them."

"Who? Whitney and Malina, or Lyra and Malina?"

"All three of them."

"That's interesting, because Malina came up to me earlier in the night and claimed that Whitney wasn't as nice as everyone thought."

Nora's eyebrows shot up. "How interesting. Maybe there's much more drama than we know. Not uncommon within the private business of families. Behind closed doors and all that."

"Could Whitney have been the one who attacked Lyra?" I mused.

"I would be extremely surprised if that were the case," Nora said. "I've known her all of her life, and she has always been a sweet person who wouldn't hurt a fly."

"Sometimes people seem one way but are actually another."

"True, true. In literature *and* in life."

My phone buzzed and I saw Whitney's name on the screen, which gave me the oddest sensation, as though she'd somehow been able to hear what we were saying. I showed my aunt, and she advised me to take the call, then slipped out of the room.

"Emma, thank you for picking up," Whitney said. She sounded stuffy, as if she'd been crying. "I know this is a lot to ask, but is there any way that you could come over to the hotel right now? Nat and I need to talk to you."

I glanced at the clock. "It's after midnight. Could we talk on the phone instead?"

There was a long pause and a sniffle. "Never mind. It's no big deal."

"Are you sure? I'm happy to talk with you right now."

She hesitated again. "Let me put you on speaker."

"Hi, Emma!" Nat's voice sounded tinny and far away.

I said hello, then asked what was going on.

"Um," Whitney said, "Would it be truly and unforgivably awful if we didn't come to the gala?"

My heart thumped.

"What's going on, Whitney?"

There were more sniffles in response.

"I'll tell her, Whit. We feel like it's a recipe for disaster," Nat said. "Reputationally speaking."

"How could your reputations be affected?"

"You heard Stella and Malina tonight, right? I mean, they were both trying to tear me down. Pretty hard." Whitney's anger was clear. "I don't need that right now. My agent and I are going into talks for reupping my contract soon."

"Mine too," Nat said.

"Not to mention the press. If they cover the horrible accusations that were made at the party tonight? I cannot deal with that."

I thought fast. "Don't you have to deal with that all of the time, though? Things that somehow get into the press, real or not? You know that by the next cycle, it will be gone."

"Yes, but this is different. This is coming from my co-star sister and my real sister," Whitney said. "Right on the heels of my niece dying. That's already a lot, you know. Paparazzi have been competing with each other to get a shot of the grieving movie star around the clock."

I hadn't seen any paparazzi on the streets of Silvercrest, but I did know it was something she dealt with on a daily basis in LA. Probably better not to debate the point.

"And I can't use any more negative rumors either," Nat said.

"What other negative rumors are you talking about?" I asked, then winced. People didn't usually like to report such things.

"That I'm a crap actor," Nat said.

That didn't seem to fall into the category of a rumor, but I wasn't going to argue with him, either.

I had a brainstorm. "But the gala is to raise money for the library. Philanthropy is *good* for reputations."

"That's true," Nat said slowly.

"Yes, though I'm actually afraid for my safety this point." Whitney said. "First my *niece* is killed, then my *friend*"—there was a microscopic pause, as if she'd heard it come out of her mouth and realized that it wasn't quite the word she meant—"was pushed down the stairs. We've only been here a few days. Law of averages says I'm next. And the slashing of my dress was probably a warning!"

I could understand her perspective on the law of averages, but all of the celebrities bowing out would be considered by Tabitha and Trevor and perhaps even Nora as a catastrophe.

"But it's not as though you are necessarily next. There's a logic to what's happening." I stopped. Was there? Or was it someone plowing through the cast of *Chasers* at any opportunity? But if so, that was a kind of logic, wasn't it? Now I was going around in circles. "I mean, for all we know, Nat could be next."

I could hear Nat's gulp over the line.

Oops.

"We will hire additional security," I added quickly. "Though I'm sure someone as strong as you, Nat, typically doesn't have to think about that."

"Right on," he said. I would have bet a hundred dollars that he was flexing as he said that.

"More security would be great," Whitney said. "Though I'm still not sure it's enough."

Anne Shirley trotted delicately into the room, leaped onto the bed—curling up on the contracts from Tabitha's folder—and meowed.

"Maybe Whit's right," he said. "Maybe it's time for us to bow out."

"Contracts!" I exclaimed, sending silent thanks to the cat for reminding me.

“What?” They spoke in unison.

“You signed contracts. To appear at the gala.”

There was an extended silence during which I imagined them staring at each other, having a wordless conversation.

“So between that and the philanthropy aspect . . .” I willed them to finish the sentence the way I wanted.

“Yeah, I see where you’re going with that,” Nat said finally.

Whitney sighed. “Do you promise you’ll get more security?”

“I promise,” I said, texting Tabitha simultaneously. She could deal with this one. I knew she would take action if the alternative was to lose her stars altogether.

* * *

I had just fallen asleep when someone touched my arm. I shot upright, arms flailing, heart racing.

“Whoa,” Lucy whispered. “It’s me.”

She was sitting on the edge of my bed, dressed in a sweater and jeans. Disoriented, I looked at the clock. “It’s one thirty. Why are you wearing that?”

“You have to get up and get dressed. We have a problem. A big one.”

“What’s going on?”

“I don’t even want to tell you, Em. I’m so sorry.”

“Is Nora okay?” My body turned to ice at the thought of anything happening to our aunt.

“Oh! Yes, she’s fine. She’s sleeping. I don’t think we should wake her. It’s . . .”

“Say it, please.”

"Baxter Ballroom is on fire. Ryan called me—I don't know how he found out."

I stared at her, then scrambled up and pulled on a sweatshirt over my thermal shirt and yoga pants. I felt around under my bed for my hiking boots and laced them up. "I'm going over there right now."

"I'm coming with you."

In a matter of minutes, we had scribbled a note for Nora and got into the car, shivering until the heater began to blow out air that wasn't arctic.

"Are you sure about this? Going over there?" Lucy asked, after I'd turned onto River Street. "We can't do anything. Are we being like those people who intentionally go to look at accidents?"

"No." I gripped the wheel and increased my speed. "We're going to look at the place where the gala is supposed to take place tomorrow night. I have to see with my own eyes what's going on."

"Are you going to call Tabitha?"

I thought about this. She was so proud of the work she'd done on the renovation—and rightly so—and was not going to take this well. On the one hand, I wanted to be sure that she heard it as soon as possible. On the other, I didn't want to be the one to tell her.

"The police probably already did . . ." I glanced at my sister.

"Surely they have," she said. "Or will soon."

"It's not our place to make that call, right?"

"Right."

I turned onto the main road of campus, and we passed through the open wrought-iron gate. Blue and red lights were cutting through the darkness beside an inferno.

Chapter Twenty

I got as close as I dared, then pulled over to the side of the road. The flames were several stories high—as we watched, the ceiling of the ballroom caved in, then two of the walls crumbled.

"Oh no," Lucy murmured. "It's collapsing."

I couldn't even speak. All of that time and effort to create a beautiful space and it was disappearing right in front of us. Tabitha was going to be heartbroken. I felt terrible for her as well as the college, which had valued not only the remodeled space but the fact that it had been one of the oldest buildings on campus.

"You don't think anyone was inside, do you?" Lucy asked, her voice trembling.

"I truly hope not." I opened the door. "Let's go see if we can find out what's going on."

Lucy's eyes widened. "We probably shouldn't."

"You're right," I said, climbing out of the car. After a moment, she did the same.

We walked closer to the row of police cars, staying out of the way of the firefighters to the left. The heat grew stronger as we edged closer, and the roar of the fire was punctuated by thumps as objects fell to the ground. The acrid, smoky air smelled of unidentifiable chemicals.

I aimed for Jake, who was directly in front of us, speaking to an officer in uniform. He nodded twice, then caught sight of me. His lips tightened but he dipped his head in acknowledgment. After he extricated himself from that conversation, he hurried over.

"What are you doing here? You two should go home. It's not safe."

"What happened?" I asked.

"It's looking like an accident that got out of hand."

"How do you know that?"

"Conversation with eyewitnesses."

"Who?"

He shook his head. "You'll hear the full story on the news. I can't say anything more than that."

"Is anyone hurt?"

"We won't know until everything is said and done," he said. "And please move farther away. This is a fluid and unpredictable situation."

Just then, a chunk of wood on fire came sailing toward us and landed about ten feet to the right of where we were standing. Jake put his arms out to the side and began moving toward us. "Really, you *have* to leave."

We were both walking backward, following his orders, when I noticed two people perched on the back of an ambulance not far away. The smoke made it hard to see them clearly.

"Thanks, Jake, we'll move away," I said. I turned around and walked straight for a while. I could feel Lucy following me. When

I peeked back to be sure Jake had gone to work and wasn't watching us anymore, I cut across the road to identify who was underneath those blankets. I was guessing it was the eyewitnesses.

"Em, where are we going?" Lucy took a few extra steps to catch up to me.

I pointed at the ambulance. She matched my fast pace and we had almost reached the vehicle when Tabitha came around the other side, yelling.

"I can't believe you did this!" She got right in the face of the shorter figure. The taller figure in the blanket put an arm up as if to stop her.

As I hurried over, I recognized Melody and Mackenzie in the blankets. They were both staring at Tabitha, who was in full-on rant mode.

"Do you know how much time I spent working on that ballroom? Years and years! How *could* you?"

As usual, she was making it about herself, but in this case, I could understand her position.

"Why are you yelling at them?" I asked her.

"*You*," she said, infusing the word with disdain. "Of course you're here. Why are you always *everywhere* that something horrible happens to me?"

"Tabitha!" Lucy said. "What a terrible thing to say!"

Melody and Mackenzie appeared relieved that the rage was no longer being directed at them.

Tabitha took a deep breath and readjusted her black leather gloves. "It *is* a strange coincidence, you have to admit. But okay, maybe I'm displacing my anger a little, which should be directed at *you*!" She pointed at Melody, who squirmed.

"I'm so sorry," she said. "I don't know what else to say. I am completely, utterly sorry. I would understand if you never forgave me."

"Consider that done," Tabitha said. "There will be no forgiving."

"What are you talking about?" I asked.

Melody ducked her head and looked up at us through her lashes. "I started the fire."

"It was an accident," Mackenzie said. "To be fair."

"Tell Emma how you did it," Tabitha commanded. "I'm dying to know."

She hung her head. "I lit all of the candles. You know, the tall holders on the ballroom floor?"

"Why would you do that?" Tabitha crossed her arms in front of her. "You know they weren't supposed to be lit until gala night! No one likes a used wick."

"I know. But we never got to do the program rehearsal, and I needed to see how the candles looked in order to adjust the lighting to perfection. Then one of them fell over and knocked another one over and soon they were all falling and fire was everywhere. We were up at the light board and couldn't get down fast enough to stomp it out before it was out of control." She burst into tears.

Mackenzie patted her on the back.

"How did you even get in?" I asked.

"I have a key," Melody said, wiping her face and sniffling. "Tabitha gave me one. I've been part of the team during the renovation."

"Barely," Tabitha sniffed. "You didn't actually contribute anything of note."

"The filigree doors were my idea."

"No, I'm *quite* sure that they were mine. I remember flipping through that interior design catalog—"

"Whatever," Melody said. "Take credit like you always do. No one believes you, anyway."

Tabitha looked as though she'd been slapped. "What did you say?"

"You heard me. I've done nothing but try to help you for years! I just wanted you to see me as capable, but every time I made an opportunity, you gave it to her!" She glared at me.

"What does that even mean?"

Melody laughed. "You really don't know?"

Tabitha thought for a moment. "You canceled the restaurant and the band?"

"Yes, I did," Melody said, in a sing-song voice.

"You tried to sabotage my gala!" Tabitha snarled at her.

Melody threw off the blanket and stood to face Tabitha. "*Your* gala? Seriously? You are the most self-centered person on the planet. I can't believe I've spent my entire life doing whatever you said. That is now officially *over*."

Tabitha took a step back.

"Guess what else?" Melody said smugly, "I *didn't* vote for you for prom queen."

Tabitha gasped.

Melody strode off triumphantly. Mackenzie slid off of the vehicle and sidled away. Lucy jerked her head toward the car, clearly ready to leave. It didn't feel right to leave Tabitha there alone, though.

"Are you okay?" I asked Tabitha, who was staring after Melody.

She turned her head toward me. “No, I am most certainly *not* okay.”

“Do you want to sit down?”

“No.” Tabitha delicately touched her face as if blotting tears, though I didn’t see any there. She patted her hair and was quiet for a moment. “I suppose we need to come up with an email to cancel the gala.”

I had an idea. “Do you want me to ask Vivi if we could use the Silver Blossom Catering space again? If we opened the walls, it would be twice as large. And it’s already set up from the party tonight.”

Tabitha caught her breath. “Do you think she would let us? That would be fantastic. Though where would we put the auction?”

I waited for her to realize that the antiques, memorabilia, and glossy packages with spa treatments, curated trips, and other adventures had been in the ballroom building.

“Oh no . . .” She trailed off as she looked at the fire.

“I’m sorry,” Lucy said softly.

“I’ll go home right now and send out a call for new donations,” I said. “It can’t hurt to ask, right?”

The only thing it was going to hurt was our ability to get some sleep, but that didn’t seem like a very strong possibility anyway. I for one had too much adrenaline from racing down here.

“You would be willing to do that?” Tabitha asked quietly.

“Yes.”

I continued pulling ideas out of thin air. “How about asking members of the Business Owners Organization to donate services in the form of gift certificates that we could print out ourselves? I know that a good many of them were supporting the gala already."

"You think we should ask everyone in BOO?" Tabitha looked doubtful.

"Yes. In fact, I'll write an email to everyone on the gala mailing list. That will cast a wider net, and others may be inspired to contribute as well."

She looked away, perhaps a little embarrassed that the last time we went to a Business Owners Organization meeting, she'd accused Nora and me of murder in front of the whole town.

At least I hoped she was embarrassed.

Probably not, though.

"Hold on," I said, pulling out my phone. "I'll text Vivi right now. She mentioned that she was going to get up early to start working today. Once we have the new venue confirmed, I can send the ticketholders an email with the new details."

"I'll help too," Lucy said. "I'll text Mackenzie and let him know not to book something else, in case he has another offer. He's in pretty high demand."

"This could work," Tabitha said approvingly. "Seems like we have a clear path forward."

The only thing that was clear to me was that the good people of Silvercrest were going to awaken to a whole lot of begging from us this morning.

* * *

I got a text back from Vivi as the sun was rising.

Of course you can have it here. I'm awake, so call me any time!

Setting down the to-do list, which had quadrupled in length since I'd gone to bed for what had turned out to be my one hour of sleep, I picked up my phone. Vivi answered on the first ring and assured me that she had it under control.

"We've already got the food here and can use Ryan's decorations. He was going to pick them up today but we just texted—he's an early riser too, which I know because I run into him at the gym all the time—and he's going to pick them up tomorrow instead. He also asked if he could add more things to fill the larger space, so don't be surprised if it looks a little different. I didn't think you would mind, considering the timeline we're working with."

"No, I don't mind. In fact, I love it. Ryan can do whatever he wants. You can do what you want. Carte blanche for everyone! And thank you so much, Vivi. I can't help but feel like we're taking advantage of you."

"Not at all! It's a million times easier because we don't have to pack anything up and lug it to the ballroom now."

"You're not just saying that?" I tried to analyze the tone of her voice.

"I'm actually thrilled." She hesitated. "That didn't come out right. Not about the ballroom, of course. But about being able to stay here."

"I understand," I assured her. "You've saved the day again. I'll be sure to remind Tabitha that your price needs to reflect that you're now providing the venue too. And at the last minute."

"Thank you, my friend."

"What would you think about doing cocktails, along with the silent auction or whatever the fundraising element ends up looking like, at Starlit Bookshop? The proximity might be useful in terms of giving the guests two different experiences and wouldn't interfere with the gala setup."

"Yes! We can put a bar in the usual spot this afternoon"—Vivi had done a bunch of readings for us, so she knew that we preferred the food in the back of the store—"and I'll send over the bartenders any time you want."

"Sounds perfect. Let's touch base later. Anything I can do to help you today in the meantime? Other than procuring you a very shiny halo because you're our guardian angel?"

"Just focus on what you need to do and remember to breathe. We'll get through this, Tabitha will pay us, and then we will sit down and have an expensive glass of wine and look back on how stressed we are right now and laugh."

"Okay, Viv, but right now, we're overwhelmed and operating on zero sleep. What could go wrong?"

"I have to confess that I slept for three hours last night. Don't hate me."

"Lucky you! But if I fall asleep in my soup tonight, please rescue me."

"You're safe. We're not having soup."

We wished each other good luck with our prospective duties ahead and hung up. I let Tabitha know that we had a venue, emailed the guests, then pulled out the file she'd given me to find a donation list that I could cross-reference with the Business Owners Organization membership list. If there were any people who weren't members of the business organization, but looked like they had a business that could donate something, I would reach out to them separately. It couldn't hurt.

I flipped through the paperwork—past the contracts from our celebrities that included a hefty no-show penalty, I was glad to see—and extracted a stapled packet with "Auction" at the top. Pulling up the list of members on the Business Owners Organization website, I began to check the donors off as quickly as I could. At the end of the list, I stopped, stunned to see Melody's name written next to a particularly interesting donation: one pair of art deco vases.

I stared at the wall ahead of me, pondering what this meant. If she was the one who had donated the vases, did that mean she was the only one who knew about them, besides Tabitha? Had Melody pushed me into the cage and stolen them? If so, why would she do that? And why had they reappeared in a different box before it was time to set out the auction items?

Then I remembered that the vases had burned up with the ballroom.

And I had more pressing things to take care of today.

I stared out the window at the river rolling slowly past our house. Today, its peaceful flow didn't quench all of my anxiety.

If we managed to pull this off, it would be a miracle.

Chapter Twenty-One

I spent the better part of Friday morning at the bookstore organizing the donations from folks who had promptly sent gift certificates that I printed out after a quick trip to the office supply store, where I bought new clipboards. I then re-created the bid sheets that Tabitha had made, at least as much as I could remember about the format. Having the bidder's contact info would be enough to follow up later if we had to. Some Friends of the Library members also dropped off new gift baskets adorned with cheerful bows and filled with jams, jellies, and scones or soaps, lotions, and candles. I thanked them profusely, stressing how much their contributions mattered to the cause.

The original antiques had sadly gone up in smoke along with the ballroom. I didn't envy Tabitha having to let the owners know about that, though they probably had put two and two together after receiving news of the fire. But still: that must have been a difficult email to write. And Silvercrest as a whole was lamenting the loss of the historic ballroom building.

By lunchtime, I had completely rebuilt the auction. It wasn't going to look anywhere near as lavish as Tabitha's original display, with her gorgeous calligraphy cards, breathtaking photographs, and enchanting stories about each piece, but people would still be able to bid on something, and we actually had more items up for auction than we had before.

The large station clock said that it was a few minutes after noon.

"Hungry?" I asked Lucy, who was shelving books after story hour.

When she affirmed that she was, I returned to the office and opened the refrigerator, pulling out two yogurts along with the container of fruit salad and pecans we'd put in there earlier this week. I set out bowls and spoons, then poured two waters from the filter pitcher.

My sister sat down across from me at the farmhouse table that served as our conference area as well as our lunch room; the office was big enough that it could serve multiple purposes, thankfully. Lunching next to the tree outside the window was far preferable to sitting in the dark stockroom.

"What do you need me to do for tonight?" Lucy asked after she'd finished her yogurt. "I already put up a sign saying we were closing early today so we'd have plenty of time to get ready and set up anything that needs setting up."

"Could we do a trial run of the auction layout? I want to make sure there's enough room to place all of the clipboards on the tables."

"Sure," she said. "When Bella gets back from lunch, I'm going next door to see what Ryan's up to. He said he was swinging by Vivi's to recalibrate the decorations from last night."

"I don't know what I would do without you two—we wouldn't have music or decorations."

"Those are the best parts of *any* gala," she said.

I spooned up the last of my yogurt and dug into the fruit.

"Aside from the dancing and the love in the air . . ." She sighed happily.

"The love in the air? You might want to temper your expectations on that part. Tabitha and Melody were at each other's throats, you may remember."

"What was that about? It was so over the top, and I didn't see it coming at all."

I speared another chunk of cantaloupe. "Maybe three decades of playing second fiddle to Tabitha finally got on Melody's nerves? Maybe Tabitha crossed some line that made Melody think enough was enough? They've been kind of testy with each other throughout this whole week. But last night was definitely over the top, I agree."

Lucy considered this. "You don't think they were fighting over Mackenzie, do you?"

"Didn't look like it. Though do you think he really is interested in Melody? She doesn't seem like his type."

My sister laughed. "I thought you didn't care about Mackenzie."

"I don't. Other than as a perfectly nice human being."

"A perfectly nice, unbelievably attractive human being."

"I guess."

"Facts are facts," Lucy said. "He's objectively gorgeous. He could be a model. But he's not all caught up in his looks, which makes him even more amazing. He's a very sweet person. Which is why I think he would be such a good person for you to date."

"How did we get back to the idea of me dating Mackenzie?" I held up my hand to stop my sister from pushing her matchmaker agenda. "Thank you for looking out for me, but I was asking about whether you thought he was smitten with Melody for *other* reasons."

"What other reasons?"

I took my time chewing a piece of melon. "Curiosity, mostly."

Lucy rolled her eyes.

"I mean, I don't really care what he does, in a personal sense."

"Do you care what *anyone* does in a personal sense?" Lucy winked. "Like how about Jake Hollister?"

I actually pshawed.

"Okay," she said pleasantly.

I didn't get the feeling that she believed me, somehow.

* * *

Sometime later, I reviewed our work. The wooden tables in the back of the store were now in two straight lines with spaces for browsers to move easily between them. The parson chairs had been relocated along the wall, which would provide seating. We'd left the damask chairs in conversational groupings since cocktail parties were amenable to that sort of thing.

I placed the item descriptions and clipboards on the tables, spacing them out evenly. I used the wicker gift baskets as centerpieces since those were the only physical items we had. Once I'd finished, I stepped back to judge the overall effect.

"What do you think?" Lucy said, coming over from the checkout counter.

"The baskets are so nice that they almost make the clipboards look worse in contrast. It kind of looks like it's set up for people to take final exams. What do you think?"

Lucy giggled. "I think it looks fine."

Bella came in through the door, calling out a hello. Her eyes fell on the tables full of clipboards. "Are we doing a survey?" Then she took in the baskets. "About picnics? Or are we having a picnic?"

Lucy laughed but stopped when she saw my face.

I went to the opposite side of the room, but that vantage point proved just as disappointing. I looked around the room, thinking hard. My gaze caught on the colorful stained glass panel my father had made that divided the upper and lower levels. It gave me an idea, so I went into the stockroom to gather up small glass vases that we had used in the front window for our spring display.

Lucy looked at me questioningly when I returned.

"We need some bright colors. I can run over to the flower shop, and we can fill up each one of these. That should liven it up a little, yes? Maybe unify things?"

My sister applauded.

"Back in a bit," I said, stopping at the coat rack in the office and preparing for the chill outside. The snow had melted—which was good news for the hems of ball gowns everywhere—but it wasn't quite spring-level temperatures yet. Our plan for this evening was to have the stockroom act as a coat check; Vivi had said she had racks and tickets and everything else that was necessary. Her crew was going to be split between the two buildings, but once the cocktail and auction portion of the evening was over, we'd all be at Silver Blossom Catering for the rest of the night. I marveled at how smoothly she had shifted gears between one plan and the next. Her personality was the type that easily accepted change and rolled with the flow. It was such an admirable quality.

Outside, I hustled across the street to Bloom, the town's only flower shop. It was fairly new to Silvercrest—previously the only place where we could buy bouquets was either the grocery store floral department or the flower farm several miles outside of town. Bloom had been opened a few years back by two of the members of my writing group, Alyssa Clarkston and Tevo Akina, who I hadn't even realized were married until after we'd met a few times.

When I walked in, Alyssa was tying a ribbon on an arrangement that stood nearly three feet tall. She always looked as if she'd come straight from a run, with her brightly patterned athletic wear, pink cheeks, and light brown hair pulled back into a messy bun. After she'd gotten the bow just right, she waved at me and said something to Tevo.

He flashed me a grin, his dark hair covered, as usual, by a slouch hat that matched his fleece—today they were red—and picked up the bouquet. We chatted as Alyssa came out from around the counter, then he left to deliver the item.

"Emma! What a nice surprise. How can I help you?" she asked with a smile.

I explained the situation and soon we were moving around the store together. One side across from the counter was taken up by a cooler full of a vibrant collection of different kinds of flowers in metal buckets—half were arranged loosely by type and half were already grouped into elegant arrangements. There were small tables in between offering enchanting little gifts as well as chocolates to entice shoppers. I was pointing at some blossoms that I thought would work when the door opened and Jake strolled in.

"I need a bouquet stat," he said toward the counter behind which Alyssa usually stood as she worked. Realizing that she wasn't there, he swiveled his head in our direction. "Oh! There you are . . . all of you."

"Help yourself to any of the premade ones in the cooler, or I can put something special together after I help Emma."

I wondered idly who the lucky recipient of the gift was, making a note to tell Lucy that he was off the market. Maybe *that* would put an end to her incessant matchmaking efforts.

Jake came over to join us and perused the cooler, hands behind his back. He pointed to an arrangement with roses. "That'll do, but I'll wait until you're done with Emma."

"You can pick out a card if you like." Alyssa pointed to a rotating rack at the end of the counter. "Or there are small complimentary ones next to the register."

She turned back to the cooler and removed the bucket that held the wildflowers I'd pointed out. As she passed me on the way back, she leaned over and said under her breath, "I didn't know he was seeing someone."

I returned to the counter quickly so I could buy the things and be gone.

Preferably before the conversation went on any further.

Jake, who should have been out of earshot, called out, "It's for my mother. I always get her a bouquet for the New Year."

Something in my chest eased a little when he said that, though I hadn't even noticed that it was tight.

Alyssa laughed. "You have very good hearing."

"I've been told it's my best quality," he said. "By my otolaryngologist."

I laughed.

"So *are* you seeing anyone else?" Alyssa asked, attempting to come across as casual but landing somewhere between eager and excessively keen to know the answer.

"I don't think Tevo would appreciate you asking me that," Jake said, spinning the rack slowly.

"It's not for me," she said. "It's for other interested parties." She gave me a meaningful look behind Jake's back. My face warmed.

"Not me," I said loudly. "I'm not the interested party."

Jake shrugged and turned around to face us. "Story of my life: no interested parties."

"C'mon, surely you've had lots of interest," Alyssa said, gesturing vaguely toward him. "Looking like that."

He grinned and approached the counter. "You're too kind."

"Really, I was hoping to sell you two bouquets instead of one," she teased. Alyssa removed the flowers from the water and began to cut the ends. "Do you at least have a date for the gala?"

"What gala?" He elbowed me. "Just kidding. It's the talk of the town. Especially with the last-minute change of venue. Speaking of which," his tone grew serious, "how are you doing, Emma?"

I'd been so busy trying to fix problems all day that I hadn't even stopped to think about that. "Hanging in there," I said, which was true.

"If you need any help, give me a call. I'm off duty right now." No wonder he seemed so chipper. I wished I was off duty.

"But are you attending the gala, is what I asked," Alyssa said, ripping off a sheet of paper and wrapping it around the floral bundles.

"I was invited, but I'm not sure."

"Maybe you and Emma should go together," she said, focusing intently on the register.

My cheeks went from warm to hot and I was suddenly numb all over. I tried to cover it up by smiling enigmatically at him, but my mouth had also gone rogue in my panic, and I wasn't sure what shape it was making. For all I knew, I was smirking or sneering.

Or both at once. Egads.

He raised an eyebrow and smiled enigmatically back, like it was easy. "I wouldn't be opposed to that idea."

All of our conflicted moments in high school flashed through my mind, one right after the other. I tried to summon up the old potent and consistent sense of outrage that permeated my usual thoughts of him, that fed my competitive streak, that made me want to keep tabs on what he was doing while I wished that he wasn't so darn compelling.

Wait. *Compelling?* What was happening right now?

I reached deeper into those memories until I became aware of something that shook me to my core: what had been between us hadn't only been annoyance and frustration.

I *was* an interested party.

Jake's green eyes were trained on mine. I looked away, breaking his gaze, and fumbled with my bag. Taking my time to extract my wallet, I opened it slowly and removed my credit card.

Alyssa held out her hand and gave me a wink.

"Sorry, what did you say?" I asked, in no one's general direction. Not the most original way to stall for time, but I needed to come up with a plan.

"I said that you two—" Alyssa began.

"Do you want to go to the gala together?" Jake asked.

Simply. Directly. Appealingly.

"Oh," I smiled at him. "That's so nice. I'm working, though, so I don't think I can."

"No problem." He smiled. "Anyway, looking forward to the next writer's group meeting."

I nodded, but inside I was screaming. I just went through all of that soul-searching and insight-having, and when I said no, he immediately went on to the next thing? As if it didn't matter?

"Maybe we should meet for dinner first," Alyssa said. "The four of us."

She was absolutely shameless.

"Sorry, I can't swing that, though it would be fun. Have to be ready for any last-minute troubleshooting . . . you know, spit spot," I managed to say, though I immediately regretted "spit spot," which I had only ever heard used in *Mary Poppins* and knew I was using incorrectly.

"I understand. Another time, maybe."

Still flustered, I accepted the flowers Alyssa handed me over the counter. "Thank you so much for these. See you all tonight."

I went out to the street and gulped some fresh air.

That was humiliating.

Chapter Twenty-Two

"The flowers look perfect in the vases," Lucy said.

I chose not to tell her about the whole Jake Doesn't Care That I Won't Date Him experience. We didn't have time to dive into that, anyway.

The next item on my list was to check in with Vivi, so I said goodbye to my sister and went out through our back porch, which we'd cleaned and readied for tonight. Our most recent acquisition had been a gas firepit we'd bought at a yard sale. It was a wonderful addition to the space—which had been newly made over this fall with couches and tables and lanterns. If any guests wanted to spend a moment out back admiring the river view, at least they'd be warm.

Vivi's back door was ajar, and I knocked before pulling it open. Inside, there was a bustle of activity as everyone inside was focused on preparing delicious things, judging from the delectable aroma. I edged along the side, not wanting to bother them. Emilio, one of the chefs, pointed toward the front. I waved and mouthed "thank you," then hurried to the business office, where Vivi was working on a laptop, her hands flying across the keyboard.

"Come right in, Emma," she said. "I'm almost done." With a few more clicks, she closed the computer and tucked it into a drawer. "We've got the party all set up. Have you seen what Ryan's done?"

When I shook my head, she hopped up and led me through the lobby and the door on the opposite wall. I took two steps inside and stopped short.

"I had the same reaction," Vivi said.

The huge room was full of circular tables covered in white cloths, with candles in glass holders on top. In addition to the columns, flowers, and ferns from before, a central stone fountain now burbled softly as water cascaded from one tier to the next. Trees wound with fairy lights dotted the room, and glowing metal lanterns with ornate cutouts hung from the ceiling, casting pretty shadows onto the floor. The effect was extraordinarily lush and romantic.

"Okay, I want to move into this space and live here forever," I said.

Vivi sighed. "Right? Tabitha is going to love it."

"Fingers crossed," I said. "Is Ryan here?"

"No, he went over to talk to your sister. You probably missed each other by a split second."

We went over the last remaining details, both checking our to-do lists to be sure we'd thought of everything. Once it seemed as though there was nothing left, I checked my watch and realized it was time to leave if I wanted to pick up Nora on time. She had some boxes to bring home with her.

"Don't worry about a thing," Vivi said, shooing me out the door.

"That's *literally* my job, to worry about all of it," I laughed.

Which wasn't really that funny, I thought, one minute later.

* * *

At Silvercrest College, where I had gone to help Nora transport books, I rode up to the top floor of the Arts and Humanities building, where the English department was now housed after Nora and some of her colleagues had convinced the school to let them move into the unoccupied space. It had been a multiyear affair and extremely complicated, but worth it: every time the elevator doors opened and I caught sight of the blue sky and puffy white clouds through the large glass windows in the lobby, it felt like stepping into heaven's waiting room. This was so much better than the cramped, dark space they'd left behind.

When I reached Nora's large corner office, a student was in the chair facing her desk. I hadn't expected that, since the college was on the winter break between fall and spring semesters, but Nora took appointments whenever she was on campus. If someone needed help, she was available.

Nora nodded at me, and I knew she'd wrap things up as soon as she could. Not wanting to intrude on their conversation, I wandered down the hallway. Most of the office doors were closed—it was, after all, a Friday afternoon—but there was one wide open. I drifted down the hallway toward it, thinking I'd say hello if it was any of the colleagues to whom my aunt had introduced me in the fall.

The nameplate next to the open door said *Gates Huddlesby, PhD, Professor of English*. I peeked inside hesitantly, but he wasn't there. His desk, a reddish wood with a high shine, was empty except for a clear box and a paperback. I took few steps inside to get a closer look at the box, which housed a boutonniere, a rose in a startlingly bright purple hue. My scholarly curiosity drew me to spin the publication around on the desk so that I could see what turned out to be a creative journal from years earlier with a list of stories on the cover. I skimmed the whole list and found, at the end, Calliope's piece, "The Spider's Web."

My mind was whirring.

Why in the world would Gates be reading the original story? And would he have stolen the script too, if he had?

I ran over to the doorway to check the halls. The last thing I'd want was for him to walk in while I was doing what I was about to do. I couldn't see anyone approaching, so I began looking through his bookshelves, which were organized by period in chronological order. Scanning quickly from Medieval to Modern, I kept an eye out for any pages wedged between volumes, but there were no such messy inclusions. When I reached the Contemporary era, I slowed down and began reading titles. At the end of the novels, plays, anthologies, and scholarly texts, there was a large collection of mysteries stacked sideways in double rows so high so that not an inch of shelf space remained. According to my online search of his work, he had written a number of articles on crime fiction and film. Which meant, theoretically, that he was an expert on murder. And he was at the screening. Could he have killed Lyra? Payback for having been excluded from the *Chasers* events?

Was the script a sort of weird trophy?

After I reached the last shelf, I peered around the room to see if I was missing anything. The only things remaining were his desk drawers and file cabinets. I had just reached out for the handle of the drawer closest to me when I heard footsteps.

Quickly, I launched myself into the chair facing his desk and raised my arms over my head, as if I were casually stretching.

"May I help you?" Gates strolled into the room and stared at me.

"Hello, Professor. I hope you don't mind my waiting for you. I'm here to pick up my aunt, but I thought I'd check in after our conversation at the shop, make sure you didn't have any questions for me about carrying your book."

His eyes surveyed the room suspiciously.

I threw in a yawn for good measure, trying to portray an utter lack of anxiety, though my body was still switching gears internally.

He seemed satisfied that everything was in its proper place until his gaze fell on the journal that was still in front of me. Facing me.

"Did you look at this?" He snatched up the text and pressed it to his chest.

"Look at what?" I summoned my most innocent expression.

He shook the journal, then clasped it in his arms again.

"What do you have there?" A drop of perspiration rolled down my back as I tried not to lie outright.

He sat stiffly in his desk chair, took out a key, and unlocked the top drawer. With his eyes on mine, he put it inside, then slammed the drawer shut. "It's a bit of reading that I'm doing."

"Something else for your *Chasers* research?"

"Why would you say that?" He leaned back and crossed his arms.

Why *would* I say that? I thought fast. Did I want to admit that I'd researched him online? No.

His eyes bore into me.

"Since you wanted to be on the panel the other night?" I tried.

His body relaxed and he leaned forward. "Ah, right. I see."

A long silence followed his non-answer.

"Did you know any of the panelists? Or, maybe, anyone they work with?"

"No. Other than chatting with them at the bookstore after the panel." His eyes lit up. "I do think they enjoyed my critical analysis of the ten most important themes, though."

Poor panelists.

"There you are, Emma." My aunt bustled into the room, arms full of books. "Sorry it took so long."

I jumped up to take the top half from the stack. "Ready to go?"

"Yes. We need to take these home and get ready for the gala."

She glanced at the clear box on the desk. Something crossed her face that I couldn't interpret. "Are you going to the gala tonight, Gates?"

"Indeed." He stroked the sides of his mustache. "Wouldn't miss it."

"See you there, then," she said. "Have a wonderful time."

She wheeled around and headed down the hallway so fast that I had to hustle to keep up. When we were in the elevator, she chuckled.

I shifted the armful of books to press the button. "What's going on?"

"Did you see the boutonniere on his desk? It's the one that my date was supposed to wear so I could recognize him tonight."

"Your Faculty Lounge match was Gates?"

"Apparently so. But that is *not* going to happen. Can you imagine working together with another professor after you've been matched up by a dating site? Oh, how awkward."

"And who knew your intellectual soul mate could have been one of your own colleagues this whole time?"

Nora stopped laughing. "That's impossible."

"But the app says—"

"The app must be broken."

* * *

We stacked the books inside next to the sofa for future reading, and Nora went off to get ready for the evening, with a new and pressing addendum to her duties: canceling the date with Gates online without revealing who she was in real life. Otherwise, she worried that all future department meetings would be unbearably awkward. If anyone could let someone down gracefully, it was Nora. She had spent the majority of the trip home trying out gentle ways to word her rejection.

After she had laughed at the possibility of him being a murderer, that is. Especially since we could see no motive whatsoever in sight.

But all future conversations about Gates would have to wait until after the gala.

Everything would have to wait until after the gala.

It was almost time to go.

I ran through the number of increased security protocols we had in place. Attendees were going to be checked against a list at the door. No one was coming in who wasn't supposed to be there. Then I remembered that the volunteers hadn't walked through the new location. I dug my laptop out of my bag and sent out a frantic email, reminding everyone that if they had previously volunteered, we still needed them as volunteers, and please get there at six thirty.

Note to self: Get there before six thirty.

I jumped into the shower, then applied appropriate lotions and potions and a touch of makeup. After I braided my hair, I donned my wonderful black gown, added the eye-catching collar necklace and simple pearl earrings, then did a little twirl in front of the mirror as I pulled on the gloves.

I truly did feel like Cinderella.

Now if we could all just make it to midnight, that would be great.

Chapter Twenty-Three

By eight PM, the gala had officially begun. Names were confirmed at the door, coats were checked in our storeroom, and cocktails were made at the whims of the guests, who were browsing the items on the silent auction tables and noting down their bids or chatting with friends. Before long, both levels of the store were full of merry partygoers mingling and laughing.

In other words, so far everything was going as planned.

I stood on the second step of our spiral staircase and looked over the well-dressed crowd. Lucy appeared in the back doorway, a vision in a pale pink gown with a beaded bodice and full tulle skirt. Her hair was pulled back in a chignon, which showed off her elegant neck, around which was a stunning crystal choker that matched her dangling earrings. Nora came in behind her, recalling the Edwardian age in a purple silk gown with intricate embroidery along the collar and along the bottom hem. A black sash circled her waist and her hair was arranged in a voluminous updo.

I went over and we exchanged compliments. Zander Flyte happened by at that moment and took several shots of us together.

"Where's Ryan?" I asked Lucy.

"He's adjusting the fountain next door—something about the water pump—but he'll be over soon."

"Look at this!" Nora gestured to the full room. "What a crowd. And people are buying books too!"

"That was smart of you to put out a sale table and add the sign informing everyone that we would gladly store their purchases at the coat check," Lucy said to me.

"It was an experiment," I said. "Figured they wouldn't want to carry a bag all night."

"Seems to be working." My aunt winked at me. "Now, if you'll excuse me, darlings, I'd like to browse the auction items. I've got a hankering for something over there, I'm sure."

"I'll join you." Lucy put her arm through Nora's and they moved gracefully through the clusters of people with glasses, who all seemed to be having a wonderful time.

Someone said my name and I turned to see Marlowe, who was breathtaking in a silver gown with a blue velvet bodice.

"Hello, gorgeous," I said, hugging her. "Wow."

"Wow yourself." She turned to the man in a tux next to her who had a friendly smile. "And may I please introduce Brandon Scott, Esquire?"

"I'm Emma Starrs. Nice to meet you," I said. His name seemed familiar.

"I've heard a lot about you," he replied warmly.

I shot a questioning look at Marlowe, who laughed. "Brandon and I dated a long time ago, when you were off at grad school. I may have mentioned him. You know . . . Mr. Tall, Dark, and Very Handsome?"

"But then I went to law school on the other side of the country and we broke up. Not my best decision," he said ruefully.

"Oh, that's right. I've heard a lot about *you* too," I told him.

They both laughed.

Marlowe took his hand. "Brandon arrived in town today and came by the store this afternoon."

"First things first," he said.

"Once I got over the shock of him showing up like that, we spent *hours* catching up," she said happily.

"And she kindly invited me to be her date tonight."

She glowed at him.

"I haven't even unpacked my suitcase," he said. "But Marlowe happened to have this tux in the store."

"It's a perfect fit," she told him.

In more ways than one, I thought.

"Will you be staying in Silvercrest long?" I asked.

Marlowe widened her eyes. She was onto my subtle fact-gathering. I was sure we would deconstruct this conversation at length later.

"I hope so," Brandon said, glancing at Marlowe, who was putting all her energy into staring at something across the room, pretending not to be listening.

They were adorable.

Over Brandon's shoulder, I saw a scowling Tabitha bearing down on us.

"Tabitha's coming this way," I said to Marlowe. "You may want to leave while you still can."

"Good idea," she said, pulling Brandon toward the auction tables.

"What's all this about?" he asked as he took a few steps with her.

"Oh, I'll reveal all later. But for now, hurry."

I took a deep breath and greeted Tabitha calmly.

"Where are the pictures?" she demanded.

"What pictures?"

"The ones that were supposed to go with the auction items. What is that . . . that list of papers on the table there? Hideous."

"It's hardly hideous," I said. "That's what I was able to pull together in less than twenty-four hours after a fire burned up everything we had ready."

"Why didn't you reprint the photographs and take them to the print shop to be mounted on display frames? I could have sent you the digital files, but you didn't ask for them, so I assumed you were on top of everything."

"Because we don't have the items that go with those photographs anymore."

"But it would have shown what we did have. Our initial effort," Tabitha said. "Not whatever *this* is."

"Don't you think it would have been confusing to have pictures of things that weren't available?"

"Whatever." Tabitha shook her head. "I can't believe you didn't *bother* to commemorate what we worked so hard on."

"Commemorate? Really? I *bothered* to email everyone for a second round of donations and buy all new clipboards. I printed out new item descriptions and made new bid sheets. And I decorated the tables with fresh flowers that—"

"I get it," she snapped. "You did some stuff."

"The auction was only a small part of what I did today to try and make this event happen, Tabitha. I also confirmed every single detail, checked the new venue—which looks fabulous by the way—and met the volunteers here early to sort out the new locations for everyone. Not to mention turning the bookshop into a cocktail party."

"In other words, you did your job," she said snippily.

"I did indeed. Where were *you* all day?" I didn't mean to say that second part, but it just flew out of my mouth.

Tabitha drew back, clearly affronted. "All of *this* requires work, you know." She indicated her vivid yellow gown, complicated hairstyle, and diamonds dripping from her ears, throat, and wrists. She looked like a very twinkly canary. If her goal was to draw attention to herself—and when wasn't that her goal?—she had achieved it.

Her eyes locked on something across the room. I followed her gaze and caught my breath. Melody Crenshaw floated toward us—with a bright red dress and even brighter red hair. The entire time I'd known Melody, she, like all four women in the country club gang, had the same hair color as Tabitha. When Tabitha added honey streaks, her besties added honey streaks. When she went full blonde, they went full blonde. And so on and so on. It was an unbreakable pattern, one of the most reliable things in Silvercrest. However, Melody Crenshaw had just broken it in the most defiant and public of ways, and she was flaunting it.

War had been declared.

Tabitha gasped and turned her back in Melody's face in front of everyone.

Melody altered her path, swerving gracefully to the left.

Collision averted.

For now.

"Are we all set, then?" I asked Tabitha. Given the demise of her ballroom and perhaps her friendship, I knew that she would be more brittle than usual, which was saying something. I steeled myself for her reply.

She took a sip from her martini glass as she considered the auction tables. It was almost as if she'd decided that Melody no longer existed, so she wasn't going to get all ruffled about it. "Although I wish the party hadn't had to end up *here*"—she barely repressed a shudder—"it seems to be going smoothly." She gave a wave to someone behind me like a beauty queen at a pageant. "But I'm noticing that our guests of honor haven't arrived yet. What do you know about that?"

"Nothing," I said. "I'm sure they're on the way, though. They wanted to go straight to the dinner part following the cocktail hour."

"*Check* on it, won't you? And report back as soon as you can," she said through clenched teeth behind the fake smile she was beaming around the room, then flounced away.

"I will," I said to her back, pulling out my cell phone from the little wristlet bag Marlowe had given me to match my dress. My calls, however, went straight to voice mail.

Glancing at the clock behind the counter, I realized we needed to alert the guests that it was time to move next door. I hustled behind the counter—where Bella and Max were ringing up a storm of purchases, happily—and pulled out the microphone attached to the updated PA system that Ryan had installed as a gift over the holidays.

"Good evening, everyone," I said, wincing as I heard my voice amplified throughout the store. "We're glad that you're here tonight. We hope that you've had a chance to bid on your favorite items in the silent auction—and thank you on behalf of the Silvercrest Library for your generosity. It's now time to move next door for dining and dancing. Please feel free to leave your coats and purchases here for now and retrieve them at the end of the evening."

The guests clapped and began to move toward the door.

Out of nowhere, Tabitha appeared in front of me and grabbed the microphone. I didn't know how she always managed to get close to any microphone anywhere so fast. Did she have a built-in sensor?

"Hello, everyone!" She turned around to face the crowd so that her back was now in my face. Melody and I had that in common. "I'm Tabitha Baxter, gala committee chair. Thank you *so* much for coming. We will be announcing the winners of the silent auction later on, after midnight. But I wanted to add that we are also accepting *direct* donations for the library—such a great cause, don't you think?—from all patrons. Come find me and I'll take care of *everything*. And if you get home and decide that you had such a marvelous evening that you want to donate even more, simply call or email me. My information is on your gala invitation but, of course, you all know *me* already." She made a sort of flourish with her hand and set the microphone down.

The guests politely clapped again.

She bowed her head, as if taking a curtain call.

I turned off the microphone and stowed it away below the counter. As the attendees went outside, an excited buzz swelled. Melody was ahead of the pack, putting as much distance between herself and Tabitha as she could, which seemed like a smart strategy.

I hurried over to the door and slipped outside, where two town cars had pulled up to the curb in front of Silver Blossom Catering. The driver of the first car opened the back door, and Nat stepped out, followed by Whitney. The crowd went wild; the couple smiled and waved their way up the red carpet between stanchion posts and velvet ropes that we'd added earlier. Then the next car pulled forward and Ariel climbed out. A pair of crutches came next, which she tucked under one arm as she leaned forward with her hand out to help Stella out of the car. Stella put down one foot but kept the other slightly bent behind her while she accepted the crutches from Ariel and began to move forward. Even the elevated second foot had a stiletto with a mile-high heel on it. No bulky elastic wrap for her.

The crowd applauded even harder as she made her way slowly into the building. When she had almost reached the door, she lurched forward in a heart-stopping motion, but somehow regained her balance and shook her head charmingly. The audience roared in approval, then when the town car drove off, they moved like a pack out into the street and along the path that the stars had followed. When the last person had gone inside, I saw Ariel on the other side of the ropes, shivering. She was listening to her phone and looking worried. When she put it back into her pocket, I approached her.

"Are you coming inside?"

"Oh, I don't usually go inside events when Stella attends. She wants me to wait in the car nearby so that I'm around if she needs me."

Ariel had to sit there all night long? In the car? That seemed like kind of an awful practice, but I didn't say anything.

"Tonight, though, because it's New Year's, she said I could go out with the squad after I dropped her off." She stared plaintively down the street, then her words came out in a rush. "But that guy drove away before I could get back in the car, and he's not answering the phone and the car service office has an after-hours recording on. And the squad members aren't answering either. And on top of it, now I'm worrying about Stella getting around on the crutches. Did you see her almost fall?"

"You can't stand out here in the cold. Please come inside. You can be my special guest at the party."

Her face lit up. "Really?"

"Yes. There's a spot at my table, and you're more than welcome to it." I had not invited a plus-one, and I was happy to offer it to her. "Dine, dance, have fun. You have the night off, right?"

A slow smile spread across her face. "Thank you," she breathed. "I can't remember the last time I had fun. And I could keep an eye on Stella from afar, just in case, so I could still be working."

"Exactly," I said. "If she calls, you would be available in a flash."

We went around the ropes and up the carpet. I said hello to the security guards we had out front. There were even more inside. We had upped the number as promised after the VIPs threatened to bail.

When we went through the door, the warmth surrounded us like a cozy blanket. A sprightly big band song was playing as the guests milled around finding their seats. We approached the check-in table, where I quickly explained that there was an addition and gave her Ariel's name. Susanna updated the list and told Ariel that she loved her dress. I turned my head to take in her muted gold sheath with a sweetheart neckline—it was old school and, with her new hair color, particularly striking.

She blushed. "It's from the vintage store down the street."

"The best clothing store around," I said, as I'd said many times before. I was so proud of Marlowe for taking her parents' business to the next level. She'd told me that Whitney had promised to hand out some cards to the LA stylists who were always looking for something fresh—a vintage piece that no one else would have certainly qualified. Such acts of genuine kindness that I heard from others about Whitney made it hard to believe the negative comments about her.

I led Ariel to our table, which was in the back off to the side—I didn't mind at all, but knew the location was supposed to come across as a burn from Tabitha—where she put her coat over the chair I offered her.

"We have a coat check next door," I said. "Do you want me to take it over for you?"

"Oh no," she replied, gathering the coat up in her arms. "You have too much to do. I'll run it over. And Emma, thank you for inviting me. You have no idea how much it means to me."

After she left, I hiked across the room to the dance floor—waving at Mackenzie in the corner, who gave me a thumbs up—where the celebrities were surrounded by guests. Ryan had thoughtfully agreed to bring in large padded chairs, originally built to seat a royal family onstage, for the main table on a riser at the far end where the celebrities and Tabitha, as the master of ceremonies, were sitting.

The stars certainly looked like royalty now, beaming down at the individuals clustered in front of their table. A fair bit of autograph signing was happening, leading to much laughter and excitement from the gala guests.

One of the kitchen doors opened halfway and Vivi poked her head out, waving me over.

"How's it going?" She cast a glance around the room. "I can't get over how beautiful it looks. There's something about the props that gives it more heft than your average gathering. Maybe Ryan should start a staging business."

"That would only work as long as people needed items that lined up with the productions they were putting on, though," I mused. "Like: *do* join us for a Happy Scottish Play Birthday Party!"

"Welcome to our *Les Misérables* Baby Shower!" Vivi fired back.

"What are you two laughing about?" Tabitha's voice cut through our conversation like a dull knife.

"Just making sure we were ready to go," I said, with a quick nod at Vivi.

"Okay if we begin serving now?" she asked Tabitha.

"Yes. Following the agreed-upon schedule would be nice," Tabitha retorted.

"Now that you're here, I'm sure you'd like to thank Vivi for saving our gala—first with the catering, then with the venue." I couldn't have ushered in a compliment any harder unless I'd pulled the words out of Tabitha's mouth myself.

"I'm sure that I will see fit to do so once we've actually *had* a gala," Tabitha said, then stalked away.

"I'm sorry," I said to Vivi. "She's so—"

"Awful," she replied. "Truly, unarguably awful."

"Please know that I hereby thank you *twice* as much to cover her half of the thanking."

She did a little curtsey and withdrew into the kitchen.

"Please find your seats, everyone," Tabitha said over the microphone, sounding gracious and friendly and all the things she had not shown to Vivi and me. I don't know how she switched personalities so quickly, but she was very skilled at it.

The music volume came down a notch, and Mackenzie started playing some classical music for dinner. The guests got themselves settled and service began. Ariel sat next to me and Nora was on my other side, along with Lucy and Ryan. Malina and Tom, the man who bought her salon, were also at our table. On the original seating chart, I'd put Malina up near the front, considering her relationship to her sister, but Tabitha must have pulled a switcheroo at the last minute for reasons known only to herself.

Nora and Malina were chatting across the table, but Tom didn't seem very interested in contributing, just in chugging his beer. His energy was so negative, it felt as if he was surrounded by invisible storm clouds.

After the service began, expressions of culinary satisfaction took the place of small talk. From the salad to the cheesecake, we savored the genius of Vivi and her team. She had a gift for combining flavors in unexpected ways and plating food with elegant touches. When we'd finished dessert and were sipping coffee, people began to lean back and relax.

Except for Tom, who was still alternating swigs of beer with gobbles of food, like it was his last meal.

"This is heavenly," Malina sighed happily. She'd matched her eye shadow to her ball gown, which was a deep purple. Although her makeup was a touch heavier than most of the women in the room, it suited her. The soft lighting Ryan had designed suited everyone. He had created an exceptionally romantic mood.

Gala attendees filled the dance floor, and the next hour or so passed quickly. I spent half of that time at the bookstore taking down the signs over each station and pushing tables back where they belonged.

When I returned, one of the volunteers stopped by the table and handed each of us a gift bag. Although the original ones had gone up in flames with the ballroom, the women had created them again. The usual thing was to give such goodies at the end of the night when everyone was on their way out, but we had noisemakers and hats tucked in among the other more expensive items since it was New Year's Eve. Balloons would fall onto the dancers at the stroke of midnight, which was not too far away. Vivi had enlisted a few of her waiters to climb up on ladders to fill the nets, thank goodness. All I'd had to do was approve the process.

Everyone around the table opened their bags and exclaimed over the contents.

"This is like Christmas all over again," Malina said. "I can't believe I'm here."

Tom gave her the side-eye and drained the bottle of beer in his fist. His bag remained unopened in front of him.

"At least take out your noisemaker, babe," she said.

"You make enough noise for the both of us already." He burped, shoved back his chair, and stood towering over the table.

"I'm going to the bar." He didn't ask if she wanted anything, just took off.

Malina watched him go, then looked down at the items in front of her on the tablecloth. "That's fine," she said, as if trying to convince herself.

"Is it, though?" Nora asked her. "My dear friend, you deserve someone who treats you like a queen. I don't get that sense from Tom. Am I wrong?"

Malina nodded sadly. "You're right. I need to break it off. I do. I've been meaning to for a long time, but I'm lonely."

"Me too," Ariel piped up, surprising me. "But wouldn't you rather be alone than be dealing with *that*? Please forgive me for intruding on your personal business. I'm only going by what Lyra said, and she was worried about you."

"She was?" Malina's eyes welled up with tears. "Really? She never told me."

Ariel nodded. "I don't know what happened between the two of you, but—"

"What happened was *Whitney*," Malina said, her face contorting into a harsher expression. "She fed her some line about me, but I don't know what it was."

"I'm not a fan of Whitney either," Ariel agreed. "All Lyra wanted to do was act. We both did. And Whitney knew it and could have opened doors like crazy, but she acted like Lyra was her assistant rather than a niece. So Lyra wasn't happy about that, but I never heard her say a negative word about you, at all. She missed you, and she was so grateful that you sent her money when you sold your salon."

This was the most I'd heard Ariel speak. Outside the shadow of work, she had a lively and engaging energy. Her eyes were bright and her smile lit up her face.

I turned to Malina. "You sold your salon to send Lyra money?"

"Yes," Malina said. "For her acting classes. Which is why I don't know who she could possibly be asking for help in that letter you found. That made me furious."

"Couldn't she have been asking Whitney again?"

"But Whitney would have recognized it when you showed it to us, right?" Malina pressed.

"If she was being honest, yes." I realized that Nora and Ariel were looking back and forth between us, trying to make sense of the conversation. I'd fill my aunt in later.

"Yeah, she would have 'fessed up. But I tell you what . . . tonight I'm going to confront my sister once and for all."

"Maybe you could wait until tomorrow?" I suggested. "She's working right now."

"No. I've had it. I'm done. Then I'm going to dump Tom too. I'm taking my life back." Humming, she returned the gifts to the bag.

"Good for you," said Ariel and Nora simultaneously.

"By the way, it's rather splendid being single these days, with online dating," my aunt added. "First dates galore, anyway. I'll show you around."

Malina perked right up.

I was still processing what had happened when Tabitha moved over behind the celebrities and asked us all to raise our glasses to our guests of honor. She read introductions for each of them that, honestly, went on far too long. My arm was getting tired by the time she started the second one. But we all gamely held our drinks aloft until she got to the end.

"Cheers!" we all shouted in unison and began clinking glasses with people around us. It was loud, but not loud enough to drown out the sound of Whitney shrieking.

Chapter Twenty-Four

All eyes turned to the main table, where Whitney was blotting the bodice of her dress with a napkin, Nat was hovering over her, and Stella was fluttering her hands helplessly as she stood nearby.

"How could you, Stella?" Whitney said angrily, her words caught by the microphone that Tabitha held down by her side.

"Oh *no*." Stella sounded as if the apology was drawn from the core of her being. "It must have slipped. I'm incredibly clumsy with these crutches."

"You aren't even on crutches at this moment, are you?" Whitney retorted. "You're leaning against the table, probably so you could have better aim when you tossed your wine right *at* me."

"No, no, honey. It was an accident. I'm so sorry," Stella said contritely.

"She didn't mean it, Whit," Nat said, trying to console her.

"Yes, she did." Whitney looked at Tabitha. "Wait, is that microphone *on*? Everyone can hear us? Are you kidding me?" She cast an anguished look around the room.

Tabitha quickly switched it off.

Whitney stood up abruptly, said something to Tabitha, and went through the door to the kitchen.

Stella grabbed the microphone from Tabitha and turned it on again. "Don't worry, everyone—she'll get herself all fixed up and we'll be *go* for more gala goodness!" She may have been slurring her words, but she threw the mic right back to Tabitha with precision and flagged down a passing server, who refilled her wine.

Nat scooted over into Whitney's chair and began speaking to Stella earnestly. Soon afterwards, Stella threw her head back and laughed. She appeared to be having a splendid time, probably due to the painkillers.

"Oh, I think she's drunk," Ariel said.

"But you're off duty right now," Malina reminded her. "You both should have some fun."

Ariel laughed. "That's true."

"And don't even get me started on Whitney. What a drama queen," Malina muttered. "She always has to have everyone looking at her all the time."

The two of them began telling unflattering Whitney stories.

"Do you think you should check on Whitney, darling?" Nora said quietly to me.

Mackenzie switched into lively dance music, reading the room and trying to lighten the mood.

Lucy gave a little hop and looked at me. "If you don't need us for anything . . . ?"

"No. Please go and enjoy."

She and Ryan headed to the dance floor.

I rushed into the kitchen. "Where's Whitney? I saw her come in here."

"She left," Vivi said, not pausing her chopping, which she was doing so quickly I almost couldn't see the blade moving. "Through the back. Said she needed some air."

"Wait for me," I heard behind me. I turned to see Jake, dressed in a tuxedo and looking exceptionally swell. His green eyes were more vivid than usual, his high cheekbones seemed higher, and if I wasn't mistaken, he was taller.

Or maybe that was the wine talking.

Or the romantic lighting.

Or my new appreciation for him that I hadn't fully endorsed yet.

"Should I go after her?" I wondered aloud. "Would she want me to?"

Vivi shook her head. "That almost doesn't even matter, whether she would want you to or not. What does matter is that there's too much going on at this party for which you are responsible. She's an adult. She can take care of herself."

The music volume kicked up a few levels and I heard some whoops and hollers.

"Good points," I said. "But—"

Jake cleared his throat. "Vivi's right. How about come dance with me instead? It's quite the scene out there. I'm seeing moves I haven't encountered before."

I stared at his outstretched hand.

And then, despite my better judgment, I took it.

He swept me through the door and directly onto the floor, which was crowded with happy partygoers. As soon as we got a spot, I realized my mistake—they were waltzing. I could recognize it from old movies—as well as the country club where I'd worked an event this fall—but I wasn't what anyone might call an experienced waltzer.

Before I knew what was happening, Jake had put an arm around my waist, taken my other hand in his, and was moving me around the circle. I turned my head from side to side and analyzed what other people's feet were doing, then tried to copy them. After a few moments of trying to sort out the steps and tripping over my own feet, I relaxed enough to realize that Jake was actually leading, which worked much better for both of us. Lucy and Ryan passed by, so wrapped up in each other that she didn't even notice until I touched her arm. When she saw who I was dancing with, she tilted her head toward him and nodded in approval.

Jake definitely knew what he was doing. After a few laps, we whirled and twirled as though we had practiced a thousand times for this moment. When the song ended, I was almost giddy.

Jake and I smiled at each other just as Zander Flyte's camera flashed and clicked multiple times. We both blinked strenuously, which made us laugh, then Jake bowed and led me off of the floor. "Nice work, Starrs. And may I say that you look radiant tonight? You should wear this getup all the time."

I laughed. "You clean up nicely too, Hollister."

"Want to go again?" He took a step closer.

I had just leaned in to reply in the affirmative when Tabitha barged up and pushed right between us. "Have you seen Whitney? I have to stay here and keep our guests and donors happy—can you imagine if they all disappeared? What a disaster! So could you go find her?"

Jake and I looked at each other.

"She's turning out to be *quite* the prima donna," Tabitha continued.

Takes one to know one, as the saying goes.

"I thought she was supposed to be the down-to-earth member of the cast. Oh well, live and learn," she prattled on. "Next time, I'll have to—"

"On it," I said, making a beeline for the kitchen again. Vivi had been right about Whitney being an adult, but now that Tabitha had asked, there was no question about what needed to be done. I went first, zipping around the perimeter, with Jake close behind. The back door was cracked to let in some cool air, so I pressed it open all the way. Passing through the porch and down the steps, I hurried along the riverwalk and had just turned left to go up through our porch to Starlit Bookshop when I heard a cry.

I stopped suddenly. "Listen," I said to Jake.

We stood in the dark. I spun around to face the riverwalk, which was lit up by streetlamps, and something beyond—on the dark banks of the river itself—moved in my peripheral vision. Squinting, I could barely make out two figures in silhouette a few blocks down. They were facing each other, gesticulating angrily, moving gradually together.

"Over there!" I said, pointing. Jake and I ran toward them, our breath puffing out in little clouds. As I watched in horror, one of them shoved the other into the river. There was a scream and a splash.

The person who did the pushing ran away before I could tell who it was.

* * *

We pulled Whitney out of the icy water where she was clinging to a rock, completely dazed and unable to speak. Jake ripped off his coat and put it around her.

"My car is parked in front of the coffeehouse," he said. "I can turn on my lights and get her to the emergency room right away."

"I'll go grab some blankets," I said, veering over to the back door and pulling out the ones we kept in the storeroom in case people became chilly sitting on our back porch.

By the time I returned to them, Jake had settled Whitney in the passenger seat and was fastening her seat belt. After he stepped aside, I moved in and tucked the blankets around her.

"You're going to be okay," I said.

She didn't respond, staring straight ahead with vacant eyes. Her teeth were chattering so hard I worried she was going to crack one.

Jake climbed in and turned on the engine, then sped off, using both siren and flashers.

As I watched them drive away, I tried to recall the specifics of the silhouetted shape we'd seen. It was someone in a dress, which could have been half of the people at the gala. And Whitney was no help on that front: the freezing cold water seemed to have erased any memory of what had happened, or at least she hadn't been able to tell us anything. At the thought of her pale face and blue lips, so much like Lyra's, I sent up a fervent wish for her recovery.

Vivi came out of her place and began repositioning the velvet ropes so that they were flat against the building rather than leading up to it.

"What are you doing out here?" She rolled one of the heavy metal stanchions.

I added my muscle power, such as it was, and before long, we had finished the project. I told her what had happened.

She looked at me in horror. "So someone inside that party tried to kill Whitney?"

"Looks like it."

"And you don't know who it is?"

"No. It was too dark."

"Wow."

"Not yet anyway," I added.

"Can I help with anything?"

"No, but thank you for offering."

"Then I'm going to hide in the kitchen, okay? Let me know when this party is over." She pulled on the door. "I'm kidding. Kind of. I mean, I'm here for you so don't hesitate to ask for anything, but also, yeah, I don't mind not attending the rest of the gala with a killer on the loose."

"That's very sensible."

She went straight back to her team, and I turned right into the gala. Everything seemed calm and magical in here. People were still dancing—Mackenzie had switched to more contemporary pop and the floor was full of less structured, but no less joyful, moves. Others were clustered in clumps off of the dance floor or dotting the now-cleared tables. I found myself scanning faces for signs of guilt, as if it would be as easy as that to identify a perpetrator, but came up short.

Malina was sitting at our table alone. She gave me a small smile when I sat down next to her, but it faded as I explained what had happened to Whitney. I watched her face closely, but she seemed genuinely surprised. I tried to smoothly ascertain where she had been for the past half hour—after all, she'd declared that she was going to confront Whitney earlier—and she explained that she'd been breaking up with Tom and pointed across the room. He was sullenly slumped at the end of the bar. Suddenly he lifted up his drink in mock salute and made an ugly face in her direction.

"See?" she said. "Break-up achieved."

After thanking me for letting her know about her sister, she gathered up her gift bag and left immediately. Over her shoulder, though, she asked me to have Nora call her.

"One minute until midnight," Tabitha announced. "Everyone please find a spot on the dance floor or in the vicinity. If we were in the ballroom, you'd be watching the ball drop on our gigantic video screen, but hey, we can count down together anyway, can't we? Which reminds me—we'll be reaching out to you about sponsoring the rebuilding of Baxter Ballroom, so do check your emails this week—but for now, ooh, here we go!"

The crowd counted backwards from ten and when they reached one, burst into jubilant cacophony. The noisemakers were blown and the balloons descended, after which there was playful hitting them back up into the air and toward other guests. There were hugs and kisses around the room, including a fairly passionate one between Nat and Stella.

I wondered in passing what would have happened if Jake and I had been dancing at midnight.

Tabitha was watching the celebration and looked—dare I hope?—gratified. Thank goodness something had gone right tonight in her book, though I was about to ruin that feeling, about which I didn't feel very good. I went over and updated her on the Whitney news. Her expression froze.

"I'll take it from here," she said briskly. "I'll let the *Chasers* group know. Could you bring me the auction winner names, please? After we announce those, I'll be sending people to collect their coats from the bookstore. Then if you could check in with Vivi to make sure that nothing else is needed from us, that would be helpful."

I ran back to Starlit Bookshop and scooped up the clipboards, noting the highest bid on each of them and typing the names quickly into a document that I had prepared ahead of time. I included the amount that each item had sold for and totaled it up so that Tabitha could share that information.

As the printer spit out the pages, I heard my sister's voice calling me.

I poked my head out of the office to see Lucy and Ryan rushing toward me.

"Em! We're engaged!" she screamed, showing me her hand that now sported an elegant oval diamond set in a white gold band with baguettes on either side. "Ryan asked me to marry him by the fountain at the stroke of midnight! So romantic!"

"Congratulations! I'm so thrilled for you both!" I hugged her, then him, then her again. My heart swelled with joy.

"Of course you'll be my maid of honor, Em. Right?"

"Right!" I hugged her again.

Bella came over from behind the register and squealed when she saw the ring. "This is so exciting!"

Max followed her, not squealing, but extending his congratulations as well.

"I know we haven't been dating that long," Lucy said, looking down at her ring, "but we've been friends forever and we just know. You know? We know."

"We know." Ryan nodded proudly.

"Have you told Nora yet?" I asked.

"We'll go do it now," Lucy promised.

They scampered off and I grabbed the printed auction list and stapled it. My emotions were roller-coastering—tremendous worry for Whitney, tremendous joy for my sister.

One thing at a time, I told myself. *Be steady.*

I thanked Max and Bella again for working such a long shift.

"It was a blast," Bella said. "We've been watching old movies on my laptop. Vivi came over with food too, which was super nice."

Max nodded. "Also, I ordered my books for spring term. Checked that off the list."

"Always working, this one," Bella elbowed him.

He grinned.

Although the two were opposites—she was bouncy and outgoing while he was quiet and shy—there was a palpable affection between them. Lucy had said a thousand times that she thought they made the cutest couple ever, but as far as I knew, they weren't dating. Then again, everyone around me seemed to have paired up without my noticing lately, so what did I know?

I left them to prepare for the onslaught of coat requests and returned to the party. After delivering the pages to Tabitha, I waited while she skimmed down to the bottom to see the grand total.

"Fantastic," she breathed. "More than I'd hoped for, even without the antiques!"

"What happens to those, anyway?"

"People had insurance policies on them, so they'll be able to claim it."

"Even though they had donated the items to us?"

"But we hadn't sold them yet, had we?" Tabitha tapped the side of her head to suggest smarts. "We technically just *stored* them for the people. The transfer of ownership had not yet taken place because that happens after the sale. Now that the items are lost, the owners will simply receive money instead."

Which seemed like a pretty good motive for . . . something.

Chapter Twenty-Five

Wheels started to turn in my mind as Tabitha announced the staggering amount of money we'd raised and read off the names of the highest bidders. She informed them that we would be mailing the items this week after receiving the payments, or that they could pick them up from the bookstore—news to me but fine, whatever—if they preferred. There was much applause and cheers. Trevor looked like he was going to faint when he walked up on stage and began thanking everyone for their donations.

Soon afterward, Tabitha ushered Nat and Stella through the lobby, heading for their town cars. I spoke with Mackenzie, who turned the music way down, and the room began to empty out. Once it had cleared, I did a final walk-around, picking up a few discarded gift bags that people had forgotten, and I checked in with Vivi, who told me to leave anything that remained behind for her crew to clean up. We made plans to meet in the morning to do a final invoice for Tabitha.

I was on my way out when I caught sight of Nora and Gates near the front door, deep in conversation.

Thinking she might need a rescue, I walked over, catching the tail end of what Gates was saying.

". . . I knew it was you and it crushed me to think that you wouldn't want to spend an evening together. I've always thought we had a lot in common, Nora. I would have done anything to get you to see me. I even wore this darn purple flower all night." He tapped the side of his jacket, where the boutonniere we'd seen on his desk earlier drooped crookedly from his breast pocket. "It's not exactly my style."

Nora smiled at him. "Thank you, Gates. It was a difficult decision to cancel, but please know that it's not that I didn't want to be your date tonight. It's just that I didn't want it to be uncomfortable at work. Why don't we get a coffee and talk?"

His face lit up.

What was happening? I hurried faster and joined the duo. The last thing my aunt needed was a thief for a boyfriend.

"Hello, Dr. Huddlesby," I said while waving at my aunt. I was hoping that my wave conveyed an urgent need for her to make an excuse and leave, but she seemed oblivious.

"Hello, Emma," he said.

"It's Dr. Starrs," Nora told him. "She has a PhD too."

"Congratulations. Well done," he said heartily, lifting his glass in a toast and taking a drink. When he wasn't mad about not being on a panel, he had a much nicer demeanor.

"Your aunt was inviting me to coffee," he said happily.

Oh dear. I couldn't really yell "Run, Nora! He's a crook!"

Could I?

Probably not. Instead, I looked him directly in the eyes. "May I ask you a question?"

"Sure."

"Did you happen to notice the *Chasers* script on display at the bookstore?"

His bushy eyebrows drew together, creating a caterpillar effect. "I'm not sure what you mean. When?"

"The night of the panel."

He started to shake his head back and forth.

"The script was based on a story by Calliope Nightfall."

He stopped shaking his head.

"And that was Calliope's story in the journal on your desk,"

"I *knew* you looked at it," he said victoriously.

"And I *know* you took the script," I said.

His look of triumph faded, and he hung his head. "I did."

Nora waved both of her hands. "Wait, what's going on? I'm confused. Who is stealing scripts?"

I waited for Gates to speak.

He waited for me to speak.

"Do I need to repeat my questions, you two?" Nora inquired.

"He took the *Chasers* script from the bookstore," I told her. "The night of the panel."

"No—" he said. "I took it from the English department."

"Wait, what? How did it get there?"

He shrugged. "It was just lying there on an end table next to one of the sofas in the lounge."

I must have looked confused because Nora clarified. "It's what we call the waiting area, right when you get off of the elevator. That's the lounge."

"Are you writing something more on *Chasers*?" I asked him. "On Calliope's story?"

He looked down. "Yes. So this was like a gift from heaven. I didn't try too hard to find the owner, though. I should have."

Someone tapped my shoulder. I turned around to see Calliope herself, who was clad from head to toe in layers of black velvet. A hat perched high on her head boasted a huge feather that appeared to be waving at us.

"Colleagues," she said in her gravelly voice, "if I'm not mistaken, I've heard my name three times. According to fairy tale rules, that is a *summoning* . . . so here I am."

We all greeted her warmly as she bowed her head.

"Goddess at your service. How may I help?"

"We were just talking about the *Chasers* episode based on your story," I began.

"Ah yes. Everyone has been simply raving about it. I am proud of it too," Calliope said. "How kind of you."

"And we were wondering if you had perhaps taken the copy that we displayed at the bookstore on the night of the panel."

Calliope tapped her chin with a gloved finger and looked around the circle, widening her kohl-rimmed eyes. "Was I not supposed to?"

Gates sagged in relief and Nora made a reassuring noise.

"I thought it was a gift from the universe. Recall that once, in the same location, I bestowed upon you a name, *Raven*." She looked meaningfully at me. "It's a magical bookstore. Anything can happen there. Remember that."

"Thank you, Calliope," I said. "My sister and I appreciate it."

"Where is Romance, anyway?" She turned her gaze around the room, then refocused on us. "Never mind. I'll find her if I'm meant to. As it always has been and ever shall be."

After a beat, Gates cleared his throat. "So, Calliope, I found your script in the lounge. I was hoping to use it while I wrote my next article on *Chasers*. Would that be acceptable?"

"Of course you may use it, Gates." Calliope smiled benevolently at him. "And let me grant one more wish before you even think of it: I'd be happy to participate in an *interview* with you. Which you could easily publish in any respectable journal or magazine. And yes, you're welcome."

"Oh." He was obviously stunned. "Thank you."

Calliope readjusted her hat, waved at someone across the room, and swept away without another word.

Nora took his arm. "Shall we get that coffee? We have a lot to talk about, Gates."

"We do," he replied, patting her hand and looking at me. "Will you excuse us?"

"Yes," I said distractedly, trying to process everything I'd heard.

Now it was his turn to look directly into my eyes. "And I want you to know that I've never stolen anything before, and I'll never steal anything again."

"It doesn't sound like you *did* steal something," Nora said. "Right, Emma?"

I nodded. And even if he had just wanted to hoard the script for a little while so no one else could read it, I would have understood the impulse: academics could be notoriously territorial about the topics on which they wrote critical work. And who could blame them? Everything depended on their ability to find something original to write about. The last thing they wanted was for someone to scoop them. Publish or perish was quite real.

It was a relief, knowing that he wasn't actually a thief. My aunt worked with him every single day. There wasn't a lot I could do to keep them apart, when you came right down to it.

* * *

I hustled back to Starlit Bookshop, which still had a long line of guests in front of the coat check. Lucy and Bella were going as fast as they could while Max kept an eye on the register. Making apologies, I made my way to the front and helped retrieve coats. It was a blur of tickets and coats and bags, but eventually, we returned everything to the owners except for one long black wool coat.

We all breathed a sigh of relief, I thanked Bella and Max again for their help, and before long, I was the only one left in the store. Nora had left with Gates—though I'd texted her a warning to be careful—and Lucy and Ryan were going to meet some friends to celebrate their newly betrothed status. I was turning off the printer when I heard the front door open. Stepping out of the office, I said hello to Ariel, who was looking around as if she were lost.

"Your coat?" I asked, smiling.

"Whew. I thought I was too late for a second there."

I went into the storeroom and got it for her. As she slipped her arms into the sleeves, I asked how everyone was doing.

"You mean Whitney?"

"Yes." We moved along the aisles toward the front.

"Everyone is freaking out, honestly. Whitney was worried that something would happen to her, and it did, despite all of the security she was promised."

I didn't say anything. She was right.

"Do you want a ride to the hospital? I was heading over now to check on her."

Ariel's expression softened. "That would be great, thank you. Nat and Stella are probably there already. Once again, the town car left me behind. That's what happens when you're only the assistant."

"How long have you been working for Stella?"

"Years," she said. "And don't get me wrong, I love working for her. She's a blast. There's just a big line between the star and everyone who works for the star, if you know what I mean. At least that's what I've always found to be true."

I switched off the lights and flipped the sign on the door to "Closed." My car was right out front, and I unlocked it so she could climb in. Once I warmed up the car and pulled out, we headed to Silvercrest Hospital, which was not far away.

"Have you been an assistant to anyone else?"

She hesitated, then spoke quietly. "Whitney."

"What was that like?"

"It was fine." Ariel said it with finality, but I asked my next question anyway, sensing a story there.

"Why did you leave?"

This time, the hesitation was longer.

I waited.

Ariel brushed something off her coat sleeve. "It wasn't right for me."

"What do you mean?"

"Our personalities didn't match up too well. I'd known her for a long time, but she was different than I thought she was. Plus,

Lyra needed a job in between her catering gigs, so it made more sense for me to go work with Stella when she needed someone, and Lyra worked as Whitney's assistant. I was glad to go. It all worked out for the best." Her sadness at the mention of Lyra's name filled the car, invisible but heavy. She turned and looked out the window, remaining silent until we parked at the emergency room.

We hurried across the lot and through the sliding doors.

Jake was surrounded by Malina, Nat, and Stella. They were all talking at once, seemed like. Ariel joined them and was swept up into the conversation. I hung back, and Jake broke free and steered me away from the group, over into the corner.

"She's getting treatment for hypothermia. They'll be keeping her here overnight. The doctor said that he didn't want, and I quote, 'that crowd' to go in and see Whitney yet, but they're plotting to bypass that plan like they were in an episode of their show or something." He shook his head. "Do you think you could convince them to leave and come back in the morning?"

"Would be happy to try." I went over and raised my voice, throwing out something vague and mysterious to get their attention, something I'd learned from teaching. "Hey, everyone, I have something to tell you."

They stopped speaking and eyed me expectantly.

"We can't see Whitney tonight. The doctor said to come back in the morning."

"Jake *already* told us that," Malina said. "But we're not leaving—"

"You can sit here in the waiting room, it's true," I interjected, "but they seriously won't let you go back there. Surely it makes more sense to get a good night's rest and return in the morning."

"Fine by me," Stella waved one of her crutches. "I'm exhausted from hauling myself around on these infernal things."

"If you're going, I'm going," Ariel said. "In case you need anything."

"Me too." Nat rubbed his eyes. "Going too."

Malina sighed. "I probably should get some shut-eye. The next conversation Whitney and I have is going to be a big one."

"Even if she's in a hospital bed?" Jake asked quietly.

"She never makes things easy, does she?" Malina muttered, drawing herself up and peering around the circle. "Yes, I said it. Don't look at me like that. You have no idea what she's really like."

There were some indistinct murmurs.

"It's just . . ." Malina looked at her feet. "I've had a lifetime of it."

No one spoke, though everyone was clearly uncomfortable. Eventually, the group members broke apart, going their separate ways.

And here I thought that the two sisters might reunite after realizing that one of them had almost lost their life tonight. Maybe when an emotional current runs so very deep, such a reunion would have been a little too much like a television show.

* * *

I was almost home when my phone rang.

What now? I couldn't bear any more drama tonight.

Jake's name was on the screen, though, so I punched the accept button and said hello.

"Can you meet me at Silvercrest Castle?"

"Why?"

"Tabitha is heading over there now. She got to the hospital right after you all left. I was on my way out, but she cornered me and told me some story about how she suspects Whitney was faking the accident to get out of attending the gala."

"But she *did* attend the gala."

"Not the whole time."

"And she *is* in the hospital."

"They wouldn't let Tabitha in, so she got suspicious."

"It doesn't make any sense," I said.

"But it's Tabitha. Who knows what she's got stuck in her craw. Anyway, I thought you'd want to be there."

We said goodbye and I did a U-turn.

* * *

It was quiet in the lobby of the hotel, with a sole figure at the registration desk and another person vacuuming the carpet near the bar. The elevator ride was one sustained whoosh and a subdued ding upon arrival at the penthouse level.

The door to the suite was open, so I walked in and closed it behind me.

The stars were strewn about the sofas, holding glasses full of a green liquid and talking quietly among themselves. Ariel, who was holding a pitcher, asked if I would like some.

Stella waved me over. "It's a fruit shake with mega vitamins. Hangover prevention."

"No thanks," I said, sitting down next to her.

"We're waiting for Tabitha to arrive. Supposedly she has something very important to share with us. And I hope it comes with a check." She wasn't slurring anymore. In fact, she sounded quite sober.

"Any word about Whitney?"

"No." She took a sip and grimaced. "Ugh. Freakin' kale."

At the knock on the door, Ariel answered. Tabitha came in, followed by Jake. She sat down next to me but gave him an admiring glance as he took a seat on the opposite couch.

What was that about?

"Will we be going to sleep soon?" Nat asked wistfully.

"Do whatever you like, but I'm here to check on Whitney," Tabitha said. "Was she released?"

"Are you kidding me? She's still in the hospital." Stella snorted. "I thought you were coming to deliver a *bonus*. I mean, I showed up *on crutches* tonight."

"Thank you for that," Tabitha said tightly. "And really, thanks to all of you for fulfilling your contracts, especially given what's happened this week."

"We're professionals," Stella said.

Nat nodded.

"Now I'd like to look in Whitney's bedroom if you don't mind," Tabitha said.

"For what?" Stella said. "She's not in there. What's wrong with you?"

"I find it suspicious that the doctor wouldn't let *me* back to see her. I mean, Tip donated so much money that they almost named a wing after him."

"That doesn't give you the right to cruise into patient rooms whenever you feel like it," I said to her.

She glared at me. "I want to take a peek."

Jake opened his mouth to speak, but Nat offered to take her to Whitney's room. His was adjoining and they'd kept the door unlocked for the duration of the visit, he said. "Anything to get this over with faster," he said.

"Are they a couple?" I asked, after the duo had left. "Whitney and Nat?"

Stella and Ariel burst into laughter.

"So . . . no?"

"He *hates* her," Stella said. "With a seething passion. We all do."

Jake and I exchanged a glance.

"Really? She seems so . . ."

"Sweet?" Stella said. "Yes. It's called having two personalities. The one that plays the part and the real one underneath."

"That's what Malina said too."

"So did Lyra," Ariel said, looking sad like she did every time she mentioned her.

"But she and Nat seem so close."

"Yeah, he is *actually* sweet. It's hard for him to be mean to anyone. As you have observed, I don't have that same flaw," Stella said, with a wink. "What you see is what you get."

Ariel nodded. "That's true."

Jake's phone rang and he went out on the balcony to speak to whoever was on the other end.

Stella watched him thoughtfully. "He's incredibly hot. Are you two a thing?"

I shook my head. "What makes you think that?"

She shrugged and lost interest. Grabbing her crutches, she navigated the space around the sofa. "Can you help, me, Ari? I need to get ready for bed. Oh, but where is that lavender lotion you said you would use on my feet?"

"It's downstairs," Ariel said. "Let me go grab it."

"I can help with one or the other," I offered.

They both took this in.

"You help me get ready for bed, Ari, and let Emma get the lotion. Give her your key and tell her where the lotion is."

Ariel looked like she was going to say something but thought better of it. She pulled a flat door key card out of her pocket, gave me the room number, and told me the lotion was in the tote on a chair by the window.

"Do you want me to bring up the whole bag?"

"Just the lotion is fine."

The two of them moved toward the bedrooms and I promised to come right back. I used the stairs to get to the next level.

Ariel's room was pristine. Nothing was out of place and the tote was right where she said it was. I opened it carefully and saw the lotion next to what looked like a contract. A card with the red bird graphic was stapled to the top.

I paused, then pulled it out and skimmed it.

Suddenly, everything made sense.

Chapter Twenty-Six

The women were still in the back when I got to the suite. I delivered the lotion to Ariel, who quietly thanked me and closed the bedroom door again.

I raced over to the balcony and motioned for Jake to hang up his phone.

"What's going on?" he said, as he came over near the door.

"I have to show you something right *now.*" I unfolded the pages and held them up in the doorway where it was lighter, so he could read them.

He took one look and his eyes widened. "Why does Ariel have a contract offering her Whitney's role?"

"Why indeed?" I asked. "And why hasn't she signed it yet?"

"Maybe she's negotiating it?"

"That's correct," Ariel said, appearing in front of us and holding out her hand for the pages. "We're still talking. Whitney's re-up, however, is not happening."

I gave her the packet.

"Re-up?" Jake repeated.

"Renewing her contract," Ariel clarified. "Everyone at *Chasers* is sick of her demands."

They were aligned in describing Whitney's personality, though it was hard to correlate the person I knew with the supreme diva they all described.

"What kind of demands?"

Ariel looked over the railing toward the pool, which was lit up and glowing green in the darkness. "She has to have everything her way. The most lines, the most flattering camera angles, the most money—and don't even get me started on the press demands. She is greedy and unwilling to share even a little of the spotlight with anyone else."

"And you would?" Jake asked. He pulled himself up to sit on the railing as if it were nothing. Then again, maybe to him it wasn't. You had to be brave to do his job and of course he worked out. A lot.

"I *will* do that," Ariel smiled at the contract in her hand. "And everyone will be the happier for it."

"How did this all come about?" I asked.

"Right before we came here, Stella and Nat talked to the director and the producers about the dynamics on set and about how they could take a big risk by going in a new direction. During that conversation, she suggested me as a replacement."

I flashed back to the *Variety* article in Stella's room, which, it seemed, had been one step ahead of the rumors.

I pointed to the card at the top of the contract. "Did you by any chance have a card with this logo at the tea with an appointment for February?"

She cocked her head. "Yes. I was looking at it in the kitchen and dreaming of what was to come, but then Lyra came in and I shoved it into the closest drawer. I must have forgotten to take it out."

"What was the appointment for?"

"Dr. Cardinal. He's a plastic surgeon. My taking the role came with expectations. I don't look much like Whitney. Yet."

"So if you took the role, you'd have to agree to having some things done?" I clarified.

She nodded. "I mean, they're not going to make me her clone or anything, but just make . . . improvements."

I kept pressing, hoping to confirm my theory. "Does Whitney know?"

"She knew that someone had been suggested as a replacement, but she thought it was Lyra, who had been trying to get onto the show for a long time and who also happens to look just like her. Whitney was going to confront her here."

"How do you know that?"

"Because Whitney told me that. She demanded that I tell her if it was true about Lyra replacing her. I said no, of course. I didn't talk to either of them about the plan. It was too tricky, and I didn't want to hurt their feelings."

Jake sat up straighter. "Wait, do you think Whitney killed Lyra?"

Ariel's eyes filled with tears. "I do think that. Can you imagine? Killing your own niece?"

"Is that why you pushed Whitney into the river?" I asked loudly, hoping that everyone nearby would hear. I had a plan.

Her mouth fell open. "I didn't."

I raised my voice. "If it wasn't you, who could it have been? Nat?"

"No," she said, sniffling. "He would never. He is the sweetest person alive."

"Then who?"

Ariel began to cry harder.

"You can tell us," I said.

"You *did* push her, didn't you?" Jake picked up the thread. "And you killed Lyra too, right? Obviously, she was a threat to you. Especially since she looked more like Whitney than you do."

"No," Ariel wailed.

"Just admit it," he said louder.

"Stop torturing her!" Stella commanded from the doorway. "She didn't do it."

"Do what?" Tabitha asked, from behind her.

Stella moved onto the balcony. When Tabitha and Nat followed her, she came toward us.

"Where are your crutches?" I asked.

She paused and looked down, as if just now realizing that she didn't have them with her. When she lifted her head, her face was transformed into something approaching awe. "I didn't even know I could walk without them. I was trying to hurry out here when I heard you grilling Ariel."

I took a step closer and spoke softly. "That's not true."

"What do you mean?"

"You didn't have them when you pushed Whitney into the river." Until that moment, I wasn't positive that it was her, but the fact that she didn't need her crutches a second time that night confirmed my suspicions.

Stella laughed, then strode toward me. "Good girl. That's right. I didn't."

Jake gasped.

"Really? We're going to have drama from you now? Don't need that." Her arm shot out and pushed against his chest hard. He tumbled over the railing. I called his name and reached desperately out for his feet but couldn't get there in time.

I've never been so glad to hear a splash in my life.

But when I looked over the railing, he was face down in the pool, motionless.

"Stella, what are you doing?" Ariel shrieked.

I raced out of the room and over to the stairway. Pushing the metal door open so hard it bounced off the wall, I took the stairs three at a time until I reached the ground floor. I burst through the exit door, slipped off my shoes and tossed my phone on a chair, then dove into the chilly water of the deep end, where I flipped Jake over and dragged him out of the pool. After the first few seconds of administering CPR, he coughed up water and was breathing again. The concierge appeared with a first-aid kit and blankets, followed by the hotel doctor, who knelt down beside me to take over.

"Thank you," Jake croaked as I began to edge away.

I paused and rubbed his arm, hoping he didn't notice how much I was shaking. "I'm glad you're okay. The doctor's here to take a look at you."

"Emma," he said, sounding stronger, "go get her."

* * *

On the way upstairs, I called the police. They promised to send someone. I hoped that the Hollywood crew hadn't already cleared out while I went after Jake.

When I returned to the room, the door was standing open.

"How is he?" Tabitha asked from the sofa, where everyone was sitting as if nothing had happened. Wow. Way to help out, everyone.

"He's in good hands," I said, as the pool water dripped on the penthouse floor. "No thanks to you, Stella."

"I'm sorry," she said. "I just get mad sometimes."

"You can't push someone off a balcony," I said to her. "That's assault, at the very least."

"He's fine, though, right? You said so." Stella tipped her glass to finish off the rest of her green juice and seemed wholly unconcerned.

"I didn't say that, and I don't know if he is."

She set the glass down carefully on the table. "I'll make it up to him."

"Can we get back to you pushing Whitney into the river as well? It's looking like a pattern."

Stella sighed. "I have a temper. What can I say?"

"You're pushing people into frigid water in the winter. It's dangerous." My voice was rising.

"She's right, Stell," Nat said quietly, as he wrapped a blanket around my shoulders.

"I won't do it again. Promise." Stella said to Nat, batting her eyelashes.

"Never again?" he asked.

"Never." She crossed her heart with one hand.

"What were you talking about?" I asked.

"I was telling Whitney what she needed to hear. That Ariel would be a better fit for all of us."

Ariel wiped at her eyes.

"I didn't even know I was pushing her. She came toward me and the next thing I knew, she was in the water."

She seemed to be the kind of person who indulged in brutal honestly as long as it didn't reveal any of her secrets while also not believing there would be any consequences for her actions. She perhaps needed a little metaphorical push of her own. Might as well go for it. Now or never.

"You can't push people, and you can't knock them out either," I said.

"What are you talking about?" Stella tilted her head.

"Are you talking about Lyra?" Ariel's voice quavered.

I nodded.

Stella fixed her eyes on Ariel.

"Wait, you killed Lyra?" Nat said incredulously.

"No. Quite the opposite. I tried to *help* her," Stella said, enunciating clearly. "She wrote to me, you know, since her own aunt wouldn't lift a finger to help."

I flashed back to the note in Lyra's jewelry box.

She fidgeted a little, tossing her hair over her shoulder.

"I've seen a draft of that letter," I said. "I believe that she asked for your help. And in exchange she gave you money, right? The money from Malina's salon. That's what you wanted." I held my breath.

"Needed." She gave me a long look. "It costs a *lot* to stay young and beautiful, which Hollywood demands."

Ariel blanched.

"I understand. How were you planning to help her?" I couldn't help but lean in, as Stella sat up a little straighter, practically purring to find herself the center of such intense attention.

"Stella," I said, "We all want to know. Please tell us what happened."

"No!" Ariel walked toward her. "It's not true. You would never kill Lyra—"

Stella recoiled. "Not on purpose. It was an accident."

Ariel put her hand over her mouth.

"I thought it was Whitney," Stella continued blandly, as if she were discussing the weather. "They were wearing the same clothes. They looked the same from the back."

Everyone stared at her.

"What? It wasn't planned. I happened to find her alone and thought it would be more expedient for the show if Whitney had a little accident. Then she'd be out for a while . . . and Ariel could step in more quickly while Lyra could be her understudy. I didn't know anyone was going to *die*." She looked around the room, pausing at each face and taking in our horrified expressions. "Come *on*. I'm not, like, a murderer. There was no intent. That was an unfortunate side effect. I was trying to do something good."

"Good? Then why didn't you tell anyone, if it was an accident?" Nat demanded.

She laughed. "Oh sure, yeah. The tabloids would have had a field day with that."

Nat shook his head.

"How could you do that?" Ariel asked. "You put her in a *freezer*!"

"Honey," Stella looked at her. "I did it for *you*. You deserved the part."

Ariel's face contorted, and she ran out of the suite.

The police filed into the room. After long conversations with each of us separately, they took Stella into custody.

* * *

"This entire trip, wow." Nat shook his head. "Feels like we're cursed."

"And don't forget that my ballroom burned down," Tabitha replied. "So the curse wasn't limited to the *Chasers* cast."

He smiled sadly at her but didn't say anything else. He may have reached his limit of what he could process for the evening.

I was almost there myself.

Tabitha looked none too pleased at his lack of robust response. She turned her head in my direction. "Let's go, shall we?"

We got into the elevator together.

"I'm sorry about the ballroom," I said after the doors closed.

"Thank you." She jabbed the ground floor button.

"And about the antiques that were lost."

"Oh, most of them weren't wanted by the owners anymore, and now they're being reimbursed for them, so that's not a problem. The vases, however, are a great loss."

"Because they belonged to Melody?"

"What?" Tabitha spoke sharply.

"I saw the donation sheets in the file. She donated them. Why wouldn't she acknowledge that when I was asking about them? Does it have something to do with the divorce?"

I could see her mind going a mile a minute.

"It does, doesn't it? Was she donating the vases to keep them away from Bruce, or perhaps to make him angry?"

She went pale. "The vases were in Melody's home during their marriage, and she deserves the payoff. If Bruce is angry, who cares? He's treating her horribly during this divorce."

"So she needs money."

"Doesn't everyone?" Tabitha sniffed.

"And on top of that, she's the one who shoved me into the cage and stole them, isn't she?"

"I don't know if she shoved you—that's your word against hers—but she did come to me later to explain that she wasn't sure she could go through with the donation. She was afraid Bruce's lawyers would come after her. I told her that was nonsense and that she should give them back to us if she knew what was good for her. They were the show-stopping pieces of the entire auction! And, as we both saw, she did."

"No offense, but the tension between the two of you was visible to all of us. Do you think she might have wanted to make you angry by taking them?"

She thought about this for a minute. It may have been the first time she seriously entertained the idea that her friends were no longer willing to do whatever was in Tabitha's best interests to the detriment of their own.

I pressed on. "And what happened the night of the fire?"

She hesitated, then spoke rapidly. "You heard what she said when they were by the ambulance."

"Do you believe her?"

"Do I believe that Melody told Mackenzie that they needed to do a music and lighting run-through? Yes. But *obviously* she wanted to hook up with him—who wouldn't? I've known her forever. She can't lie to me." She snorted. "Not that he was actually interested in *her*."

"But what I'm asking is: Do you think there was any other intention to lighting the candles?" I watched her face closely as she processed the question. "Especially with the vases back in the ballroom?"

"Absolutely not. She would have known that I'd never forgive her. Which I'm not doing."

I felt like I had to spell things out a bit more clearly. "Tabitha, now she's planning to submit a hefty claim to the insurance company."

Tabitha lifted her chin. "Yes. Like everyone else."

"So she'll get a lot of money from the vases."

"Yes," she said again, though she sounded uncertain.

"Because of the fire."

Her eyes widened slightly. "Are you suggesting that she set the fire because of the vases? Intentionally?"

"It's plausible, given the context, isn't it?"

"Hmm. Well, how about you let me take care of that?" Tabitha jabbed the elevator button again. It seemed like she hadn't thought through the possibilities before, but I suspected that Melody was about to get an earful.

Chapter Twenty-Seven

On the first day of the new year, I was sitting on the back porch of Starlit Bookshop, enjoying the balmy weather.

Balmy for winter, that is. The sun at high altitude could make it feel like springtime in the Rockies on any given day.

As I watched the river moving, I thought about how much had changed since this time last year: I'd left academia, moved back home to work at the bookstore with my sister, and confirmed that I loved living in our charming little hometown. Lucy had found the love of her life, and I had found a writing group.

"Such a nice surprise to discover your thank-you note and gift card first thing this morning. Thank you, Emma." Vivi set a tall paper cup down on the wrought-iron coffee table in front of me.

"It's only a small token of my vast and infinite gratitude." I reached for the cup, removed the lid, and happily breathed in the steam. "And bless you again, Viv, for bearing coffee!"

She laughed. "You really enjoy your skinny caramel lattes, don't you?"

"Or as I like to refer to them: pure bliss."

"I've never seen anyone who loves coffee as much as you do." She took a sip of her drink.

"Wish I could find a perfume that smells like a caramel latte so that even when I'm away from one, I would feel like I'm not."

"I'm sure that exists out there somewhere."

"Haven't found it yet. But in the meantime, I will fully enjoy drinking this."

She nodded and pulled a folder out of her bag, then passed me one of the stapled packets inside. "Here's the bill. Would you please take a quick look before I send it off to Tabitha? Did I forget anything?"

I scanned the pages and passed them back. "Only a generous tip for yourself and your crew."

"I was going to let Tabitha add that."

"Normally, I'd agree with you, but with her, specifically, you may not want to leave it up to chance. Can you include an amount you think is fair, then see if she adds to it? You know, like the fancy hotels do when they hand you the room service bill with tip included and hope you don't notice."

Vivi nodded thoughtfully. "Twenty percent would be great."

"Maybe do thirty." I smiled at her. "You've earned every penny. Remember all of the extra scrambling required with a few days' notice—and you saved the entire gala. Or if you're not comfortable doing a pre-included tip, you could add a special you-gave-me-such-short-notice fee."

"Do you mean a rush fee?"

"Exactly. That sounds more professional."

"I'll think about it. Thanks, Emma."

"My pleasure. Thank you again so much for saving us, in so many ways."

"Any time," she said. "Happy to help. So what happened last night? I heard something about Stella being taken downtown, or whatever it's called when your town is so small that there isn't really a separate downtown to go to."

"Taken into custody," I murmured, before drinking another delicious sip.

"Oh, there you are," Lucy said, popping her head out the back door. She came over and plunked down on the loveseat next to me.

"What is that flash?" Vivi asked, pointing to her hand.

Lucy gave her left hand an affectionate look before holding it out for Vivi to see. "Ryan and I are engaged," she said shyly. "As of last night."

"Congratulations!" Vivi said. "I was hoping something wonderful would come out of that romantic atmosphere. He did such a terrific job setting it up."

"Come to find out that he was sort of inspired by that," Lucy said, giving her ring another happy look. "He'd been carrying the ring around for a week. First, he was going to propose on Christmas Eve. Then on Christmas. But he didn't feel like it was exactly right. When he was setting up the fountain and everything, he decided to create a perfect setting not only for the gala but for the proposal too."

"So happy for you, Luce," I said, giving her arm a squeeze.

She leaned against me for a moment.

"Please consider me for your wedding needs," Vivi said. "I love to make huge cakes."

Lucy laughed. "You're hired."

Vivi sat back. "But I didn't even prepare a pitch!"

"You've been so good to us," Lucy said. "It's the least I can do. I'd be honored for you to take the job. Plus, your food is amazing, so it's kind of a win-win."

Vivi smiled. "Let's get together soon and come up with a plan."

"Sounds great," my sister said.

"Wait, have you already set a date?" I asked her. "It will have to be an enormous venue because the whole town is going to want to attend."

"I'll call around and find a location—neither of us are too picky about that. Somewhere pretty will be fine. But we don't want to wait too long, so whatever is available soonest. Wait, is 'soonest' a word? In any case, what I mean is that we'll probably take the first available place. We just want to be married as soon as possible."

Her joy was emanating off of her in waves. I was surprised that she was being so relaxed about things—she'd been dreaming about her wedding day her whole life. I'd seen the album of wedding ideas that she'd put together in college, bursting with dresses, cakes, and floral arrangements. But now that the opportunity was here, she was more focused on the marriage part.

Or maybe the wedding fever hadn't kicked in yet.

"There you are!" Nora said, echoing Lucy's earlier statement. Had I known everyone was looking for us, I would have left a note on the door.

She joined us, sitting down next to Vivi and looking back and forth among us. "What are we talking about?"

"Lucy's wedding," Vivi and I said together.

"Oh, I can't wait." Nora clasped her hands, her sleeves gracefully swooping through the air. She wore a down vest over an artsy tunic jacket, which was layered over a thick sweater. There was not a season cold enough to persuade her to trade in her flowy style.

"Speaking of which, would you walk me down the aisle, Nora?" Lucy asked her quietly.

My aunt put her hand to her chest and blinked rapidly. Fighting tears, I was sure; we were all registering the same pang at the thought of my parents not being here to see their daughter get married.

"I'd be honored," she said finally. "Thank you, darling."

Vivi closed her folder and stood. "I should let you all talk. But remember that I'll be next door if anything juicy is said, so do come get me."

We laughed and said our goodbyes.

After the door closed behind her, I took another sip of my latte and waited for Nora to tell us why she'd come searching for us. It didn't take long.

"Trevor Fontaine called to say that they made more for the library this year than they *ever* have before. He was talking a mile a minute, but here's the gist: he's absolutely thrilled and has promised to hire Starlit Bookshop to provide books for all of the library's speakers this year. Congratulations!"

"That will help us so much," Lucy said. "Emma, I can't tell you how grateful I am for everything you've done."

I shook my head. "Everything *we've* done. It's a team effort."

"You're the captain, then," she said.

"And you're the co-captain," I replied. "Nora too."

"Fine, we're all captains," my aunt said. "Do you think we should get matching hats?"

Lucy tilted her head, pondering.

"Definitely not," I said. "No hats."

"Not even a pirate hat, Emma?" Nora asked. "Our library sleuthing session suggested that you are all about—"

"What did I miss?" Lucy asked. "Sounds fun."

"More fun than a barrel of rum," Nora said, winking.

"You missed nothing," I said. "Promise. Though I'm curious to hear what happened last night with Dr. Huddlesby . . ."

Nora fluttered her hand at me. "Oh, you. Gates and I just had a little coffee date."

"Do tell."

"He was much more charismatic than I'd expected. And he already reached out to someone who might be interested in adapting my work. Wouldn't that be marvelous?" Her eyes softened. "To think I've worked down the hall from him for years and never once actually *considered* him."

My sister and I shared an eloquent glance like characters in an Austen novel, then she looked down at her engagement ring again, shifting it slightly so that it sparkled in the sunlight. "I can't believe I'm getting married!"

We all cheered.

Nora leaned forward. "How did he pop the question? What exactly did he say?"

Lucy smiled. "He brought me over to the fountain and said that he knew we hadn't been dating very long but that he loved me and couldn't wait any longer to ask if we could spend the rest of our lives together. Before he even finished saying the last word, I was saying yes."

This time, we all gazed happily at the ring together.

* * *

A week later, I received an email from Whitney, letting me know that she was feeling better and thanking me for everything during the visit, especially for figuring out what happened to Lyra. She gave me a brief update on the latest with *Chasers* and told me that if I ever visited Los Angeles, I should come to a taping. Malina had written too, saying that she was putting her house up for sale and would be opening a new salon. I was, she said, invited for a free cut and color, and she'd even throw in a makeup lesson if I wanted. Hint, hint.

I closed the mailbox and joined the West Side Writers—Tevo, Alyssa, and Jake—at the wooden table in the back of the bookstore. Jake's flannel shirt in forest green beneath a black puffer vest complemented his eye color.

"Thank you for agreeing to meet on a weekend. I know you could be watching any number of sporting events."

"Taping them. Which is better because I can fast forward through the commercials." Tevo readjusted the purple slouch cap that matched his fleece vest.

Alyssa, whose yellow jacket and matching pants were yet another great athleisure gear combo, smiled at her husband. The couple had arrived first and were ready to begin, their edited pages in front of them. "And working on our writing is such a great way to start the year. One of my resolutions is to get this book finished and start looking for agents."

"When you're ready, I'll introduce you to mine," Jake said, digging around in his bag. "That goes for all of you. I can't promise that it will be a match, but I'm more than happy to put in a good word for you, however I can."

We thanked him, then fell silent. We were all probably imagining getting to the point where an agent would be willing to represent us.

"I guess I'm up first?" Jake looked around the group.

"Marlowe should be here any minute." I was thrilled that my friend had agreed to formally join the group—everyone had been impressed by the pages she'd shared at the last meeting and was eager for her to be a member—and excited for her to finish her PI novel. When we were in middle school, we used to spend hours talking about what it would be like to be A Real Published Novelist. Nothing would feel more right than both of us going after our goal together.

Jake stood up from the seat beside me, positioned another chair from a nearby table at the end, then sat down there.

"Very thoughtful. Thank you," I said.

"I love that our group is growing," Alyssa said happily.

I removed my copy of Jake's chapter from the vintage black messenger bag that I'd bought at Marlowe's shop in the fall. It had called to me while I was there to pick out something else, as often happened in her store. Shopping there was like going treasure-hunting.

"I like that," Alyssa said, gesturing to the black fisherman's sweater that went down halfway to my knees. "It looks so cozy."

"Thanks. It belonged to my father."

"How nice." Alyssa did what people do when they realize they've unintentionally tiptoed onto sad territory—she smiled and busied herself by straightening the papers in front of her. I had done something similar before in such situations.

The front door opened and Marlowe came hurrying in, followed by someone. "Sorry I'm late, all. This is Brandon Scott. He's . . . we're . . ." She looked at him and laughed.

"Dating," he said. "Officially. And when Marlowe told me she was joining your group, I asked if I could tag along, see what it was like."

Introductions were made all around.

Marlowe slid into a chair next to me.

"So you two enjoyed the gala, I hope?" I said, tilting my head toward Brandon.

She nodded, her eyes bright. "We need to have lunch soon and catch up."

"Can't wait. So happy for you."

She squeezed my arm and began to unpack.

"Are you a writer too?" Alyssa asked Brandon, who was bundled up in a dark blue ski coat.

"Yes," he said with a broad smile. "Sci fi, mostly."

Jake grabbed another chair and gestured to it. "Nice to meet you. Please join us. The more the merrier."

Brandon peeled off his coat, sat down, and looked around the table expectantly.

"Welcome to West Side Writers. If you like, you can read these pages before we begin the discussion." I slid my pages with comments over to him.

He began reading as Marlowe pulled her pages from the briefcase that matched her red wool dress and jacket.

Tevo looked at Jake. "Before we get started, what's going on with the movie-star-murderer thing?"

The detective dipped his chin. "The trial is going to be a media circus. I'm not sure we've seen anything like that around these parts before."

"And Whitney's going back to the show and Stella's going to get fired," I said.

"Stella can't play that role from jail, obviously," Alyssa said.

"If that's where she ends up," Tevo replied.

"How could she not?" Marlowe asked. "She killed Lyra and admitted it."

"And she didn't even seem the tiniest bit remorseful," I added.

"Maybe Ariel will end up playing Stella's role," Marlowe mused. "That would be quite the irony. Stella made a space for her, just not the space she intended."

"Why did she do it?" Tevo persisted.

Jake looked at me. "You're the one who put the pieces together. Do you want to explain?"

It all looked complicated on the surface, but as I recounted the details, I saw that what it truly came down to was simple: pure jealousy along with a strong desire for control. Stella simply wanted things the way she wanted things and that was enough of a rationale—for her—to do horrible things, even if she had a tendency to classify them as "accidents."

"It's tragic," Marlowe said, shaking her head. "Lyra probably would have had a real opportunity to make her dreams come true eventually, with her connections. She was just in the wrong place at the wrong time."

"Was she talented enough to make it as an actor?" Tevo wondered.

"She deserved to try, anyway," Alyssa said.

"Everyone deserves to try," Brandon said.

"Agreed," Jake said quietly.

The sound of the cash register slamming shut snapped us out of the somber silence that followed.

"All this talk about dreams is making me want to chase our own. Should we start working on our stories?" Alyssa asked brightly.

So we did.

Chapter Twenty-Eight

It was business as usual at the bookstore, which seemed almost impossible after the intensity of the previous weeks, but somehow things were settling down quickly in Silvercrest.

When Tabitha came through the door, Lucy and I looked at each other for a long moment, as if gearing up for battle.

Paisley was draped over Tabitha's arm and keeping a watchful eye on Anne Shirley, who was curled up on a nearby bookshelf and dozing in a sunbeam.

"I should thank you for stepping in at the last minute and helping with the gala," Tabitha announced.

"Of course." I smiled at her.

She held my eye. "It may interest you to know that Melody and I are no longer friends. Not only did she ruin our fabulous gala by canoodling with Mackenzie and setting the place on fire, but she obviously destroyed my entire ballroom."

"I'm truly sorry," I said. Which I was.

"Cannot believe we have to do it all over again." The way she ran her hand across her brow wouldn't have looked out of place in a melodrama. "But we'll begin the rebuild just as soon as the insurance clears. Some of the original stone walls are still standing, so not all has been lost."

"So glad to hear that," Lucy murmured.

"Anyway, this should conclude our business." She pulled an envelope out of her bag and slapped it down on the counter, twirled around, and departed.

After the door closed, Lucy burst out laughing. "Wow, that was a short one. At least she said that she *should* thank you. Someday maybe she'll actually do it. And considering what you just did for her . . . seems like she could be a bit warmer toward you."

"It's fine," I said. "I prefer short tepid visits to long icy ones any day."

Inside, I found a check and a note from Trevor, gushing about our contributions to the gala. He also formally invited us, as Nora had mentioned he would, to become the official bookseller for Silvercrest Library and suggested that we brainstorm additional activities to do together throughout the year.

For the rest of the day, we had a steady stream of customers, many of whom congratulated Lucy on her engagement. She was delighted all over again every single time and absolutely glowing.

Shortly after Tabitha left, Calliope made an entrance.

Gone were the dark femme fatale getups; instead, she was dressed in filmy layers of white and gray, with some kind of sparkles catching the light, beneath a long fleece vest and a necklace made of bells that emitted soft chimes from time to time.

"Raven! Romance! I am thrilled that you're both here," she said, moving at a rapid speed across the bookstore, her jewelry softly chiming. "We must form an energy circle, my beloveds. Quickly, quickly." She held both arms out, wiggling her fingers to indicate that we were to take a hand. We did as she said, standing one on either side of her.

She smelled like peppermint.

"I'm moving into my next creative phase," she reported, closing her eyes and humming loudly.

I didn't dare look at my sister, for fear of sparking giggles, as had always happened whenever we were somewhere that we were supposed to be quiet.

The humming increased until the melodic sound seemed to ricochet off the star lanterns hanging from the ceiling and wrap around us.

"Angels, angels everywhere," she murmured. "Darkness vanquished by light."

After another humming session, she squeezed our hands once, released them, and whirled away.

We stared after her.

Just before she went through the door, she called out, "That was an incredibly powerful vision. We are all going to have a *very* interesting year."

* * *

After Calliope left, I asked if Lucy felt that I could keep my appointment that afternoon.

"What are you doing?" she asked, as she handed a customer a bag full of books.

"Nothing really. I can cancel if you need me to stay here. It's pretty busy for a Monday."

Lucy turned around. "Wait. Isn't this your big coffee date with Jake?"

"I wouldn't call it a *big* coffee date. We're having coffee. Just two friends, catching up."

Her eyes sparkled. "Oh, you're going. No excuses. Maybe did you want to go put on some lipstick?"

I gave her a look. "I'm not putting on lipstick for coffee. It's just Jake. You know, Jake whom I've known forever, and to be honest, I'm not even sure how much I like him."

She nodded.

"Like him as a *friend*, I mean. He's actually kind of exasperating."

Lucy nodded again, though for some reason, it appeared as though she were trying not to laugh. She reached under the counter and slid something across toward me. "Before you go—did you see this? Zander Flyte sent it over."

I opened the envelope to find a picture of Jake and me at the gala, smiling at each other during the waltz.

He looked handsome.

I looked elated.

It looked like the end of a Rom Com.

Lucy grabbed it out of my hand and whistled. "Wow. A picture *is* worth a thousand words!"

"Very funny," I said, tucking the picture back into the envelope and handing it to her.

"I'll keep it safe for you," Lucy said.

"Whatever." I slung my bag over my shoulder. "I'm going. Call me if you need anything."

"No worries. I've got everything covered here. Have so much fun," she called after me.

As if that was going to happen.

* * *

Even though the menu at Riverside Coffee offered a cornucopia of magical drink possibilities, Jake turned out to be a straight-up house blend kind of guy.

Should have guessed it.

He did add a splash of cream, though. Watching the liquid turn a rich brown as he stirred it gave me hope that someday I might be able to entice him to experiment with something more adventurous.

As friends, of course.

"So . . . where should we begin?" Jake leaned back in the chair.

"We already apologized to each other about all of the competition stuff in high school," I said. "So let's not go back there."

"And we already know what each of us does for a living," he said.

"I guess we're caught up, then," I said. "Should we call it a night?"

He took a slow sip and put his mug down. "Not yet, Starrs. I want to hear more about your life. We went to college together, that part I know."

"How do you know that? We never ran into each other on campus, as far as I can remember."

He looked down at the napkin and folded a corner of it, then smoothed it out again. "Let's just say I kept tabs."

I registered a small warmth inside my chest.

"So tell me what happened next." Jake leaned forward. "In graduate school. What were your favorite classes? What was it like writing a thesis and dissertation? How did you pick the topics? I want to hear everything."

"No, you don't." I took a sip of coffee. "No one wants to hear about that."

"I do. I really do."

I took a deep breath and started talking. Tentatively at first, but much to my surprise, he seemed wholly engaged. He asked more questions and I found myself enjoying telling him about the highs and lows of grad school. Rather than being the awkward meeting that I'd dreaded, it soon became an absorbing and interactive conversation. After a while, I asked him to tell me about the academy and his work on the force, and he obliged. It was fascinating.

After an hour or so, Jake looked up. "By the way, I wanted to tell you how much I appreciated you jumping into the pool. I can't believe I ended up in the water."

"You did pull a Gatsby there. Which, although terrifying for the rest of us, probably does enhance your street cred as a crime writer."

He laughed, then stopped abruptly. "Hold on. *The Great Gatsby* isn't a crime novel."

I put my coffee down. "You don't see it?"

"No."

"Not even a little bit?"

Jake crossed his arms over his chest as he pondered the question.

"Think about the ending."

His eyes widened. "Oh. Body in a pool."

"Not to mention all of the other crimes committed—theft, fraud, hit and run, et cetera."

He gave me an appraising look. "I'm starting to think that I should sign up for one of your classes."

"If I were teaching one, you'd be welcome to join us. In the meantime, I'll be over here selling books and solving crimes."

"You could just leave it to the professionals," Jake said, with a wink.

"I could." I smiled at him. "No promises, though."

Before I knew what was happening, he reached his hand out and put it over mine. "Seriously, Emma, thank you for saving my life."

Part of me wanted to pull my hand back immediately.

The other part wanted to sit there holding his hand for a good long while.

Before I could decide, he let go.

Like I said: exasperating.

Acknowledgments

Deepest gratitude for the wonderful and supportive family, friends, colleagues, students, writers, and readers whom I am lucky to have in my life. Additional shout-outs to those who contributed significant energies and/or specific kindnesses during the creation of this particular book: Terri Bischoff and the entire team at Crooked Lane Books; Lesley Sabga and the Seymour Agency; Greg Bourgeois, Julia Rifkin, and Christopher Oliver at UC Health; Ashley Birger at Aspen Care; Craig Svonkin, J. Eric Miller, James Aubrey, Elizabeth Kleinfeld, Andreas Mueller, Wendolyn Weber, Vincent Piturro, Renée Ruderman, and Elsie Haley at MSU Denver; Ellen Byron, Jennifer Chow, Becky Clark, Marla Cooper, Vickie Fee, Kellye Garrett, Leslie Karst, Lisa Q. Mathews, and Kathleen Valenti at Chicks on the Case; Natalie Guessas; Ann Perramond; Wendy Crichton; William Guerrera, Dorothy Guerrera, and new friends at Aston Gardens; and Kenneth, Griffin, and Sawyer Kuhn—thank you with all of my heart.